MW00381103

Millennial Piece of Shit
John-Paul Wolfe

All rights reserved. No part of this book may be reproduced in any form or by any electronic or mechanical means, including information storage and retrieval systems, without written permission from the author, except in the case of a reviewer, who may quote brief passages embodied in critical articles or in a review. Trademarked names appear throughout this book. Rather than use a trademark symbol with every occurrence of a trademarked name, names are used in an editorial fashion, with no intention of infringement of the respective owner's trademark. The information in this book is distributed on an "as is" basis, without warranty. Although every precaution has been taken in the preparation of this work, neither the author nor the publisher shall have any liability to any person or entity with respect to any loss or damage caused or alleged to be caused directly or indirectly by the information contained in this book. This is a work of fiction. Names, characters, places, and incidents either are the product of the author's imagination or are used fictitiously, and any resemblance to actual persons, living or dead, events, or locales is entirely coincidental.

Acknowledgements: God. Goggins. Mike Weber.

About this book: I am not a writer.

Chapter 1. Life or Death

I can't move. Any motion and I'm worried I'll be uncontrollably drawn to one of the two guns in the room. The thought of lifting my head off the pillow is unimaginable, as I know it will lead to greater movements and those will eventually lead to my death. I must remain absolutely still. If I move it will only be towards the gun. I can feel every inch of my body squirming under my skin as tears slide down my face. I lay here, arms and legs splayed out, recognizing only the sound of my own breath; breath that is shallow, short, and filled with hopelessness and despair. I want to reach for my cellphone on the nightstand to call Fred and tell him to come get the guns and take them far the fuck away from me. I would call him, but again; I can't fucking move. I'm paralyzed by fear and the unexplainable desire to end my own life for reasons that I don't even begin to understand. Normally, being in my own bed, alone, in my empty apartment is one of the more comfortable places to be, but not tonight, the only night I have ever wanted to kill someone so badly. I can't call for help, I can't do anything, so I just lay here motionless and frozen, hoping that if I can just wait it out things will be different in the morning.

Chapter 2. Xavier

My neighbors are friendly and rarely complain when my friends and I are drunkenly making noise at inappropriate hours, not that we do that often. We're always nice and polite, so we all get along pretty well. The building has around 40 units, I would guess. A variety of people live here, not many families, mostly couples without kids or single people. I chat regularly with the property manager who also lives here, but I've never been 'friends' with any of my neighbors. A few of them make attempts at connecting more deeply than simply exchanging pleasantries in the hallway or parking lot, but I eschew them entirely. Not out of rudeness or any sense of superiority, I just have this weird thing about that.

See, I'm a bit too cautious about mixing relationships. I suppose this is due to worries about the potential conflicts that could occur. For some reason my whole life I've liked to keep things separate; I know it's not logical, but it may have something to do with an undiagnosed, but extremely obvious to everyone, case of OCD. It doesn't affect me so much anymore, and it didn't really change my life in any meaningful way that I can recognize, but back in the day I was OCD'ed the fuck out.

As a kid I would have to go around and check all the doors and windows before bed, several times. I'd have to touch the door a certain way so that there was an even numbered amount of contact points with the door handle and my body; two or four, normally the thumb and index finger, possibly both fingernails as well. Everything had to be an even number, even things that had no numerical value. That's how fucked my head was in those days. I would sit there like a fucking retard, flicking my ears and counting to myself, trying to rebalance whatever imbalance in my head had manifested itself as an obsession with 2s, 4s and other numbers that seemed orderly and predictable to my brain.

Back then it was an impulse I couldn't control. I guess that should've been a sign about my overall lack of self-control. See, the way I see it, self-control is entirely different than discipline. Discipline, I have. Self-control, I do not. Discipline is being able to motivate yourself in the present moment for an expected future payoff. Self-control is about not doing something you want or are drawn to in the present moment because you know it will lead to problems down the road. And, man, I felt drawn to some stuff that I knew would screw me over eventually, but I just couldn't stop... drugs, women, money, wanting power over everything expect the one and only thing in this world that I might actually be able to control...myself...

Anyway, that whole thing about mixing relationships, I never liked to do it. I always felt I needed to compartmentalize my life. People from this area of my life do not need to know shit about people from the other areas of my life. I've always just preferred it this way.

I took this obsession so far that it even played out on my Thanksgiving Day plate. One year, my sister saw me trying to appear normal as I reshuffled my food and carefully grouped it into safe, separate, sections; so that no one type of food would in any way be touching another. She caught me doing this despite my attempts to conceal my actions by hunching over the table and casually moving the food around my plate as if I were aimlessly playing with it. She commented, "What are doing with your food? Just eat it. Are you trying to make sure it doesn't touch or something? You're such a freak."

"Uh, yeah," I said, in a rush, knowing that I was caught red handed and trying to quickly think of an excuse, feeling as shitty about myself as the words directed at me.

"I like to keep it separate. It tastes better that way," I said, while staring down, feeling powerless as to how the world perceived me, and assuming it must be with the nasty intentions that were so often present in those who were supposed to convey the opposite during my confusing lonely youth.

I was used to lying about my motives because I was constantly doing ridiculous shit that needed an explanation other than, *'my heads making me do it,'* or *'it feels good,'* so I would fabricate something that I thought would explain away my bizarre behavior without eliciting further inquiry. I was embarrassed when people noticed the manifestations of my OCD, but the embarrassment wasn't enough to make me stop.

By now it should come as no surprise that with the circus show going on inside my head, I didn't find much success at school. I barely got by academically. At one point I had a .7 GPA, not 1.7, just .7. The good news, I suppose, is that grades and school didn't matter to me in the least. And, unlike some kids who had to perform at school or else there would be consequences at home, by the time I had reached High school the people who were supposed to be my family had lowered their expectations so far that I could do just about anything short of murder, and I would barely hear about it.

Fast forward to today, and with no useful skills, education or value system, I've actually managed to carve out a seemingly good little life for myself. I have a job selling shoes at a high end department store and consistently side hustle so that I have more than a few bucks left over at the end of the month.

Chapter 3. A Good Morning

I wake up feeling refreshed. Considering the suicidal episode the night before, I'm rather surprised at how good I feel today. Maybe it wasn't such a big deal after all. I mean, everyone has bad days, right?

After staring at the ceiling for maybe ten minutes, I decide to roll out of bed and make my way to the bathroom. There are two times during the day when I don't feel rushed; when I wake up and haven't gotten dressed yet, and when I take my clothes off and get into bed. The other hours of the day need to be filled with productive activity, and if it's not productive, it better be stimulating, or else I'm just wasting time. In the bathroom I sit on the toilet and let nature take its course while I stare at my phone and scroll through useless social media bullshit that somehow makes itself a priority in our lives. I should probably use this time to read something worthwhile, but the draw of the phone doesn't allow me to.

I don't have to be at work for another hour, but I'm already not looking forward to going in. I pass the time giving likes and comments, analyzing the lives of others through the small snippets that they use to paint a false picture of their fantasy-reality on the internet.

My place of work, Northgate Mall, is only a few miles away from my apartment; the drive takes maybe ten minutes, if that. I park in the employee section of the massive lot, all the way at the far end, in the absolute last row.

"If you drive to work make sure you park in the last row, if not you might get towed. Drive all the way to the end and there's a yellow line, so be sure you park behind that yellow line at the very, very end. If you're injured or need to park anywhere other than the last row behind the yellow line for any reason, then please clear it with us first so that your car doesn't get towed. Again, be sure to be behind the yellow line, please and thank you," was the direction given ad nauseam when hired.

Obviously, I park behind the stupid fucking yellow line.

Walking from my car I pass through empty row after empty row of parking lot before arriving at the employee entrance on the backside of the building.

Wearing my most colorful suit does nothing to dilute the melancholy distain welling up inside me as I prepare to spend another eight hours selling overpriced shoes to rich assholes and broke idiots going into debt for clothing in order to create the illusion that they're rich assholes.

Up the elevator I go, to the fourth floor, where all employees must pass before entering the holy land of the sales floor. The sales floor; where we interact with the customer messiah. As I exit the employee area I paint a phony smile on my face, as is required by management. Strolling onto the escalator in a blue jacket, khaki pants, tan shoes and paisley gray tie I think to myself ...

'What do I have to complain about? There are starving people in Africa for God's sake. Oh I'm sad, oh I'm depressed, boohoo, poor me. Get over it.'

Going down from the fourth floor to the first I ride the escalator and wave occasionally at familiar faces and wonder about the lives' of strange ones.

Riding up the other side of the mechanical staircase is Joe from the Men's Furnishings department. I lock eyes with him and say "Hi, Joe. Good morning."

"I heard about your Saturday. Nice work, big numbers," he replies.

"Oh, thanks. Mike helped me out with a lot of those sales. Have a good one," I say, as Joe drifts up and out of earshot.

The first floor is naturally the busiest, but at this early hour it's fairly deserted. My keys and wallet go into my mailbox in the stock room just behind the wall of the sales floor. I take a breath and get ready to go out there and sell. At the point of sale, a.k.a. the computer/cash register, I log in to clock my hours and commission. Colby, the assistant manager, is standing close by. He's carefully adjusting his hair in the mirror and smiling at himself with pride. I envy Colby's ability to be, or at least appear to be, totally self-satisfied with trivial nonsense like matching his socks to his outfit or having his hair perfectly styled. I don't think Colby likes me very much on a personal level, but I sell, and that's really all that he, or the other managers, care about. A few weeks ago they fired a girl named Mary because she didn't 'make draw'. Making draw means selling enough so that the commission you earn on sales is greater than your hourly wage. This way the store knows that you're making them a profit instead of just hanging around chatting with customers all day. Usually, a sales person is given some grace and could miss making draw once in a while; maybe they would get some harsh words or, if the manager had any sense, some coaching on how to boost their sales. But, not this time, one miss and she was gone.

Because of the firing and the fact that no one really knows much about our new manager, tension has been high, but it doesn't really affect me. I'm an island at work, and that's fine for me and fine for them. I show up, I sell, and I leave. Besides the yellow line rule in the parking lot, I don't follow much of the other procedural bullshit that the store holds sacred. They have dozens of rules and protocols for how to handle every little thing. It's almost like they would prefer to have robots working here instead of real humans with minds of their own. One of their commandments states that every customer must see at least three pairs of shoes, even if they only asked for one specific item. I sometimes do this and sometimes don't, but I always make draw and am usually one of the top three sales people in the department; so what's it really matter if I don't fall in line with each and every rule that they try to shove down our throats? The new manager occasionally pesters me about not following these procedures to a 'T,' but I don't care. I have job security because I do the one thing that's actually important; I make the company money.

Pacing back and forth on the sales floor while waiting for a customer to appear, I suddenly feel a hand come to rest on my shoulder. I know it's Shane; a forty-something year-old who speaks three languages, has a college degree, but for some reason has been selling shoes for the last fifteen years. He starts in on one of his infamous sexually explicit ramblings.

"Oh, man, look at Holly" he says, as I adjust my glance to match his, and see Holly bending down as she slides a shoe onto an elderly customer's foot. Her blonde hair is hanging straight down her back, making the top of her large breasts visible, although less displayed than usual due to her conservatively cut sweater; her posture, however, revealing more than enough to attract Shane's attention.
"Man, if I was with her I wouldn't even want her to suck my dick. I'd just sit down in my big LazyBoy recliner, get out the Astro-glide, and go to work fucking those titties, man," he says, leaning in close so that I can hear his hushed tone. He says all this while wearing a comically huge smile on his face that makes his words seem friendly and not quite so creepy.
"Hmm, yeah," I say, unsure how to respond.
"I think they're real too. They look real," he says, as he lifts his hand from my shoulder, turns and walks to the other side of the sales floor.
Shane is by far my favorite co-worker simply because he's friendly and makes the day interesting by saying outlandish shit. On another occasion, Shane came up to me and started the conversation by casually stating, "Sure, I've smoked crack a few times."
I've barely been on the sales floor for five minutes and here comes the new manager, Mike. Mike is a nice enough guy, and by nice enough guy I mean a disingenuous dope like nearly all the people I'm forced to interact with for reasons other than genuinely enjoying their company. But, hey, I'm sure a lot of those same people would say similar, or probably much worse, things about me.
"Xavier, can you follow me to the office? I need to speak with you privately," says Mike, before turning and walking away without waiting for a response.
It's still early morning so the sales floor is pretty much dead, no customers in sight. Sure, I'll go listen to some spiel from Mike the manager.
"Have a seat."
I notice Colby is here as well, half standing half leaning against a filing cabinet as if he doesn't have a spine. I can tell he's trying to wear a serious expression, but he can't

seem to wipe the ever present shit eating grin from his face. This throws me. The energy in the room is off, it's too tense. This is not going to be a normal conversation about following monotonous procedures.

"Hi, Xavier," says Colby, as he straightens up and begins talking to me like we're old friends and he's confessing to fucking my wife while at the same time castigating me for somehow having made him do it.

"I think you can probably figure out why you're here. I mean, you know what you've been doing. You showed up two hours late for one of the biggest sales of the year. You..,"

I cut him off and direct my full attention to Mike.

"I thought we talked about that and were on the same page?" I say, in a jumble of words spoken too quickly, before continuing on at a slightly slower cadence. "It was a different schedule for the sale and I assumed it was my normal start time."

Now, switching my eyes back to Colby, I hope this plea will somehow change the current trajectory of the conversation, but it's too late, there's no hope.

The reality of what is happening begins to sink in. I'm getting fired. Fuck. I immediately launch into a frenzied monologue inside my own head...

Yes, I showed up late during the sale. No, I didn't follow all the rules. But, Yes! I sold shoes! What more could they want? I mean, come on. Their rules are designed, so they say, to make sure that we're selling as much as we can and, well... I'm selling! Selling well. Just let me sell and keep my fucking job.

A sense of panic washes over me. I can barely hear their words over the script that is now continuously playing over and over in my mind while Colby and Mike take turns double teaming my apparently shitty job performance.

I try to bring myself back to the present. *What are they saying now?*

"What we are trying to do here is build a positive work environment. Part of that is showing up on time, following procedures, engaging meaningfully with your coworkers.

These are things you've demonstrated that you're just not willing to do," Mike says, as he concludes The Great Firing. They both wait anxiously for my response, but the best I can muster is...

"Well, I'm sorry you feel that way. I thought I sold pretty well."

Colby steps forward, opens the door, and holds his arm out in a gesture resembling that of a butler ushering guests. He lets out an uncomfortable chuckle as I walk by. The store security guard is waiting just outside the office. I see him and he sees me. It dawns on me that he's here because of me. These idiots think I might fly off the handle or some shit, so they send this rent a cop to make sure I leave without making a scene. Jesus fuck Christ, what just happened? I guess they see me a lot differently than I see myself...

I grab my wallet and keys from my mailbox and walk straight towards the main exit. I don't pause to look around for one last time or say good-bye to anyone. What would I say anyway?

'Hey, Shane! I really enjoyed our talk a few minutes ago about titty fucking Holly, but unfortunately it will be our last. I just got fucking fired. Bye.'

Yeah, I think I'll pass on the good-byes.

Empty row, empty row, empty row, yellow line. In my car I feel numb. There's no desire to share this news with friends or family, not just yet anyway. The thing is I'm not that mad. Not even all that disappointed. I mean, I wasn't in love with this job. It was all day dealing with snooty customers while wearing a suit, tie, and dress shoes. And besides, the stuff I've been doing with Fred lately has been so profitable that it makes selling shoes, for maybe $200 on a good day, seem like a waste of time.

Right now I just want to go home, but after last night's episode and today's firing, I'm not sure that home alone with two firearms and a freezer full of whiskey is the best place for me to be. Even though I don't have the emotional energy to explain what just happened, I have to. To her at least I do, because with her is the one place where I can lose myself and disconnect from this shit reality. I know

Sarah will be home because her new job doesn't start for another few weeks. I assume she'll be thrilled when I show up, unannounced, especially considering how absent I've been since the arrival of her brother.

Chapter 4. Sarah

I met Sarah only a few months ago while aimlessly looking for lust on a dating app, but somehow I feel like I've known her my whole life. On our first date we must have passed three hours doing nothing more than talking and sipping cocktails tucked away in the corner of the Octopus Bar; a trendy place in Seattle's Wallingford neighborhood, it has dim lighting and music at the perfect volume to drown out any conversation at the next table without being obnoxious. We talked about our lives; the conversation flowed like a steady stream from one topic to the next, it was like conversing with an old friend even though we had only just met. The first date ended with no kiss, no sexual tension to speak of, at least none recognizable to me. Part of me felt that this was all too good to be true.

Yeah, she must just be lonely and needs someone to go out with, to talk to; she has no family or old friends here. She must see me next to her the same way I see myself, beneath, unworthy, just a convenience without any hope of developing into something more.

I mean, come on, here she was; a gorgeous, smart, educated girl who could have any guy she wanted. And then there was me, a shoe salesman and small time hustler with nothing more to offer than a quick wit and funny stories about the trouble I used to get into as a kid. She's been in Seattle about four years now. She moved here from Egypt to study architecture at Seattle University when she was eighteen, and now that she's finished college she plans to stay. Already she has a job offer with one of the big tech companies helping to design their newest campus over on the east side. Sarah is too perfect, not just for me, but in general. She makes me believe in the old saying that if something seems too good to be true then it probably is. But, so far, she has been nothing but perfect. Any great flaw she is concealing must be buried deep, because I see no sign of it.

Anyway, it wasn't until our fourth date that we actually kissed, and things escalated quickly from there, her unique sexual interests overpowering any attempts at modesty. We had planned to go out to a movie that night, but she texted suggesting that I come to her house instead, because she was running late and thought it would be better to stay in. She made her intentions clear as soon as I arrived.

Within a few minutes we were laying on her bed, exchanging playful kisses and exploring each other's bodies with our hands. She was in cotton shorts and a light tank top. She had taken my shirt off, but was intentional about not addressing my lower half. Lacking a gentlemanly patience I, probably too quickly, began tugging at her shorts, but she resisted.

"I don't really do this with guys unless we're dating," she said.

I pulled her close so that we were pressed chest to chest, lying on our sides, and whispered into her ear, "Don't do what? Let guys kiss your neck?" as I began kissing, licking and biting her soft caramel skin. Her hips reflexively opened and she slid into me as she relaxed, momentarily giving into desire. I could feel her willingness and pressed her onto her back. Slowly, my mouth started making its way down from her lips towards her...

"I can't!" she gasped, the words barely escaping the grasp of her throat, tightening with nervous anticipation.

Feeling the need to back off a bit and slow things down, I floated up to her face and gazed playfully into her almond brown eyes. Hovering over her I kissed her lips, then fell beside her, and at once lifted her body into the air and placed it softly back on top of mine.

"You're in charge," I said, smiling up at her and hoping that this change in our physical position would put her mind at ease and allow things to move forward at whatever pace she was comfortable with. It quickly became clear that this was not what she was looking for. She let out a disappointed sigh and allowed her body to slip off my chest, coming to rest in the cove of my side, my arm wrapping around her back. I closed my eyes, trying to hide the disappointment, assuming things had reached their end and would advance no further. Sarah pulled herself closer, nuzzling her head into my neck, and after a few moments of cuddling in silence, she spoke softly into my ear. "Will you spank me, please?"

Chapter 5. Downtown Intercom Calls

Arriving at Sarah's building in Seattle's Belltown neighborhood I see an open parking space right in front, lucky me; fired one minute and find a great parking spot the next. You'll see that my emotions and moods tend to change with the wind. In this moment I feel the warm wind of joy and optimism as I prepare myself to see her, Sarah, the one and only person who can make me feel the way she does. It's like she's a drug that I can't resist and that nothing and no one else can compare to.

My unplanned visit should be a pleasant surprise. Sarah has been asking me to do a lot lately; basically she wants a committed relationship where we share each other's lives. I'm more of a lone wolf and not really looking to share every waking moment with another person, but at the same time I want to be with her and I worry about losing her due to my insistence on keeping much of my life separate from hers.

Her brother is in town for a few weeks, and she has already asked at least three different times that I meet him and we all go out for dinner or drinks or whatever it is people do when introducing family members to boyfriends. I really don't want to do this, so I keep making excuses. I feel bad about not giving her what she wants in terms of my time and perceived seriousness of our relationship, and I can tell that her patience is beginning the wear thin, as does everyone's after spending sufficient time attempting to interact with me as if I was one of those nice normal people whose motivations are vanilla and whose lives run according to societal norms. I love this girl, or at least I'm so blinded by lust that I can't tell the difference. Regardless of what it is making me want her, I do want her and I want to try and make it work out between us. Anyway, we haven't seen each other in almost a week because she's been playing host to her brother, but he is gone visiting Vancouver for the next few days and I can't wait to be alone with the best part of my life.

I pay the parking meter and walk up to the intercom system. We've been dating for a few months, but I've never shown up unexpected like this before. I can feel butterflies in my stomach as my finger hovers over the intercom call button. Suddenly, the terrifying idea that I'll hear the voice of a strange man on the other end of the line disrupts my thinking. I try to put this thought out of my mind, but it seems stuck, pestering me like a hovering insect.

No way, she's not like that. If there was another guy, she would have told me, or at least made it clear that she wasn't looking for anything serious.

Click. The speaker connects and I hear her warm, beautiful voice on the other end.

"Hello..?"

"Yes. Uh, Sarah, this is the police. Open the door immediately."

"Xavier...uh, what are you doing here?"

"I said this is the police. You've been a very naughty girl. Now open up."

Giggles.

Buzz.

I'm in.

I walk into the classically furnished lobby and press the elevator call button. I hope it's empty. I don't want to see anyone other than her. The elevator door opens, empty. I enter. Reaching into my pants I begin to warm myself up a bit. I'm not sure if we'll get right to it, but if we do I want to be ready. The sex with her is amazing, for me at least it is. She seems to enjoy it too, or she says she likes it, and she asks for it non-stop so I assume she's telling the truth.

Ping.

The doors open and I remove my hand from under my pants. I'm not erect, but not fully flaccid either. This way, if she happens to be waiting on her knees in the doorway I'll be prepared to give her mouth something substantial. I know, I know, what a gentleman I am.

It's a long walk from the elevator to her apartment. My heart is beating slightly faster than normal in anticipation of one of life's great gifts; being completely at ease and vulnerable with your partner, giving yourself fully, without apology, without shame or embarrassment, without hesitation, sharing in desires that we dare not speak of outside the protective walls we've built on trust and taking chances.

I've always said that I could know someone for a decade and not really know shit about them if we've never gone through anything difficult together. On the other hand, I could know someone for five minutes, and if those five minutes were intense enough I'd know everything I would ever need to about that person. That's how it is with Sarah, we haven't known each other long, but the time we've shared has been so concentrated that it transcends lineal time and has connected our spirits at their core.

As I approach her apartment I can see the door has been left slightly ajar.

Tap, tap, tap.

"Hello..."

There's a teapot whistling on the stove.

"Hello, anyone home?" I say, slightly louder this time, into the void of the dimly lit apartment.

I know she's here, but I can't see her and I don't hear her voice or any movements from inside. I'll go in and see where she's hiding. The door creeks as I push it open. The whistling teapot grows louder while I make my way through the living room and into the kitchen. I swivel my head around the corner, hoping to see her standing there. No luck. I start to turn around and head towards her bedroom, and then- my body becomes entangled by arms and legs that seem to have formed out of thin air. She must have been hiding in the coat closet by the front door.

"Are you here to arrest me?" she asks, embracing me and looking up in to my eyes.

"That depends. Maybe you can convince me to let you go with a warning," I say, trying to remain stoic, but unable to control the smile spreading across my face.

She's clinging onto me with all her might, and then, boom! Her foot slides in behind mine while bear hugging my waist and driving into me with all her strength, she leans in hard and I go crashing to the ground with her on top of me.

We're both momentarily stunned by the fall. I swing my legs to the side, unsettle her balance and reverse the position, so that I am now the one on top. Kissing her makes all my worries fade away in an instant. Our tense bodies loosen and we relax onto the floor.

"Why are you here? I thought you had to be at work today," she asks.

"I got fired, but I don't really want to retell the whole story right now."

"Oh my God, what happened?"

"Honestly, nothing happened. I guess me being late for the sale a few weeks ago was too much for the new manager to handle. I don't really care, to be honest, and I don't want to keep running through it in my head, so let's talk about it later, okay?"

"Okay, fine. Then let's talk about when you're going to take my brother to jiujitsu class with you?" she says, while laughing and stroking my neck with her fingertips.

"Maybe I should leave," I respond, sarcastically, hoping that she picks up on my tone and doesn't think I'm serious.

"Shut up," she says, rolling her eyes. "I really want you two to meet. It's important to me, so will you do it when he gets back from Vancouver? He'll only be here another few days before going back to Egypt."

"Yes," I say, knowing that deep down I have no intention of doing this. It's not even that I really don't want to. It's just that I feel like I can't. I feel like if I meet her brother then everything will change. Then I would become one of *those* who meet their girlfriend's family and friends, and get married, and have kids, and buy a house, and drown in a mortgage, and grow old never living *their* life because they've sold out to society's expectations. No, that I cannot do, I'm sorry.

"Thank you," she says, as she nuzzles into me the way she often does, somewhat puppy like.

Laying on the floor I think to myself,

Am I a piece of shit for lying to her? I just want to make her happy, but at the same time I want to make myself happy, although I'm not quite sure what happiness feels like, I think that's what I'm looking for and I know that lying to her isn't going to get me any closer to that sought after sensation, but...! But, is it lying? In the moment I want to believe that I will meet her brother, but I know that when it comes down to it I'll make an excuse and back out. Or, what if I tell her that I won't meet her brother and it's due to a deep down unexplainable compulsion to separate everything in my life...well, then what? No, I have no choice. I must gloss over the topic with a simple 'Yes' for now, and later I'll address the matter -and by addressing the matter I mean fabricating another bullshit excuse.

We have sex and somehow in the chaos of it all end up on her bed. Laying here, sweating and out of breath, my hands find her throat and begin to gently remove the belt that's tightly wrapped around her neck. Some red marks are visible on her soft caramel skin. I run my fingertips over them so that my touch is barely perceptible.

"Are you okay? Your neck is a bit red. Was that too hard?" I ask, with genuine concern.

"No, it wasn't too hard. It was fine. You could even go a little harder next time, if you want." And she reaches up, pulling me onto her, holding my head and stroking the muscles of my back as I caress her hair and connect with every sensation; her touch, her scent, the beauty of her body, the softness of her voice and the taste of the sweat on her neck.

The idea of *'going a little harder next time'* seems utterly insane to me, but I say nothing, not wanting to disrupt our time with my incessant thoughts.

We rest on top of the covers, naked, sexually satiated and satisfied with everything about this perfect moment, free of judgment and worry.

"It's not even noon and I just want to fall asleep in your arms," she says.

"At least now when I leave you won't get mad that I'm not staying the night."

And in the next moment.

"Ow!! That was too hard," I shriek, as she bites into my arm, playfully, but with just enough force to illicit her desired response.

Sarah always wants me to spend the night and I almost never do. And I rarely have her over to my place, well, ya know, with the pounds of weed stashed in the dishwasher and various cupboards; I just don't think it's a good idea that she stumble upon it, so we don't really hang out at my apartment. Obviously, she doesn't know what Fred and I have been up to these last few months- actually that all started around the same time Sarah and I met. And speaking of all that, I've got to once again disappoint her by cutting our time short.

"What are your plans for the day?" I ask.

"Oh, nothing really, I have some online trainings to do for the new job and I'm calling my parents back in Egypt in..." She reaches for her phone to check the time, "fifteen minutes." Her laugh causes her body to bend forward without warning and she accidently head butts me in the chin.

"Stop beating me up," I say, while she continues to giggle at my exaggerated reaction.

I stand from the bed and start getting dressed.

"Are you leaving?" she asks, sounding surprised and a little hurt.

"Well, yeah. You've got to call your parents. Also, I have to go see Fred before he heads out of town."

She looks up at me from the bed with sharp, seductive eyes. I know where this is going. She's good at getting what she wants.

In the sexiest way possible, she whines, "But I don't want you to leave."

Looking down at her on the bed, I stand barely back from its edge. Her stare doesn't leave my eyes as I watch her finger tips dance on the border of her skin and the lace edging of her grey panties, she allows her fingers to drift lower as she moans, "Daddy, please don't go."

"I have to," I lie.

I can feel myself becoming aroused once again. She's the only woman who could have this effect on me only a few minutes after climaxing, and she's done it without even touching me. I know what she wants and I'll happily give it to her, but what she wants will require some acting on my part. I put my shirt on in an attempt to show that I'm serious about not staying any longer.

"Don't go! I'll do anything," she cries out at the sight of my shirt being pulled down over my head.

"I'm leaving," I say, as matter-of-factly as possible.

"Please," she begs, as she starts crawling closer to the edge of the bed, reaching out her hand towards her favorite bedroom accessory that is now fastened around my waist.

I grab her by the throat with one hand and lift her head up, so that we're looking into each other's eyes only a few inches apart.

Slap. It's hard. Hard enough that it shocks her and she seems genuinely surprised, although I know she probably expected it. I unzip my pants and pull it out through the opening.

"Open your mouth," I command.

"I won't suck it."

Slap. Harder this time. Slapping Sarah in the face used to make me a bit uncomfortable, but she tells me she likes it and I suppose by now I've gotten used to it, although at times it still weirds me out, more so when I'm sober.

She opens her mouth invitingly and arches her body forward. Her mouth fits perfectly over the enlarged head of my penis and she begins to moan and move rhythmically while on all fours. She tries to go deeper, chokes and lurches back spastically allowing some space to breath. Barely a second passes and she takes a breath and continues. We don't have much time, and honestly, this one's for her, not me, so I decide to move along quickly. Once again, using her neck as a handle I remove her head from my waist and push her back into a kneeling position.

"You're perfect," I whisper into her ear, before flipping her face down on the bed, pushing her head into the mattress with one hand as I use the other to guide myself inside her.

"Fuck!" she screams, as I begin thrusting violently. I'm fucking her with my whole being. She begs me to spank her.

"Harder!"

I spank her until my hand begins to go numb. I can feel she's getting close to climax because it seems someone has turned on a faucet inside of her. She used to get embarrassed about how wet she gets during sex, but now she knows that I love it and she seems to have embraced it too. I love everything about her and I wish she would share more with me because I know that knowing every little detail that makes her who she is will only cause me to fall more deeply for her.

I turn her over; scooping my arms under her knees I extend my hands for her throat. No belt this time. I begin pounding her as my hands grip tighter and tighter around her neck. Her face begins to change color just slightly, her leg twitches and her toes and fingers curl uncontrollably. She's coming and I must continue exactly as I am so as not to disrupt her moment. I feel her body go limp, not from asphyxiation, but from the empty feeling that washes over us after giving full exertion. I'm still erect, but I don't have the time or energy to finish. Once again, sweating and panting, we are exactly where we were fifteen minutes ago. I kiss her face, neck and breasts all over before quickly getting dressed.

"I'll call you tonight."

"Thank you for coming over," she says, still slightly short of breath.

I can't believe she thinks I'm doing her a favor by coming over and fucking her brains out at 10am on a weekday.

"Thanks for coming over?" I ask, in a dumbfounded kind of way. "You don't have to thank me for coming over. Jesus. I wish I could do this every day."

Her response, once again, shows cunning intelligence and perfect timing with words to get exactly what she wants.

"Then why don't you?"

I can see where this is going and I don't want to get into another discussion about the seriousness, or lack thereof, of our relationship.

"Okay, we'll talk more about all this stuff later, I have..."

"About what stuff?" she asks, tersely.

"Relationship stuff," I say, with a tone that sounds tired and unwilling to engage in the current topic.

"We're in a relationship?" she questions, with plenty of attitude mixed in with sincerity.

"Yes, obviously we are. Listen we can't do all this right now. I'll come back tonight or we can meet out somewhere if you want."

"Can I come to your house?" she asks.

"Uh, maybe. I'll text you in a bit," I say, wanting to escape before we end up having an hour's long discussion about 'us'.

I lean over the bed for a parting kiss before making my way to the door.

Chapter 6. Weed

"Oh happy day! Oh happy day! When Jesus washed, oh when he washed, yes when Jesus washed, oh when he washed! HE WASHED MY SINS AWAY. OHH GOD MY PUSSY! WASH MY PUSSY OH JESUS! HAHAHA. F.M.P incorporated how may I direct your call?" asks Fred, at the end of his usual singsong telephone greeting.

'F.M.P.' is Fred's fictional corporation. It serves one purpose, to allow Fred to answer the phone like this... 'F.M.P. incorporated how may I help you?' or sometimes simply 'F.M.P.'

In case you were wondering, F.M.P. stands for fuck.my.pussy.

"Yo, Fred, where you at? Please tell me you haven't left yet?"

"Nah, I ain't left. You comin' by or what?"

"Yeah, I'm leaving downtown. Be there in fifteen."

Fred and I go back so far that when we first met we were just kids and neither of us had had any exposure to the type of fucked up world that we're currently creating for ourselves.

Fred was nine and I was eight when we stumbled upon each other at the mailbox and began an everlasting friendship. Fred is bulky, black and brash. I'm slim, white, and reserved. We're opposites in many of the bullshit categorical ways that society likes to impose on people, but we've always had a few things in common that connect us deeply. We're both ruthlessly individual, with no scruples, and a thirst for adventure and the uncommon. Sometimes we went looking for trouble, and at other times trouble found us. And we're about to find ourselves in a fucked up predicament that neither of us saw coming.

Fifteen minutes, I now realize, was a bit of an under-estimate. I've forgotten that I need to make a quick stop on the way to Fred's. I want to get high and I'm going to try to make some money at the same time. Weed has been medically legal for a few years here in Washington State, and I've been taking full advantage, as a smoker that is. Everyone needs a medical card to buy at the stores, so I got one from a guy named Dr. Gotti. Yup, just like the old gangster. But this guy is no gangster, just a hippie doctor making easy money selling, uh I mean, 'prescribing', medical marijuana licenses to anyone over twenty-one years of age who can utter the words, *I've got pain, Doc.'* For the last few months, I've only bought weed from one place. It's run out of a shack on Lake City Way, the main throughway in the north Seattle neighborhood where I live. I buy here because it's close to my apartment and competitively priced. Compared to the larger, more professional operations, this place looks like a dump, but the esthetics don't concern me. Arriving at the shack I take a few moments to think about how to play this. I don't even know this guy's name. He and his wife own and operate this place and they've always been cool with me, but I get the sense that they don't exactly do everything by the book.

I need to introduce the idea of selling him large quantities of weed under the table, without raising suspicion or incriminating myself too badly.

Should I tell him my name and try to get his? No, I've seen this guy at least twenty times and we haven't exchanged names yet. I'm not going to start off with something out of the ordinary, keep it simple, just like it's a normal visit to buy a few joints.

It appears as though there's no one in the waiting area. This is good; I couldn't bring up the topic of an illegal buy in front of other customers, even if they were out of sight but possibly within earshot.

There's a clearly defined objective that's directing my actions as I approach the door to the shack. This sense of purpose has put me into state of focus that calms my mind and releases me from all other concerns in life, there's only one thing that matters now, a mission; and that's convincing this nameless weed dealer to buy pounds of marijuana from me without being a legal seller, potentially putting him and his business at risk. Game on.

Inside the waiting area there are chairs, a coffee table, several cameras, a window cut into the wall, and a door, and not much else. The waiting room is empty, so I proceed to the door that leads into the inner area where the business goes down. I press the buzzer to alert the owner that a customer is waiting. Knowing the protocol, I stand there in anticipation of the little window sliding open, my hand holds the necessary documents, ready to pass them to the man on the other side. Whoosh. It opens and I hand my ID and medical license through the opening. The window closes shut with my cards still on the other side. He doesn't take long inspecting their authenticity and a moment later the door opens. I step into the small room and stand across from a man in his fifties who I've seen at least twice a week for the last few months. We're separated by a wooden counter made out of particle board. Behind him is an assortment of cannabis products. I buy a few joints and edibles each time I visit, and today will be no different.

"What'll it be for you today, my friend?" he asks, in his usual gummed up, quasi friendly, phony manner.

"What are those? Full gram joints? Give me four of those and two twenty-five milligram Cheebachews."

"Alrighty, anything else today, young man?"

Here's my opening. Be cool.

"Nah, that should do it. Ay, but, I did have one other question for you..."

"Shoot."

"Well, a friend of mine, more of an acquaintance really, recently had a deal fall thru and he was left with a bunch of weed, and he's not really the kind of guy to sell it on the street... So I was wondering if you, or anyone you know, would be interested in it. I mean, this would obviously stay just between you and me, ya know, and it would just be a onetime thing, ya know, I don't want to make you think, uh, nothing."

Fuck, fuck, I fucked up the ending and came off as nervous. I need to shut up and let him respond so that I can gauge what he's thinking.

He pauses before answering, his stare attempting to penetrate my mind, he's analyzing everything about what I've just said. I can't tell if he's intrigued or pissed off. Say something goddamn it! I can feel sweat starting to drip down my underarms. I look at him with an expression that begs for some response.

He finally speaks, "How much? And how much?"

"Sorry, how much of or how..?" I say, stuttering like a nervous idiot.

"How much can you get your hands on? And how much is it going to cost me?" comes the answer. An answer that is more promising than anything I had imagined. At best, I expected to be giving this guy a hard sales pitch, but he didn't need it. Okay ,Okay, stay cool and don't fuck this up. Now I have to play the fool and seal the deal.

"Hmm," I pause for effect. "I think he said he has a few pounds, maybe more, but I'll find out for sure. Will you be here this evening? Maybe I can swing by with some of it later so that you can check it out."

"Yeah, sure, I'm here all day kid; but the price?"

"I think he said he wanted to sell it for around two thousand per pound, but don't quote me on that. Does that price seem about right to you?" I innocently inquire.

"Two thousand, wow, well, we'll have to see what it's like. I close up and leave at eight, so come before then if you're coming at all."

He hands me a small paper bag containing my purchase. I smile wide and bow my head as I turn and walk for the exit door.

Little victories will win great wars, and in the war of life I feel like this little victory deserves a reward. After starting my car, but before shifting into drive, I set the mood with some music and unsheathe one of the perfectly rolled, cone shaped joints. Smoking helps me shift my perspective and see things in a new light, usually in a silly, fun, lighthearted kind of light. I enjoy the physical sensation that cannabis gives me, too. Whenever I hit the gym I always hit a joint first, this way I can feel my body working, the muscle fibers ripping, my heart and lungs burning as I push them to their limit. Anyway, I'm high now and only a few minutes from my best friend's house, ready to continue plotting our latest scheme.

Chapter 7. Fred

I walk into Fred's living room to find him sitting on the couch in dim light, listening to The Temptations on an old record player.

"Sorry for the longer than expected fifteen minutes. I stopped at the weed shop," I say, for no reason at all.

Fred is probably the tardiest person I've ever met, so the fact that I'm apologizing for showing up a few minutes late to get high and shoot the breeze seems completely ridiculous.

"So, I've been thinking. I want to try to move as much of that weed as we can while we still have the connection," I say.

Fred is listening intently as he balances a book between his knees, using it as a platform on which to roll a joint of his own. Fred has always rolled the best joints; I, on the other hand, am lucky if the thing stays lit long enough to get high, but the pre-rolled joints at the medical marijuana stores have made this a non-issue.

"That connection ain't goin' nowhere," Fred says, while lifting his eyes from the task between his fingertips.

"Oh really, I thought we had a finite supply? That it was a onetime thing and when it was sold, that was it, no more. What changed?" I ask.

Fred briefly looks up, then returns his attention to the partially rolled joint before answering.

"It was, but shit changed up. You wanna hear the truth? I think you're the reason he wants to re-up. You've sold what, damn near twenty pounds for him in the last two and a half months? That changed his thinking, and he says he already has an order in for another shipment. You're right, he was gonna get rid of the fifty-whatever pounds he got from his boys, but you made it disappear so fast that he wants to keep it going."

This is obviously great news from a financial stand point, but the idea of becoming more intertwined with this nameless cartel associate is a bit troubling, to say the least. I know next to nothing about this guy other than that he plays football with Fred and Cam, has tons of cheap weed, and walks around his living room brandishing a firearm while openly sharing his desire to murder his ex-girlfriend's fiancée; and the way Fred and Cam tell these stories, it does not appear to be a joke.

"Hmmm, okay, okay, interesting. This could be perfect. I think I've got the weed shop owner convinced to pick up a few pounds and my buddy Adam who bought some before has this idea about driving a shit ton of it to Florida where he says these pounds could sell for five grand each, easy. Let's see what happens. You're headed back over there today, yeah?"

"Fuck, man, I don' even know. You wanna hit this?" Fred asks, as he lights the joint.

"Nah, no thanks, I'm going to see Adam at his work and I just smoked, I don't want to overdo it. But hey, talk to your guy and see how many and at what price I can get it at if I head over there this weekend."

Fred's eyes open wide with the look of someone who just remembered a good piece of news and is ready to share it.

"Oh shit, you're coming this weekend, that's right, it's Halloween. You're gonna trip when you see the costumes; they're too good."

Fred plays football at Washington State University, which is about a five hour drive from Seattle. It's located in a little college town that is purportedly the greatest consumer of Busch-lite beer in the country, despite its relatively small population. Those college kids can drink, and Fred is no exception. He's a sixth year senior linebacker, after red-shirting his first two years due to a mix of bad grades and injuries. Fred and his teammate, Cameron, are all excited because they have a bi-week, so they can party all weekend, with the added bonus that Halloween is on Saturday. I was already planning to go over there this weekend because I need more product, then a few days ago Fred called in a frantic state and added a new wrinkle to my latest trip east over the mountains...

"X! X! Can you hear me?" Fred yells as soon as I answered the phone.

"Yeah, what's up, man?"
"Yo, what are you doing Halloween weekend?"
And without waiting for my response he continues.
"Jefe, you've got to come over here. We got a bi-week..."
He's cut off as Cameron wrestles the phone from him.
"Hey, you big bitch, are you coming or what? We need you! You're the boom-mic guy," Cameron shouts into my ear.
"Put Fred back on. What the fuck are you guys talking about?"
Fred regains control of the phone.
"Okay listen," he says, struggling to contain himself and get the words out. "You, Cameron, and I are going out on Halloween as a Girls Gone Crazy camera crew."
"Isn't it Girls Gone Wild?" I ask, still not understanding what the fuck these two are giddily blabbering about.
"Yeah, but they're out of business. We're going as a new start up called Girls Gone Crazy."
"You guys are fucking idiots. But yeah, I'm coming over to pick up more product anyway, so, yeah, sure, I'm in."

And thus was born 'Girls Gone Crazy', a one night, three man production that demonstrates the dramatic effects that alcohol and a video camera can have on seemingly nice young college girls, but more on that later.
I've got to say peace to Fred and go find Adam. It isn't yet noon and I've gone to work,
gotten fired,
made love to the woman of my dreams,
potentially negotiated the clandestine sale of several pounds of medium strength marijuana to a crooked medical supplier,
confirmed my business/amateur soft core porn making trip across the state this weekend,
and now I'm off to try and convince a childhood friend to buy more weed and that he should drive it to Florida in a risky move that I certainly wouldn't attempt; but hey, I've got to look out for myself first, right? He's smart; he can make decisions on his own. I'm just giving him a little nudge, an opportunity to make some money in a somewhat sideways way. I'm not forcing him to do it.

Sitting in my car, again, this time with the half smoked joint from earlier unlit and put away in the center console, I take out my phone to call Adam.

Ring. Ring. Click.

"Hey, Adam, are you on your lunch break? Want to smoke?"

"I'm taking lunch at Magnuson. Can you meet me here?"

"Yeah, I'm five minutes away. Leaving Fred's now. I'll see you there."

We've danced this dance enough times that little communication is needed to set up a meeting.

Adam works for the city as a parks maintenance person. The way he describes it, he gets paid thirty bucks an hour and has to empty a few trash cans, but mostly he spends the days getting high and reading in his work truck. Adam graduated from the University of Miami the year before, then traveled the world and found himself back in Seattle working his old Summer time job and contemplating what kind of life he should pursue. A few weeks ago I told him that I needed to sell a cheap pound and inquired if he knew anyone who'd be interested. To my surprise, Adam bought it himself and flipped it pretty quick to a couple frat boys from the University of Washington who had the disposable funds to each buy a quarter pound at eight hundred bucks. Adam was amazed at the unbelievably low price, as was I the first time I learned how cheap it was. He kept telling me that he could sell these back in Miami for a huge profit, I assume to all the fraternity kids he still knows back there. Anyway, I don't have a job anymore and I want to make some money and not have to worry about it, maybe get the fuck out of town for a while, or maybe I just want to see how far I can take this whole part time drug dealer thing before it blows up in my face. Whatever the reason, I'm going to tell Adam that he needs to buy at least ten pounds and drive it to Miami.

Just one time, man. Then that's it. Take the money and run. This is a once in a lifetime opportunity. I mean, neither of us can believe how cheap it is.

So, let's say that Adam agrees to buy ten pounds at fifteen hundred a pound. Let's assume I can get the pounds for eight hundred each. I could make seven grand in a weekend, more than I'd make in a month selling shoes, it's just too easy and profitable. I have to do it.

Chapter 8. Adam

I pull into the repurposed naval base turned city park, and drive to Adam's usual perch, located behind a set of abandoned barracks. There he is, book in hand, sitting in the driver's seat of a green Seattle Parks truck.
I approach from behind hoping to sneak up on him unnoticed. "Working hard or hardly working?" I say, as I lean into his window, disrupting his reading.
"Holy shit, man, you spooked me. I'm on my lunch break. I've actually done some work today if you can believe it; painted a few soccer fields."
"Great, I'm happy to know our tax dollars are hard at work here. But anyway, I came over because I have an idea."
"Oh, yeah? What's that?" he asks, with a touch or arrogance in his voice.
"Remember you were saying you thought you could drive a car with some of the weed to Miami and turn it for a nice profit?"
"Hypothetically," he adds, sharply.
"Well, hypothetically..." I'm trying to sound as non-pushy as possible; by the end of this I want *him* begging *me* to sell him the weed.
"Well, check it out," I say. "I think I could get maybe ten pounds, and if you bought that much I might be able to get it cheaper, like fifteen hundred instead of two grand, and like you said, you could flip it for 5k a pound back in Miami. So you'd make like what, thirty-five grand? Shit, you'd make a lot more than I would on the deal..."
"Yeah, but I'd be taking a fuck of a lot more risk driving a truck load of weed across the country!" he says, while maintaining the condescending tone that accompanies his voice more often than I think he realizes.
"Oh for sure, but you'd be making in a week what some people make in a year. It's up to you but, I mean, I don't know how long this connection will be around. Make hay while the sun shines, right? Anyway, think about it and let

me know. I'm going over there to get some more this weekend, so no rush. Just let me know by Friday, cool?" "How the fuck am I supposed to get that kind of money?" he says, his voice now rising nearly to the level of a shout. "Oh, I'm sure you can figure something out. Maybe the fraternity brothers could pool their money and split the cost with you, I don't know. But, hey, I've got to go. I'll hit you up in a few days if I haven't heard from you. No pressure, just let me know."
"I'll let you know," he says, leaning slightly out the window for an awkward departing bro-hug.
I turn and walk back to my car contemplating the conversation, looking for clues to meaning and motivation. *'How the fuck am I supposed to get that kind of money?'* So, he's going to buy it if he can get the money. This seems promising, but I expect that in the next day or so he'll call with an idea of his own- he'll want me to front him the product and pay me upon his return from Florida; this I will not do. I trust Adam, I just don't trust all the other greedy fucks out there who wouldn't think twice about robbing his soft frat boy ass, and then he and I would both be fucked. Nope. People have asked me to front in the past and I've always said no, this time will be no different.
Pulling out of the park my check list remains long: I need some coffee.
I need Fred to talk to the connection and find out if ten or more pounds is even doable and what it would cost.
I need to continue convincing the pot shop owner to buy.
I need Adam to come up with a shit ton of money and give it to me.
I need to fully digest the fact that a few hours ago I lost the job that I'd had for the last few years.
I need Sarah to love me and at the same time continue to let me be my selfish, lone wolf, unlovable self.
I've already done too much today and there's more to come, but of all the things I need right now there's just one that I can actually attain, so I head to the Rooster's espresso stand in front of the I5/Lake City onramp.
Coffee, check.

Before I can negotiate price with anyone, Fred needs to confirm with his guy how many pounds I can pick up this weekend and what it's going to cost me. I can't make a hard offer to anyone without knowing how much product I can actually get this time. From my understanding, this guy, the connection, plays football with Fred but has some 'in' with drug cartels and thus ended up with like fifty fucking pounds of weed in his small town college apartment.

It was supposed to be a onetime thing, but now it sounds like he's going to get another shipment from the cartel and try to keep this little operation going. I've made at least five trips to Pullman over the last three months to pick this stuff up and bring it back to Seattle to sell.

Each time the price changes a little depending on... who knows what.

I've bought it as cheap at eight hundred a pound and I think the most I ever paid was twelve hundred. I usually pick up between three and five pounds depending on the price and the interest of my customers back on the west side. It goes like this- I talk to Fred, Fred talks to this guy, I drive over to Pullman, from there Fred leaves and comes back with the weed about a half hour later. I've never met the connection and I do not want to meet him. Again, I like keeping shit separate.

Ring. Ring. Ring.

Pick the fuck up, Fredrick. He does.

"Fred, what's good? I'm fucking exhausted and we need to get things moving for this weekend. Talk to your guy and find out if we could potentially buy ten or more pounds, and if so what the price would be, alright?"

"Yeah, yeah I'll call him."

From the droning slur present in his voice I can tell that he's half asleep, there's no chance I hear from him within the hour.

It's midafternoon now and I'm already looking forward to getting into bed. I need to go back to the pot shop to show the guy I'm serious and reliable, but I don't have hard numbers for him. Fuck it, I'll just wait until I'm back from Pullman and actually have the stuff. So what if I show up a few days later than expected, I don't even know this guy's first fucking name.

Having this whirlwind of changes and challenges should make someone frantic and nervous and stressed out, but I suppose that because my natural state is frantic, nervous and stressed out the addition of these things seem to have the opposite effect. I feel driven and with purpose and the need to check these to-dos off my list fills the space in my mind that would usually be filled up fretting about, well, everything. It's like I need to ruin my life just to stay alive, to tear everything down just so that there's something to build back up. Deep down I know I will never be content or happy or fulfilled and the best medicine seems to be to continually inject new fucked up things into my life just to keep me occupied.

Anyway, I'll be running around all week trying to make this shit happen. More importantly, I've decided to spend some real time with Sarah. I'll take a nap, then pack a small bag and head over there, stay the night, hang out in the morning, act as if I'm a nice good normal boyfriend type who does those things, or at least in this instant that's my intention. However, I know that it's not likely to play out this way due to my constantly changing thoughts that force my decisions to change along with them, leaving me in a perpetual state of purgatory and worry about what will come next, but without the ability to commit to anything beyond the present moment.

Chapter 9. To Pullman

It's early Friday morning, the week has been filled with rather bland occurrences, and some, but not nearly enough, time with Sarah, and I'm filling up the gas tank in anticipation of the several hours of driving that lay ahead. I'm going to Pullman to buy another shipment of weed from Fred's football teammate/Mexican drug cartel member, or if not member then at a minimum a loose affiliate. I'd rather not know too much about this guy and I'd most certainly prefer that he not know shit about me. I'm somewhat lost in a tornado of thoughts and emotions this morning.

The other night I slept at Sarah's, and that seems to have earned me some points with her, but those points are sure to fade into a forgotten oblivion of disappointment at what is headed her way. Today I'm letting her down by leaving with no real reason that I can offer; I'm sure she'll assume that I'm simply preferring time with Fred and the guys over her, even though that's not really the case.

I still haven't met her brother and he'll be heading back to Egypt soon. I know that I'm being a total fucking asshole, insensitive, self-centered, jerk, but somehow knowing this doesn't cause me to make the right decision, to turn around and drive straight to Sarah's, tell her I love her and that I would love to meet her brother because it's important to her and thus I will make it important to me. But no, instead I will continue to create a wider divide between me and what I see as my most likely path to happiness; being with her. I know that I am fucking myself in the long run by continually demonstrating that I am not the man she's looking for. The man she's looking for certainly wouldn't be a drug dealing head case without a job, and as if that's not bad enough, add in the fact that I treat her like shit... Well, maybe I should clarify, when I'm with her I treat her like a queen, I would do anything she asked of me; but when we are apart, I am distant in more ways than physical space. I don't respond to calls or texts,

I cancel plans, I basically make it seem like she's totally unimportant to me when the opposite couldn't be more true. It's just... I seem to always make the shortsighted decision in the moment. I guess I figure that if we're meant to be, if we're right for each other, then it will just work out and I won't have to actually try, it will just happen; or at least that's what I'm hoping for so I lie to myself to alleviate the guilt and stress that would accompany facing this personal flaw with honesty.

Crossing over I-90, I light a joint and put Jimmie Hendrix on the speakers.

I have no intention of fucking another girl this weekend, but the idea somehow enters my mind and the marijuana relaxes my worries enough to let me see the world in a different light, allowing me to consider the possibility without the usual judgment I would heap onto myself.

Am I going to get laid this weekend?

If the opportunity presents itself, should I do it? I'm in my early 20s and heading to an all weekend long drunken Halloween party in what has been described by some as, *"The Curious Case of Pullman Washington."* Why is it called this, you ask? Well, just imagine thirty thousand college kids trapped in a small town with nothing to do but party within the confines of a few square blocks cordoned off by rolling farms and wilderness in every conceivable direction for miles. Shit gets crazy over there. If a hot sorority girl wants to throw some pussy my way, who am I to say no? Sarah would never find out, particularly because I've compartmentalized my life to such a degree that she likely won't ever hear anything about this weekend, unless I choose to tell her, which I won't. She won't be chatting with my friends at a holiday party because I don't go to holiday parties, and if I did I wouldn't bring Sarah and risk having my idiot friends regale her with the debauch tales of our troubled past, secretive present, and surely hopeless future.

I'm surprisingly excited for tonight and not feeling too anxious about going out and interacting with a bunch of strangers. I guess that knowing I'll be there with two good buddies who've proven to have my back makes it easier.

Not that I'm worried about physical violence or anything like that, it's just... I don't know, I suppose knowing that there's someone close by you can count on is reassuring; maybe this is something missing from most of my life. While driving I am alone as can be. Not only alone in the car, but sealed off from all others by the metal box that separates us from one another in an unnatural way. I suspect this sensation of separation is what allows for road rage to be a common occurrence, whereas walking rage is something I've never even heard of. In the car I'm left in solitude to search for the shadowed causes of anxiousness and despair as I stare off into the green mountains that engulf either side of the highway.

Off in the distance I can see the exit for Cle Elum. I always stop here on the way to Pullman to use the bathroom and get a medium coffee, two breakfast burritos, one hash brown, two packets of hot sauce, and a water at the McDonald's.

If you've done a respectable amount of long distance driving in this country, then you know that McDonald's is the pinnacle of fast food coffee quality and bathroom cleanliness. I enter the establishment, first using the restroom and then proceeding to order. I take mine to go. I prefer to eat in the quiet, controlled, separated, environment of my vehicle.

I know, I know, I bitch and complain about the phones and the cars and the damage they're doing, not just to us as individuals but society as a whole, but I'm powerless to fight against it. It's just too easy to go with the flow, the flow of deepening separation and reliance on manufactured feel good devices that are making us go insane and eroding our natural instincts by the second. But who am I to resist the collective power of innovation and technology boiled down to its most powerful and placed in the palm of my hand? Or to reject the convenience of personal automotive transportation for some less desirable, slower method? No thank you, I'd rather stay spiritually dead and comfortable, just like all the rest.

I've got about three hours left of driving, but it's easy going. No notable traffic and I'm on pace to arrive early as it is, so there's no rush.

Driving calmly and with a full stomach I watch the passing landscapes change from lush green mountains to dry rolling hills, as liberal western Washington gives way to the conservative eastern side of the state.

I've arrived.

Stepping out of my car and walking through the semi-frozen parking lot, the cold is the first thing that makes this place markedly different than Seattle. I've left home and am in a strange new land where the usual rules, customs, and societal laws do not apply. I begin to approach the door to Fred and Cameron's apartment, well, actually it's Cameron's apartment in which Fred has positioned himself as a quasi-permanent resident. Fred, much like myself, is unwilling to compromise on certain things; things like he won't give up his ridiculously cheap and well located apartment in Seattle even though he's a student athlete five hours away. He's also unwilling to pay rent at two places at once, and so he's ended up living in the coat closet of Cameron's apartment while in Pullman, rent free. Unsurprisingly, this has led to the non-stop berating of Fred for being Cameron's live in concubine. Fred takes these good-natured jibes in stride, recognizing they're a small price to pay compared to actually paying for a place of his own.

As I cross the lawn of the apartment complex, I see a pizza deliveryman carrying what can only be described as an unbelievably large pizza to one of the neighboring units. This pizza is so fucking enormous that the deliveryman has to tilt the box sideways just to fit it through the door. A group of overly eager college students meet their meal at the door, and the looks on their faces tell me that they're as equally shocked as I am, and likely just as stoned, if not more. It's novelty large. Witnessing this scene makes me feel like I'm in a modern rendition of Alice in Wonderland, but where the psychedelic scenery has been exchanged for a drunken, weed and ecstasy fueled college vibe.

In utter amazement I watch the pizza man complete his delivery before hurrying my walk as I make my way towards Cam's door. There's music blaring from the inside. My expectation is that no one will be home and that the door has been left unlocked, as was stated by Fred before I left Seattle. Fred and Cameron are supposed to be at football practice and they've either left the music on full blast while no one's home or somebody is in there.

I try the handle, locked. I knock, nothing. The music is so loud that my attempts at knocking seem futile at best. I try again, but this time using my foot, stomping the door so that the vibrations can be felt inside, but without quite enough force to do damage. Bang. Bang. Bang.

"Fred, open the door," I shout, but soon realize my voice is nowhere near loud enough to penetrate the pounding bass of the stereo system. I stomp the door hard once again. Bang.

Open.

"Jesus, X. Why didn't you just walk in? You don't need to knock."

"Uh, the door was locked."

"For real? Well, fuck it. Come on in."

"I thought you were going to be at practice. Is Cam here, too?"

"Nah, he is at practice."

"So why aren't you?"

"I told the special teams coach to suck my cock. They suspended me for a few days. Fucking jack-offs," he says, in a relaxed way that suggests this issue is of no great concern to him.

At this unexpected news a look of great surprise contorts my face, as I say, "Ah, well that sucks., but no practice, no meetings, no nothing for you or Cam tomorrow or Sunday, right?"

"Yeah, man, he'll be freed up from like 4 today until you bounce."

"Okay, okay, so what's the plan for tonight?" I ask.

Fred immediately erupts in uncontrollable laughter before stating, "Follow me."

We enter Cameron's bedroom and Fred points to an assortment of items laid out on the bed. Shirts, hats, a video camera, plastic bags full of what appear to be mardi gras style beads, and an old school fuzzy microphone on a three foot pole.

Fred puts one of the hats on his head, in bright neon pink, it reads, 'Girls Gone Crazy'.

Without invitation, Fred transforms into character.

"Del Brigham here! Coming to you from Pullman, Washington! We're looking for the craziest girls on the West Coast! Who do we have here?" he asks, putting his arm around an imaginary coed. "Alright! Show us how crazy you can get!"

Fred makes just about the most convincing character that I could have dreamed of; it's clear he's missed his true calling. He should be a carnival barking, immoral porn producer; making his living off the bounce and jiggle of drunk girls' assets being donated to his cause of decreased societal standards. Oh, and what do they get in return for being the engine of this machine? Some attention? Sure, some attention that they'll soon likely regret ever pursuing. Yeah, man, Fred, aka Del Brigham for one night only, is perfect for this gig. The gig... is still not exactly clear to me. We're in costume... Or are we wearing these outfits in a legit attempt at making a Girls Gone Wild spin-off video? I'm not quite sure, so I ask again.

"So, what exactly is the plan for tonight? Like where are we starting and when? Is it just you, Cam, and me?" My words reveal a nervous energy and Fred looks at me with compassionate eyes and sighs before answering. "Don't worry about it, man, just chill. And yeah, our guy from the team, Tommy, is coming out too. You met him last time you were out here, remember?"

'Oh, fuck,' I immediately think to myself. Tommy is a weird fuckin' dude, and I like weird motherfuckers, but this guy is on some other shit. Despite being an elite college athlete destined for the pro's, he appears to be suffering from a case of little man syndrome and, I suspect, some deep seeded issues about his sexual preferences. I see him clearly as a closeted homosexual, but no one else seems to

buy into this theory. He does a good job of masking his
true cock-loving self by acting out in stereotypical macho-
man fashion; he gets into fights, degrades women, ya
know, the good ol' boy stuff; but he makes a habit of
taking it to another level; random assaults at bars, spitting
on girls who deny him, secretly taking pictures of naked
chicks in his bed who mistakenly fall for his... uh, 'charm'.
Add in some alcohol and who knows what the fuck will
happen with this guy. I don't hate him, I just don't like
being around him because I can tell he's the least authentic
motherfucker alive. He's always trying to be something he's
not.
"Oh, Tommy. Great!" I say. "How many cocks have you
caught him sucking in the locker room by now, 10? 20?"
"Nope, none yet. Maybe you can fuck him tonight," Fred
says, smiling and getting a kick out of what he considers to
be a far-fetched theory.
"I'm sure he'd like that," I say.
I'm hungry so I change the subject. "Yo, do we have time
to eat before Cam and the fag get back? I'm fuckin'
starving."
"Yeah, let's go to Denny's. I'll drive. Alfy's working and
they have .50 cent shots until 7. We're probably going to
his house tonight, so it will be good for you to meet him."
"Good, let's go."
Pulling out of the apartment complex we have to turn left
through a four way intersection. A pedestrian is splitting
her attention, glancing back-and-forth from the real world
to her cellphone. As soon as the WALK signal is displayed
she begins strolling into the street while staring into the
abyss of her phone's screen. The car on the other side of
the intersection is waiting to turn, but sits ideal for several
seconds after the light changes, probably distracted by a
phone too. I see the woman in the cross walk. The car
starts moving and is heading right into her path. She's
oblivious; her full attention is being sucked into the light
illuminating from the palm of her hand. The driver of the
sedan isn't paying attention and hasn't braked since
starting the turn. She's going to get hit. Fuck. "Fred!"
"What?!"

"Jesus fuck Christ, that woman, that woman almost got ran over. That car! That car was like an inch hitting her."
The sedan passed just in front of the woman, missing her by the width of a hair, at least this is how it appeared from my perspective. She reacted with surprise at the impact of rushing air caused by the passing vehicle. She was shocked, but not nearly distraught enough considering the deadly consequences of the accident that just barely didn't happen. People are so fucking clueless.
The idea of life and death takes control of my mind. I can't slow my sprinting thoughts. My mind has taken off, dragging me along for the ride.
At Denny's I shake some hands, down a shot and a beer, and have no recollection of any of it. It's a blaze of red leather seats, a basket of fried comfort food and the faces of people whose voices I could hear but not understand over the words and images running though my own mind, dominating my consciousness to the exclusion of the world around me. All I can hear are my own contemplations, going over it again and again, trying to make sense of the fine line that is life and death. How oblivious we all are to our own mortality; mortality that depends on drivers paying attention at cross walks instead of giving into the unrelenting pull of The Phone. Any second it could all end in a way that is totally unforeseen and unforgiving.
"What the fuck is wrong with you, man?" Fred asks, with a slip of the tongue and a slight lisp due to the three shots and two beers that he's consumed in the last hour.
I can already tell this is going to be a strange night.
Fred knows me better than anyone in this life and when he asks *'What the fuck is wrong with you, man?',* I don't know if it's because I'm acting so weird that my actions would seem unusual to anyone and everyone, or if Fred has picked up on some barely noticeable sign of discomfort and distress.
"I'm fine. You're just drunk," I say in response, trying to play off my disturbed emotional state as nothing out of the ordinary.

"Oh, yeah, real drunk," Fred says, while mockingly waving his hands and arms like an out of control hobo about to fall over.

"I'll drive," I say.

"Fuck you," replies Fred, as he gets into the driver's seat. Luckily, he drives carefully; not wanting to get his second DUI, but also unwilling to give up driving after having a few, or several, or too many drinks. Fred has become a master at driving like a granny while intoxicated; slightly under the speed limit and coming to a full stop at every intersection. Honestly, I feel safer with a drunk and overly cautious Fred behind the wheel than I would with a distracted cell phone staring sober person. We make it back to the apartment, alive and without incident.

Chapter 10. Halloween

I'm sure that the music was off when we left, but as we approach the apartment door the bass from Cam's speakers is once again blaring out into the parking lot. I'm not one for loud music or loud drunk people but, when in Rome...

We head into the music filled apartment. The whole vibe of the place has shifted since Fred and I left a mere hour ago. Tommy is here, dancing by himself in the living room, beer in hand. He runs up to Fred and wraps him in an over the top bro-hug, probably just a cover to try and rub his semi-hard cock up against Fred's body.

Letting go of Fred and turning his attention to me, Tommy says, "Yo, Xavier, hey, bro. You guys are fucking crazy! Those costumes! What do you think is gonna happen? Ya'll gonna fuck some of those chicks on camera? Shit, I know I'm gonna get some pussy, dog! If I don't get some pussy, I'm for sure fucking something tonight. Shots?!"

I respond with a simple nod of the head, too overcome with sensory input from the music and Tommy's over the top presence to construct anymore of a reply. I feel like I need to run the fuck out of here, but I know I can't, I have to stay until at least tomorrow morning when I can get the weed and then get out of this drunken land of fucktards. As my thoughts settle, Tommy's recently spoken words begin to rise to the surface of my mind and it becomes clear that he's just confirmed my suspicions. Did he really just say, *'If I don't get some pussy, I'm for sure fucking something tonight'*? What the fuck does that mean? Did Fred hear that shit? What the fuck, man. It's early evening and this dude is bouncing off the walls in a house with three other dudes and demanding we take shots. I need to calm this scene down, for my own sake. I know it's not going to go over well, but I have to try. I stand up and saunter over to the stereo; I turn the volume down a several tics, while asking, "Tommy, where's Cam at?"

"In his room," says Tommy, with a touch of unintentional femininity in his voice.

'Please leave the fucking volume down,' I think to myself as I nod at dancing Tommy and go up the stairs and into Cameron's room.

"Mr. Cam," I say, ducking my head through the doorway to announce my arrival.

He turns and smiles, "Who let you in? No sick deviant drug dealers allowed."

"Nice to see you again too."

"You ready to get into costume? Let's get this going," he says.

"Sure, which one's mine?"

Cam hands me a hat and black shirt with the neon lettering of our fake company on the front and STAFF on the back. While donning our costumes I feel the need to gauge my suspicions against Cam's judgment on the topic of Tommy being a closeted homo, about to break free and break booty holes all across this beautiful campus.

I begin to broach the subject, and at first, Cam is just as unconvinced as Fred. I get aggressive and state bluntly, "He's a ticking fucking time bomb, dude!"

"No way," Cam responds, now sounding a little less secure in his denial.

I continue to press the case, "He just said, just fucking said two minutes ago, *'If I don't get some pussy, I'm for sure fucking something tonight.'* I mean, what the fuck, dude?! What is *something?!* A dog? A cat? A male fucking asshole; that's what *something* is, dude! It's fucking obvious!"

Cam, now laughing hysterically at my impassioned pleas to convince anyone to confirm what to me seems like unquestionable reality, rolls his doubtful eyes.

"We need a sacrificial booty hole. Someway to see for sure. Cam, tonight, you've got to try to fuck him."

"Um, yeah right. Why don't you try to fuck him?"

"Okay, okay, no one is fucking him. In fact, I need you to cover my ass tonight, literally," I say, trying to joke, but unintentionally coming off as seriously concerned.

"Sure, bro," replies Cameron, now appearing a bit uncomfortable with the whole topic of conversation. I decide not to continue down this awkward road for the time being and instead start to head back downstairs.

In the living room the music has miraculously remained at a non-deafening level. Fuck it, if I stay sober all these drunk fucks are going to drive me crazy. I might as well jump into the deep end and drown my worries and inhibitions along with everyone else.

I head to the fridge and retrieve a beer.

"Grab me one," Fred shouts.

"Everyone want one?" I ask.

"Yup. Yeah, sure," comes the communal response.

Having barely cracked our beers, we head outside because Tommy has requested we throw the football around in the parking lot.

It's cold, too cold for a casual game of pass outside as far as I'm concerned, but I'm not one to bitch about the weather, so I figure I'll just go along with it.

I suspect this is precisely how Tommy has drawn it up in his head, and now he's attempting to bring his fantasy to life. We'll all head outside, get cold standing around tossing the ball, and in a minute he'll say *'Hey it's too cold, let's head inside to warm up.'*

Once inside he'll keep insisting we warm ourselves as quickly as possible.

'Come boys! To the kitchen," he'll shout.

"Vodka! Vodka! Shots! It will warm us from the inside. Take many, lower your inhibitions.

And after the shots, he won't stop.

'Now that our insides are warmed by the booze, we must warm our skin. Quickly, off with your clothes and into the bed. Body heat, boys!" And within minutes he would be engaged in an all-out fuck n' suck with the three of us.

And so far, it looks like his plan is going off like clockwork; we're outside and it's fuckin' freezing.

I'm standing on the edge of the parking lot, trying to catch eyes with some of the better looking female tenants coming and going, while Tommy and Cam hock the ball back and forth, and Fred does tricep dips on the stairs.

Before any of us have finished our beer, I hear, "Hey, it's too cold. Let's head inside." It's Tommy, his plan is going perfectly, I can't fucking believe it.

Back inside, I wait for Tommy to initiate phase two of his fuck-n-suck fantasy, but it doesn't happen. Cam and I find ourselves waiting for Fred and Tommy to change into costume before we head to Alfy's for the first stop of the night.

Fred comes down first to complete our trio of the perverted Girls Gone Crazy camera crew, and Tommy follows close behind dressed as a doctor.

"Okay, gentlemen, let's do a quick check of the equipment," states Cam, unknowingly coming off like a genuine member of a video production team.

He turns on his video camera and begins to record.

"Del Bringham here!" exclaims Fred, as he struggles to get the words out while drinking from a can of beer.

Looking over Cam's shoulder I watch the small screen that displays what the camera is capturing. I follow the image with my eyes as Cameron turns the camera from Fred and pans into the kitchen to find Tommy, with his pants around his ankles, gesticulating in such a way that causes his penis to spin like a helicopter blade, around and around. The allure of the camera seems to affect Tommy as it has the thousands of Girls Gone Wild victims before him; the idea of notoriety associated with a video camera somehow justifies ludicrous behavior. Funny, I would think that anyone with half a brain would be more concerned with keeping their clothes on, once a stranger's camera appears, but no, not in today's fame obsessed society.

"Jesus fuck Christ," I say, while shooting sharp, accusatory stares at both Fred and Cam. My eyes clearly screaming out, *'He's gay! Jesus fucking Christ, he's spinning his dick in your face as we speak!'*

"Alright, Tommy, time to put your cock away," says Fred, trying to pass this off as if it were no big deal.

Tommy continues to hula-hoop his hips as he fascinates himself with his spinning member, practicing its use as a lure, hoping to snag some innocent freshman football fan who won't believe for a second that the macho Tommy all-star could be gay; that is, until Tommy's cock comes out late into the night and spins right into the unsuspecting fan-boy's drunken mouth.

"Fred, let's get a road beer and get the fuck out of here," I say, wanting to change environments as I feel Tommy is getting closer and closer to doing something seriously unpredictable and fucked up.

It's already dark as we make our way out of the apartment complex and walk along the semi-frozen ground towards Alfy's house. Alfy's house; where the party apparently begins and ends in an endless cycle of stereotypical college shenanigans.

"Hey, do you think anyone is going to think we're a legit camera crew, like actually making this for real?" asks Cameron, to no one in particular, as we walk briskly, trying to stay warm.

"If we see one pair of tits it will be a success," adds Fred.

"Man, if people believe this is real it could get pretty crazy," I say.

"They're gonna believe it! You guys look like a professional Girls Gone Wild camera crew. Cam, make sure you film everything," yells Tommy, as if we were all deaf and screaming was the only way for us to hear him.

Up ahead I can hear Alfy's house before I can see it. I feel the frenzied, party-ready energy of my three associates rise with each step as we get closer to the first destination of the night.

We walk into Alfy's and I can't tell if I've just entered a nightmare or a good time. The house is filled with people, many of the faces familiar by way of mutual Seattle friends. The girls are unanimously good looking and everyone seems to be racing to reach peak drunkenness in the shortest possible time. I hear shouts of "Wooo Girls Gone Crazy," followed by laughter and greetings, as everyone at this house knows either Fred, Cam, or myself and no one will be fooled by our costumes, although they all seem to be impressed and enjoying our festive getups. Kathleen, an old Friend from Seattle and current student in Pullman, comes over and compliments our attire.

"Please tell me that video camera and microphone don't actually work, Xavier?"

"Cus' they work, we're making a movie. You want to be our first guest?"

"As tempting as that sounds I think I'll pass, but I'm sure you guys won't have any problem finding willing girls, this is Pullman after all," says Kathleen, as she rolls her eyes and pats my shoulder.

"You have to be my wingman while I'm here," I say to her. "Stick with me, show me the house."

I always feel like an idiot when I'm in a group of people and don't have a purpose, and as far as I can tell, my only purpose right now is waiting for Fred to reach a sufficient level of intoxication before initiating our movement from this house party out into the untamed streets of Pullman, where our faces won't immediately betray the inauthenticity of our costumes.

"Okay, fine, if I have to," replies Kathleen, feigning irritation.

She leads me upstairs and we begin to chat with two of her friends, who I've met before, but only in passing.

It's been about fifteen minutes since we arrived and I've already finished one beer and feel I need another one ASAP, not because I really want one, but because everyone else is drinking and I don't' want to seem out of place.

"I'll be right back," I say, shaking my empty beer can before slipping out of the circle of conversation like a mouse through a crack, hoping to escape unmolested, head bowed and shoulders hunched.

On the way down the stairs I see Fred and can tell he's approaching a state of lowered inhibitions that will lead to who knows what type of behavior.

I grab him hard by the shoulders and yell into his ear, "Let's get Cam and get the fuck out of here."

"Roger that, ay vamos," comes his response.

I walk towards the front porch, only to see Tommy has beaten me there. He's got his arm around an innocent looking girl dressed as a football player and is continually using his upper body to move her around like she's some sort of puppet.

He pulls her into him, then grabs her arm, pushes her head, it all seems non-threatening and flirtatious on the surface, perhaps even cute and loving, but deeper down I can see the sinister motivations at work. He's letting it be known that her body is under his control and he'll do as he pleases; his superior strength leaving her helpless against his perverse desires, taking away her freedom of movement and making it clear that he is in charge in a frighteningly psychotic way.

Fuck, I don't like this guy. I walk right past them with hurried steps and situate myself standing in the empty, dark front yard. I take my cellphone out and start staring at it, hoping that this will make me appear busy, causing Tommy and anyone else other than Fred or Cam, to leave me alone.

Perfect timing, here they come, and great, Fred is carrying so many cans of beer with him that he can't keep them from slipping and dropping from his grip. I rush over and take a few off his hands, opening one and depositing another into my pocket for later.

"Okay, where to?" I ask.

"This way, follow me," answers Fred, before letting out a wolf like howl at the top of his lungs for no apparent reason at all.

"Let's go, let's go," I implore, wanting get out of here before we grab Tommy's attention and he decides to leave the party and follow us.

Cameron grabs a beer from Fred and drinks it in two gulps. Before he has a chance to do anything, Fred says, "Put that can in the recycling, you bitch."

"Fuck you," responds Cameron, throwing the empty can far into a neighboring yard.

"You're a bitch," retorts Fred, the drunken environmentalist.

"Let's fucking leave, guys!" I say, trying desperately to move us along as I notice Tommy's eyes now shifting between us and his unsuspecting prey on the porch.

I've seen these two hard headed human gorillas get into disagreements that lead into wrestling matches that lead into long uncomfortable feuds and I want to avoid all that shit and just go enjoy a few hours of drinking before I have to pick up the weed and return to Seattle tomorrow morning.

Surprisingly, Fred pursues no further vengeance on Cam for littering and we begin walking down the cold dark street, hearing the sounds of Halloween parties coming out of all corners of these college student infested homes.

We've been walking for no more than five minutes and, "No shit..." Are the words mumbled as I see two girls under a dim porch light suddenly stand and shout, "Oh my God, is that Girls Gone Wild?"

"Turn the camera on," Fred says to Cameron, his whole demeanor changing on a dime. Suddenly he doesn't appear like a hostile drunk, but rather the benevolent boss of a work crew giving important directions.

I can't believe this. We've barely walked a block and already there are two girls running up to us inquiring about the camera and our affiliation with a bankrupt soft core porn company that I would assume should send any co-ed with a measurable IQ running in the opposite direction, but no, the camera has drawn these two gals to us like flies to shit.

"Are you guys really with Girls Gone Wild?" one of them asks, excitedly.

Cameron attempts to answer her. "Actually we're Girls Gone Craz..."

Fred cuts off him mid-sentence and continues as the defacto spokesperson, "Girls Gone Wild is out of business, we're a new production with a similar concept. Stand over here, okay, ready?"

These two girls are hot, like really hot. They look to be about nineteen and they're laughing and hanging onto each other, seemingly waiting for one to make the decision for both about what they should do next.

"Camera check?" says Fred.

"Rolling," responds Cameron.

"Microphone, check?"

"We've got sound," I say, not even believing that this can really be happening so fast and easy. We don't really have sound, at least not any generated from the non-functioning prop I'm holding, but the small hand held camera is on and rolling with video and audio as Cam and I stand in front of Fred, who now has his arms around these two girls, positioning them to his liking. He takes a deep breath and gets ready to perform.

"3,2,1, go," says Cam, from behind the camera, signaling with his fingers as he counts.

My mind becomes still as nervous excitement focuses my attention singularly at the scene about to unfold before me. *What is about to happen...?*

"Del Brigham here with Girls Gone Crazy. Coming to you from Pullman Washington. We're looking for the craziest girls on the west coast. Who do we have here?"

The girls giggle, but after barely an instant they look right into the camera as if they've done this a million times before, naturals.

"I'm Melissa."

"And I'm Bri."

"Melissa and Bri, are you two ready to show us why Pullman is number one?"

Before Fred even finishes his sentence, Melissa pulls her top down, flashing the camera. She then grabs her friend's shirt, pulling it down with excessive force, not wanting to risk being the only one standing there half naked.

"My Dad better not see this," one of them says over fits of laughter.

Bri, the seemingly shy one, then turns around and surprises all of us by showing off her ass and telling Fred to spank it. He does so without delay.

"Del Brigham here, and wow what and ass! I think it's safe to say that Pullman has some of the craziest girls on the west coast. Ladies you've been great."

And with that, we depart the porch and leave the girls in giggling disbelief at what has just transpired.

"What the fuck, dude. That was ridiculous," I say.

Cam seems as equally amazed as I am, but Fred, due to alcohol or the sudden onset of horny-ness, seems strangely focused and professional about what just happened, and is fixated on continuing the journey of capturing more and more hot naked chicks.

I open the beer in my pocket and the other two join me in drinking as we walk.

We stroll the streets and repeat the process of filming drunken co-eds in various states of undress for hours. None of us can believe the power of the video camera. Girl after drunk girl runs towards us, or more accurately stated, towards the allure of a camera crew. Outside a restaurant, in the large and mostly empty parking lot, a group of at least thirty guys gather around watching three girls strip completely naked and make out with each other. In a fraternity house, a wanna be good guy tries to stop the filming and becomes a semi-conscious figure on the floor after being hurled out of the way by an overzealous onlooker who didn't want the party to stop. The unfortunate fellow's frat bros cheer us on with no regard for the safety or well-being of their supposed, captain-save-a-ho 'brother',who was thrown out of the way like a sack of potatoes. Oh what a night.

Now it's 2 something in the morning and the cycle of alcohol, naked bodies and non-stop walking has culminated in Fred being sound asleep in a strangers front yard, Cam crying and bleeding from a self-inflicted head injury that was caused by an ill-fated backflip attempt that his nearly three hundred pound frame narrowly missed landing, and I'm beginning to feel the spins and have no fucking idea how to get back to their apartment, and the thought of going alone is too terrifying, considering the fact that Tommy could be there waiting in the shadows for an unsuspecting drunk sleepy male ass.

I've got to get Cam up and moving towards the apartment. "Cam, you're fine, get up and let's walk home. Fred is refusing to wake up; he can sleep here until he feels better. You and me, let's go."

Cam, sniffling through partially frozen tears and mucus, manages to get to his knees and eventually stand up.

"Okay, big guy," I say, as I try to get him stable and oriented in hopes that he will lead us back to his apartment.

Now standing up, appearing confused and off balance, Cameron mumbles a jumble of incomprehensible words, none of which I understand in the least.

"We need to get back home. Where is home? Can you walk to your house, Cameron? Go home."

I feel like a hostage negotiator or wild animal tamer trying to get my instructions to be followed, and somehow, miraculously, it seems to be working. "Home! Walk home," I keep shouting.

Cameron is making strange moaning sounds and has blood dripping down his head and face to his shirt, jeans and shoes. He looks like something straight out of a zombie movie; anyone who happens to encounter us stumbling down the street will likely be struck by fear for their own safety as the gigantic, drunk, bloody Frankenstein wobbles towards them mumbling, "At bitch I aid, Fred, an cans littered, bitch," is the best interpretation I can muster from the sounds coming out of his mouth.

"You're sure this is the way home?" I ask, as we slowly stumble down an unfamiliar and unlit road.

"Bitch ass, and I got them what I got."

"Okay, good job big guy, keep going home," I say, encouragingly.

It's cold and late and the night should still be playing back in my head, I mean we just saw at least a dozen really good looking girls get naked or partially naked simply because we were holding a video camera, but right now all I can focus on is getting off the cold street and into a warm bed. I'm fucking exhausted and drunk and Sarah hasn't called or texted since I left Seattle and that makes me feel like a failed loser for some reason, like one day without her validation and I might as well be nothing. Of course, if I told that to her she wouldn't believe a word of it.

Finally, I can recognize that we're arriving back at the apartment complex. I reach into Cam's pocket and take out his keys, but I don't need them, the door is unlocked. I can hear the TV is turned on with the volume droning on low. Inside is Tommy, sleeping on the couch that I had hoped to occupy for the night, but since Fred is missing I'll just situate myself in his closet/bedroom and pass out until morning. I can hear Cam still mumbling to himself as he makes it into his room and crashes onto the bed. I sneak through the living room and into the kitchen for a glass of water, I chug two glasses hoping that they'll prevent the morning's hangover. In the bathroom I piss, brush my teeth and wash my hands and face and finally I feel ready for some peace, solitude and slumber. Before stepping into the room to sleep, I glance at the couch and look for any sign that Tommy is awake and aware that we've returned; his snoring tells me he's out for the count and I need not worry. I wrap the comforter around me like a cocoon and let myself drift off to sleep.

Chapter. 11 The Beginning of The End

The pleasant sensation of waking up and feeling the cold on my face while the rest of my body is warmly wrapped in blankets is a welcome calm compared to the chaos of last night. The house is silent. I exit the closet and see that the sofa is empty; Tommy is gone, thank God. I slip into the bathroom and find a clean towel under the sink, so far everything seems to be going my way this morning. I shit, shower, and then beat off while sitting on the toilet. I begin by fantasizing about the events of last night, creating illusions of wild orgies born from nothing more than a cheesy costume and video camera, but my mind returns to Sarah, as it inevitably has done as of late, and I reach orgasm thinking about her face and the way she looks at me when we make love, or whatever it is you want to call it.

There's coffee in the kitchen and I make a fresh pot while watching the morning news. After about a half hour, Cam wakes up and comes downstairs to join me for a cup and we begin to reminisce about the unbelievable happenings of last night.

Only after several laughter filled minutes recounting stories of depravity does the subject of our missing friend come up.

"Have you checked your phone?" Cameron asks.

"No, it's twisted up in the covers. I haven't looked at it this morning (a miracle in its own right). Fred hasn't hit you up yet?"

"No, where do you think he is?"

"Well, we left him in a yard under a tree somewhere near the frat house that we ended up at," I reply. "He's supposed to go pick up that weed for me this morning and I don't want to spend all day here waiting for it. I'm gonna get my phone and see if I can find out where he is to try and get this show on the road."

I stand up from the couch and go back to the closet, trying to unravel the blankets and locate my cellphone. Shaking

and tossing the bedding finally results in a thudding sound and I spot my phone on the ground. Four missed video calls from Sarah this morning. I should call her back.
"Hey."
"Hi."
"Is everything alright? I see you called a bunch this morning, you kind of worried me, what's up?"
"Well, I was just thinking about you and getting really horny. I was playing with myself and I wanted to see you really, really bad, like a lot. I miss you so much when you're not here. Even if it's just for one day I just can't stop thinking about you."
"Shhh! You're making me feel bad, don't do that. Anyway tell me, how was your Halloween?"
"So fun! I went with my friends to Freemont."
"Ah nice, did you do anything else yesterday or just Halloween related stuff?" I ask, feeling even lamer than I sound, but lacking the creative energy to engage in a more meaningful conversation.
"Well, I also went shopping yesterday and I really want to show you the new things I got, I think you'll like them. Will you come over tonight?" she says, seductively.
I know that when she says she wants to show me the new things she got, that what she really means is that she bought some new lingerie she wants to wear while I fuck her.
"Yeah, of course. I should be back pretty early, I hope."
"Okay sir, come over right when you get back. I can't wait to see you."
"No more touching yourself until I get there, understand?"
"Okay fine, but it's hard! When I think of you I just get so wet and I want to..."
"Stop, be a good girl until I get there."
"Okay, I promise."
"I'll see you in a few hours."
Hanging up the phone I can't help but ask myself, *How did I get so lucky to have her in my life?*
I return to the living room trying to hide my erection. Addressing Cameron I feel the need to flex my face and disguise the shame of beating off in his bathroom and

nearly beating off again in the closet/bedroom while chatting with Sarah.

"No word from Fred," I state, with no expression what so ever. "Are you down to go get breakfast?"

"Yeah, let's go," says Cam, lifting his football player frame from the couch, wasting no time.

We head outside and Cam offers to drive.

"Here he is," he says, as we approach the car.

Here who is? I wonder as I walk around the front of the car to the passenger side door.

"Oh," I say, as I see that a large slumbering body that is unmistakably Fred has found its way into the back seat of Cameron's car, who knows how many hours ago.

"Get in, let's just go, he'll wake up on the way," Cameron says with hearty laughter.

Once in the car, I ask, "Where are we headed?"

But before Cam has a chance to answer we hear a voice fighting through dry, hung-over vocal chords. "Jesus, fuck, which one of you faggots has some water?"

Fred has woken up.

"There's some in the gym bag back there," Cameron tells him.

"Stop the car or I'm going to piss in it," shouts Fred, his body and brain unable to decide what they need first, to add liquid or release it.

We pull over and Fred rolls, folds, and eventually stands half bent over, leaning against the car while urinating and moaning sounds that you'd normally associate with agony, but his words give away his true feelings in this moment.

"Ohhh, fuck, yes, it feel so good," he says, followed by more grunting and moans until he puts his dick away, pulls a hood over his head and falls back into the car, straining to reach for and close the door behind him.

"Please God, tell me we're going to Denny's and not that piece of shit Lucy-whatever-the-fuck-Diner," he adds from the back seat as soon as we begin moving again.

"I'm always in for Denny's," I reply.

"Yeah, sure. Whatever you want lord piss you pants," says Cam.

Sitting down at Denny's I'm thinking I have to push the weed buy, no matter that Fred is half asleep, I have to make him agree to go straight from breakfast to buy the weed, or else this could turn into an all-day affair complete with hours of waiting on Cam's couch for Fred to wake up from his quickly approaching, and likely very long, nap. I'll stress to him again that I do not want to spend all day here, and now, thanks to Sarah's early morning chat, I have a reasonable excuse; girlfriend, or whatever she is, needs me back before nightfall.

Coffee arrives and in un-Fred fashion he partakes. It's rare for Fred to drink coffee. Anything short of a gram of cocaine, in terms of stimulates, just doesn't seem to get his attention, but today he orders coffee, he must be deep in the hangover gutter.

"I know we've talked about it," I begin to say, but before I can finish Fred cuts me off.

"Yeah, yeah don't worry your sweet little ass; I already got it last night. It's in the back of my car."

"What?! You went and got it last night? Okay, okay, this is great, but, dude, what the fuck? How much did you get and what was the price this time?"

"There's six pounds and he needs four grand for it," he says, while lifting the coffee cup to his mouth with both hands as if he were a priest preparing it for blessing.

Yes! Yes! Yes! This is almost perfect. It's done, which is the biggest thing. I can finally check that box and stop obsessing about when where and how much. And it's as cheap, if not cheaper, than it's ever been. I mean, less than seven hundred bucks a pound, $666 per pound to be exact. If I can sell these for eighteen hundred each, I'll make plenty.

"Fred, thank you, brother. I was just going to say that Sarah wants me back early and things have been all on edge with her lately, like I've told you. So I really wanted to get it early and get out of here. Fuck, I'm glad to have it, man, thank you."

Lowering the coffee cup from his mouth, he adds, "He wants to meet you before you leave."

"What!?" My stomach turns. "I've really got to get going."

"He says you can't have it unless you go meet him," Fred says, head bowed, coffee cup now half empty, eyelids dropping like a patient heading into surgery at the point of being overtaken by anesthesia.

"Dude, you already got it. Shut the fuck up," I say, trying to drive some sense of urgency and alertness into him. His eyes drift even closer to being fully shut, and I reach across the table and give his arm a shake.

"Fred, explain this, man. What the fuck is going on?"

With eyes barely open and his words now dripping like molasses, he says, with great effort, "Here's what he said, X, 'Have him come see me before you give it to him or don't give it to him', okay?"

Fred's words send a shock through my system, this annoying obstacle is like an unexpected boulder blocking an otherwise pristine highway; if it would just move the fuck out of the way I could make it home, but it appears to be going nowhere, I'm stuck.

"What the fuck, man. I do not want to meet this guy. I thought he and I both wanted it that way. I don't even know his fucking name. And I don't want to know him. Dude, just tell him that I have a girlfriend thing and that I took off super early, that I'm already gone."

Fred, struggling to stay upright, somehow manages to say, "Don't be a bitch. I told you, he said he won't sell it unless you go meet him."

"What the fuck does he want though?!"I say, as I once again reach across the table and give Fred's arm a shake.

I glance over at Cam and see an uneasy expression on his face. He's not used to these conversations or the intensity with which I'm imploring Fred to wake the fuck up and do something to prevent this unnecessary meeting from taking place.

Unlike Cameron, my frenzied pleas do not affect Fred in the least; he is calm and clearly not going to bother arguing as he's likely to fall asleep at the table any second now. I am panicking while Fred clearly couldn't give less of a fuck. To him, it's no big deal. To me, it's meeting a faceless, nameless drug dealer with cartel connections whose mental image I carry is that painted by tales of toting machine guns in his underwear while walking around his apartment devising ways to kill his ex-girlfriend's fiancée. I, in no way, shape, or fucking form, want to be in the same room with this maniac, under any circumstances.

"Like I said, don't be a bitch," comments Fred, as he sinks closer and closer to sleep, his body sagging with each breath.

"Can we go there right after here?" I ask, recognizing that I'll just have to fucking do this, hoping that I can get it over with, quick.

"Yeah, sure." And Fred slides low into the booth, letting his eyelids close, shutting him off from the world.

I know that Fred is solely concerned with Fred in all endeavors, and thus continuing to push the issue will only have the effect of annoying him and potentially putting more distance between me and my goal of getting the weed and getting going as soon as possible.

I try to relax and drink the coffee. Bad idea. Caffeine touches me like a double-edged sword, at times it gives me the strength and energy to achieve tiresome difficult tasks, and at other times, times like right fucking now, it causes my head to spin out of control, focusing on minute unimportant details of future events that I try in vain to choreograph within my own mind while knowing damn well that none of my obsessive circling thoughts will have any impact on reality.

'Hey, how's it going?' I imagine my opening line to the still nameless drug supplier. He'll want me to sit, I shouldn't. I should make it clear from the start that I'm pressed for time. *'Hey, man, it's great to finally meet you, but I have this thing in Seattle tonight and I'm already going to be late. Let's chat more next time I'm in town.'*

Shut the fuck up in your own head and try to eat breakfast. Four scrambled eggs, hash browns and sausage. More coffee, damn, that was a mistake.

"Hey, bitch man, wake up. Nap time over," says Cam, as he reaches over and pulls Fred's wallet from his front shirt pocket.

This, unsurprisingly, gets Fred's full attention and he sits up with a quickness.

Clutching his wallet, he regains ownership of it, takes out a fifty, and mumbles, "Breakfast on me."

Fred has always been generous and rather foolish with money, acting as if dollar bills have an expiration date stamped on their back.

"Thanks, Freddy," I say.

"You owed me," replies Cam, and we take off from the restaurant.

In the car I decide to press the issue once more.

"Does this guy live close? Think he's awake? Let's just go by there now."

"He said to come at eleven," answers Fred, with a touch of irritability now accompanying his voice.

I look at the clock, 9:45.

"Okay, perfect. We'll head back to your spot and I'll get my stuff together, then we can just stop by there while leaving town, cool?" I ask.

"Whatever you want."

In the parking lot of the apartment complex there are hung-over, or possibly still drunk, students meandering around, coming and going with the ease and nonchalant attitudes that only accompany unmotivated party enthusiast college kids. Knowing that these zombie-like-creatures will in no way cause us any problems, I say to Fred, "Let's open your trunk and get a look at the weed."

"It's EXACTLY the same as the last stuff," barks an unrested and annoyed Fred.

"I'm just going to check it out a bit."

I go to the trunk of Fred's car and peer into two large paper grocery bags. Inside the paper bags are several large Ziploc bags filled with the product. I open one and take out a small sample piece. I have no intention of smoking right now, as I want to be level headed going into this unwanted bullshit meeting that awaits me in one hour's time. The weed looks to be the same, or slightly better, quality than in the past. It's all been pretty similar with the exception of one bad buy when the three pounds I bought were overly dry and filled with seeds. I had to stretch some shit to sell those less than quality pounds, but never made a stink about it because one- the price was dirt cheap, and two- I didn't want to get into a back and forth with the dealer using Fred as our intermediary. This stuff today is good enough that I need not comment on it. I reseal the Ziploc and lift the two paper bags out of the trunk and carry them to my car, where I open the spare tire hatch and deposit the product, now safely hidden and locked away and, most importantly, in my possession.

Now that I have what I came for securely stashed away, I head into the apartment and see Fred sleeping on the couch, bad sign.

We have to leave in an hour and if Fred gets into a deep sleep there may be no waking him. I put the TV on in hopes that this will be enough of a stimulus to bring him to at least a semi-conscious state. Just then, Cam enters the living from the upstairs carrying his handheld video Camera.

"Gentlemen let's see what happened last night."

Wallet snatching and titty watching have both proven to be suitable antidotes to Fred's sleepiness and he pops up, alert and ready for the viewing.

"Ah, yes, let's see," says Fred, miraculously awake and ready to review last night's shenanigans.

We watch the footage and it's even crazier than my memory allowed me to believe. The final tally was 9 girls showing their tits, 3 getting completely naked, 1 flashing her ass and wow what a lovely booty it was, and my personal favorite, a drunk frat bro begging us to gang bang his girlfriend and film it. She at no time agreed to this as she was in another room while her drunk idiot boyfriend pleaded with all his might, *'Guys, she's a slu, she'll be down. All three of you can fuck her and film it, do it my guys.'* He went on for several minutes like this, all the while knowing that it was being recorded and believing it was going to be widely distributed. What the fuck was he thinking? I mean, I've done some dumb shit in my life, but never have I been as foolish as the people who we captured on film last night. I feel kind of bad about it, but knowing that the footage will never be seen by anyone besides us makes my worries seem not so grave. We probably did these people a favor, taught them a lesson. This way they'll regret what they did, never do it again, and not have to pay the price of being seen by thousands of unknown, or worse, known, eyes.

It's safe to say that the night far exceed all of our expectations.

It's 10:45 am now and time to go meet the man.

"Alright, Fred, let's go. What's this guy's name anyway? He's been so shrouded in secrecy it seems weird going to meet him. You're sure this is all good? I don't want this guy... I donno, doing any weird shit."

"He says he just wants to meet you. His name is Juan. I told you he's impressed with how much you've sold. He probably wants you to sell more."

"Okay, fuck it, let's go. Drive your car and I'll follow you. I don't want to have to come back here and drop you off."

Fred shoots me a look that communicates he believes my last statement makes me a lazy fuck; great, he's one to talk.

"I'll follow you," I say, as we split to opposite sides of the parking lot and enter our respective vehicles.

Fred backs out and I do the same. I don't know why I'm so nervous about meeting this guy, but something tells me not to go. I have to go. I'd like to just keep driving out of town and call Fred once I'm safely gone and say, *'Listen, man, I have the weed and you'll get the money. Tell this Juan-fucko that I didn't have time to hang around and chat. I hope he enjoys the money I'm making him,'* but, deep down I know that I can't do that, that doing that would only provide a short term relief and would eventually lead to more problems.

After a few minutes of driving we reach the other side of campus where there's a house that's been converted into a number of apartment units. Here, I assume, is where Juan lives. I watch Fred pull into the driveway and I follow close behind, parking right up against his bumper so that I can fit into the space without my backend sticking out into the street.

I step out of the car and approach Fred's window, he's sitting still in the driver's seat. I tap the glass. The window lowers and I ask, "Are you ready to go?"
Although it seems impossible to be more pessimistic in regards to this 'meeting', Fred's response to my question manages to lower my already rock bottom expectations.
"Go knock on the door on the right side of the porch, it has the number three painted on it."
"What the fuck? You're not coming?"
"He said he only wants to see you."
"This is fucked. What does he even want?!"
"He just wants to make sure you're all good and see how much more of the shit you want to move."
"Fred!" I say, as my frustration and preoccupation begin to bubble over. "I don't even know if I for sure want to move any more shit for this guy after today. I'm not going to become his fucking work bitch."
Fred looks up at me with an empty expression and eyes that say *'Hey, I don't know what to tell you.'*
Further argument will only delay the inevitable, so I shake my head and walk up the steps to door number three.
I knock.
No answer.
Maybe he's gone or asleep and I'll be able to get out of here with a good excuse.
I try the doorbell against my better judgment.
"Coming," says a strangely familiar voice from the other side of the door.
I hear three locks being unlatched and then the creaking of an old heavy door sliding open.
Standing there in the doorway is Tommy. I knew I recognized that voice.
"What are you doing here?" I ask.
"Just chillin'. Come in. Juan is waiting for you."
I walk into the dimly lit apartment that smells of beer and garbage. The man who must be Juan is seated on a sofa staring at his phone.
"Hey," I say, as I step towards him, sticking out my hand for a friendly greeting.

"Hold up," he says, his eyes don't even flinch from his phone's screen, his voice carrying notes of insecurity and false bravado.

Everything about this seems contrived, like some sort of preplanned hidden camera show that I've unknowingly stumbled into. I stand there waiting for his attention. Juan is showing his self-perceived superiority through his indifference to my presence and his weakness through his attempt at intimidation, exhibited by a general air of unfriendliness. Already I can tell he's a soft bitch deep down inside, but it is precisely the man who feels weak and powerless who will use what little power he has to disprove to others what is obvious to those not fooled by his manufactured show of strength.

After an exceedingly long pause just standing there, waiting for this wanna be gangster to put his phone away, he finally cedes and asks, "You got the money?"

What a ridiculous question. I assume another attempt to put me off guard and possibly intimidate in what is already an exceedingly uncomfortable situation.

"The money?" I respond incredulously. "The money has always been delivered to you by Fred. I'm sure he'll have it for you whenever you want it."

My response, direct and without emotion, seems to have caused a moment's hesitation, and I see the wheels turning in his head as he tries to decide how best to respond.

He eventually delivers a nearly unintelligible reply.

"White boy, it aint 'bout how it used to be done, it's how it's 'bout to be."

Tommy is now sitting down on a recliner in the corner, watching this exchange with great interest. I stand in the center of the room, between the two of them. Trapped.

"I'm not sure what you mean? I don't live here so Fred has been the one getting me the weed and you the money. I mean, if you want to talk to Fred then maybe we can find a better way, but I think the way it's been going has been pretty good for us all. Wouldn't you agree?"

"Nah, nah, nigga, it aint like that no more. Tommy, bring my new shit over here."

Tommy stands from his seat and enters the kitchen. I can hear a door being opened, but I can't see around the corner to where Tommy has gone. I direct my gaze at Juan, the weak bitch won't make eye contact, he prefers to stare into soul sucking void of his phone's illuminated screen, waiting for Tommy to return with whatever his 'new shit' is.

I hear Tommy shuffling around with things, like he's uncovering some deeply buried treasure. Is this the new shipment of weed? Is it going to be different? Better? Way worse to the point of being unsellable? All the possible scenarios are rushing through my head, barely noticed, as adrenaline slowly starts to hit my system.

The ruffling noises stop and Tommy comes around the corner, exiting the kitchen. The first thing I notice is the deranged smile painted across his face, it makes him resemble The Joker's gay, half-retarded little brother. The next thing I notice is the assault rifle aimed at his own chin as he carries it without the care of practiced hands, allowing the barrel to point any which way.

I've been in the presence of criminals and guns before, and criminals with guns, but the aura of this situation is fucked beyond belief and I can tell that he doesn't just want to show off his new toy, there's something very sinister about all of this.

"Good boy, Tommy; bring that over here," he says, as Tommy passes by me and hands the rifle to Juan before standing at my side, awaiting further direction from his supposed master.

Tommy looks at Juan and then at me and his face tells me that he just fell into the same pit of uncomfortable angst that I've been occupying since ringing that goddamn doorbell and smelling the stink of Juan's grotesque personality that was only briefly masked by the scent of stale beer and garbage emanating from this hell hole of an apartment. I want to turn around and leave immediately, but I know that won't help anything. I just need to stay calm and let this psychopath play out whatever Scarface style business deal fantasy he's trying to orchestrate.

Tommy stands there frozen and I can't tell if he's one second away from punching Juan between the eyes or about to spontaneously burst into tears.

Juan gives further direction, this time dumping the home boy twang and opting for the tone of an abusive boyfriend wooing back his battered lover. "Come sit next to Daddy and we're going to talk to the white boy about our new business."

At this comment Tommy suddenly changes his posture, his shoulders slump and he stands with his weight unevenly centered, so that one hip points exaggeratedly out to the side. He stares at me, then back at Juan, then back at me. "You better not say a fucking word about this to your friends, not Fred, not Cam, no one. Understand? I'll fuck you up if you ever say a word," says Tommy, and the moment he stops speaking he transcends into full fag mode, slithering onto the couch, coming to rest with his head on Juan's lap.

Welp, I can't help but think to myself, 'I fucking told you so! He's gay as fuck. I knew it.'

"Okay white bitch, uh I mean white boy. Tommy thinks I can trust you and I know you can make some money so here's how it's gonna be. You're gonna start selling for me. You come back here every week for four pounds, the first week you don't show, we gonna have a problem."

"I mean I..."

"Shut up, I'm not asking. Dem boys are dropping off another fifty pounds and you're gonna sell it. Four pounds every week until it's gone. You got it, white bitch?" says Juan, while stroking Tommy's head that rests awkwardly in his lap.

"Man, I can see what happens with the stuff I got today, but I don't really have buyers for that much. I mean, I can try. I mean, we'll both be making some money so yeah I'll try," I say.

All I can do now is say agreeable shit without actually committing to anything, not that he's waiting for my agreement. I just want to appear to be on board, but without actually demonstrating that I've grasped the gravity of what's happening. I'm playing dumb, just buying time until this nightmare comes to an end.

"Tryin' ain't it. The first week you don't show up, I'm comin' to you and bringing my friend," he says, as he begins stroking the barrel of the assault rifle that is placed between his legs, pointed up at the ceiling. He grabs Tommy by the back of the neck and proceeds to yank his head up, giving him a momentary kiss on the forehead before harshly pressing him down again, but this time not aimed quite low enough for his lap. Tommy hesitates and Juan grunts, forcing his head down, the tip of the gun now stuck firmly in Tommy's mouth. Juan somehow looks like he's enjoying the sight of Tommy sucking the barrel of the gun more than he would be had Tommy actually been sucking his cock.

This is too much. I take a slow backwards step towards the door and I say, "Okay man, got it. I've got to hit the road." This last scene is just too much for me to endure. I've got to get out of here. Fuck it if he's not done presenting his spiel, fuck him, I'm gone.

I turn and head for the door, hoping that I'll reach it without interference. One step, two, three, I'm at the door. I hear the unmistakable sound of fist hitting flesh and then, "Owe, fuck, Juan, please don't. That's too hard, you're gonna leave a mark." Tommy's voice sounds legitimately scared as he pleads for the violence to cease.

As the door opens I pause and turn my head once more towards the two inside, the sound of a zipper being undone is surprisingly clear even as I further distance myself from its source. I suspect all my senses are on heightened alert. Adrenaline is following freely through me.

"Now!" say's Juan, with all the wrath of an upset toddler demanding his favorite toy. No need for anymore of this. I push the door open and the first thing I see is Fred asleep in the driver's seat. I barely manage to avoid breaking into a full on sprint as I make my way to his window and rap my knuckles hard on the glass. He doesn't stir from his slumber. I try the door, unlocked, good.

"Fred-idiot-fuck! Wake up! First thing, fuck you! Second, Tommy is gay and fucking your idiot fuck friend in there as we speak. And third, I'm not fucking with you or Juan or any of this shit anymore," I say, with spit and vitriol spraying from my lips.

The still mostly asleep Fred casually tells me, "Alright, man, whatever you say."

He in no way has comprehended a word of what I'm saying. He'll be back asleep as soon as I close his car door. I can't get out of here fast enough. An overwhelming sense of panic consumes me. I don't know what to do. I'm playing through every possible scenario there is.

I kill Juan and Tommy.

I throw my phone away and cut off all contact with Fred and anyone in that circle for at least six months or until this whole thing has been forgotten.

I call the DEA and tell them I have a lead.

I put the weed back in Fred's car while he's asleep with a note that says 'thanks but no thanks'.

I tell Fred that he got me into this and it's his problem and he needs to help me get out alive.

I buy a plane ticket and get the fuck out of town for a while and tell no one where I'm going.

I work for Juan and 'dem boys' and hope to make a fuck-load of money before getting killed or ending up in jail.

I don't fucking know, man. All I know right now is that I'm pissed off, scared, and I want to get my mind off this shit, but I can't.

Okay, just start driving, I tell myself. I'll smoke a joint and head to Sarah's, at least there I'll be able to use my little head and give my big head a rest for a while.

The roads out of Pullman cut through rolling farm lands that give way to rolling grasslands that give way to deserted landscapes that will eventually fade into higher and higher hills that will fade into mountains lined with endless evergreen trees.

I keep repeating the same line over and over in my head for the entirety of the 5 plus hour drive, 'It aint 'bout how it used to be done, it's how it's 'bout to be.' Obsessing about this causes anxiousness, confusion, anger. I pore over each word trying to deconstruct its meaning from every conceivable angle. My mind is racing and I can no longer try to control it. I give way to helplessness; tears fill my eyes and eventually run down my cheeks. *'White boy, it aint 'bout how it used to be done, it's how it's 'bout to be.'* "Fuck him!" I scream out, as frustration gets the best of me. This all started by me doing him a favor. Yeah! Fred called asking if I could help get rid of some weed for a friend and my answer, *'Sure, man, I can try,'* ended with me up being threatened by a fucking thug, cartel connected, psychopath who will probably rape me if he gets the chance. Great.

Chapter. 12 Back to Seattle

It's dusk as I enter my home city. I've smoked myself silly during the drive and it's honestly a miracle that I, and the lucky passersby, survived the journey. I have to go to Sarah's straight away. Showing up there in this state won't lead to anything good, but it won't be as bad as not showing up at all. Here's another example demonstrating the power of separation; I don't want to talk to Sarah about how fucked-up my life has gotten in the past week, and because she has no idea about that part of my life I really can't tell her anyway. The nature of our relationship will force me to focus on other topics while I'm with her, and knowing this begins to put me at ease, the anticipation of having my head space hijacked by her presence is my only hope for escape. Am I even making sense to myself? She's going to think I'm a high idiot when I show up, so I figure I should just embrace this and try to use it to my advantage. The thoughts pouring into my head have changed from the panicked indecision of deciding where to run and ride without a plan, to how I can fade into a stoned oblivion on Sarah's couch and hopefully be left relatively alone, allowed to pass out until the morning when I pray that this will all reveal itself as a bad dream.
The city lights shine bright in the rain soaked streets. Here it is, her building, and once again a lucky parking spot right out front, a good omen it must be.
The familiar elevator ride is a new experience; the whole interior of the building is shining in a new light, undoubtedly the strange hue of my surroundings is due to the excess of weed I've smoked in the last five hours combined with an extreme emotional state that have me feeling like I've been transported to another planet, a fairly pleasant planet in fact, a planet that pulsates with a bass drum vibration born of a beating heart that feels the fatigue after a long day filled with strife and panic, a day that has finally come to an end; relief. The long hallway has been transformed into a red carpet carnival ride that

seems to continue in perpetuity. The doors all look exactly the same, unmarked, but somehow I remain confident that I'll recognize hers when I come to it. I've managed to achieve this super-heroic task each and every time I've been here, but have yet until this very moment given myself due credit. Wow, what an accomplishment, finding an unnumbered door. Until I actually become cognizant of thinking this ridiculous thought I was momentarily diluted to the point of believing it. Maybe Colby could be self-congratulatory enough to bask in the glory of correctly identifying a door, but I, whoever I am, am not, and thankfully so. I'd rather be a miserable prick than a delusional Colby. Here it is, Sarah's door, here it is, hopefully Sarah's door, here it is, fingers crossed that this is the right one, knock, knock...

The door opens all of an inch.

Pushing forward into the entrance I see her standing there, arms crossed, looking rather miffed.

"Hey, what up? Mice, Halloween?" Did I just say 'mice'?

"You're late, and thanks for calling or letting me know when you were going to be here. You can be such a jerk sometimes, like you don't think about anyone but yourself."

"Oh, damn, I'm sorry. I forgot to text you. I started driving and... last night we drank way too much. I'm feeling not too good. I smoked quite a bit on the way here. I'm just...I'm sorry." It all comes streaming out making little sense, if any.

"You can go," she says, stretching her arm straight out to create a barrier between me the entryway.

"What?" I ask, not wanting to believe she actually means what she's saying.

"I'm serious. You treat me like shit when we're not together. I don't deserve this. It's like you don't even think about how what you do is going to affect me. It's like as soon as you leave you forget me and anything we've talked about. You're another person when we're not together, sometimes even when we are together I feel like you don't really care what happens between us. I just don't understand you." She sounds tired, stressed and out of patience. I feel like dropping to my knees and begging for forgiveness, but I know that would only result in her continuing to view me through the current lens of negativity, but with the added filter of 'soft groveling bitch'. No, it's better I stay standing and hold on to at least a shred of my dignity.

"I'm sorry it's just, I don't know what to say."

I'm fucking blowing this, man, Jesus fucking Christ, how can this day get any shittier- wait, I know, I'll go downstairs and find that the perfect parking spot was also the perfect spot for a thief to break my window and make off with the six pounds. This irrational worry makes a home in my head, bringing fear and panic to the surface with the extra boost of marijuana induced paranoia.

Nervous sweat begins to drip from my head and underarms as she speaks. "Well, I just wish you'd leave, but I can't let you drive like this. Give me your keys and I'll move your car into the garage."

"No, no, I'll move it!" The words jump from my mouth with over the top exuberance. The car reeks of marijuana and if she should decide to sniff around, her nose would surely lead her to the hidden reality of who I really am stashed in the back.

"Fine, just be safe. Here, take the clicker and my keys so you can get back in."

What did I ever do to end up with someone like her in my life? I mean, Jesus, man, she's so far beyond anything I deserve. I just hope I don't do anything too devastating to her when I inevitably fuck this up in the end.

I'd suffer a hundred days just to keep Sarah from enduring one uncomfortable minute. I wish I could just fucking do that; suffer in some manufactured way to show her my dedication, my feeling for her. This game of life doesn't give me the chance to show what I have inside and I know that my words won't do justice to what I feel and I worry that it will remain this way forever.

I make it out to the street and, ah, thank God, no one broke into the car, a fucking miracle.

The half a block drive around to the alleyway where the entrance to the garage is requires one hundred percent concentration so that I don't side swipe anything or lazily relax my foot off the break during a crucial moment due to the foggy headspace in which I'm currently traveling. I slowly maneuver the car into the undersized parking space; the garage lights also appear different than ever before, a world of orange tint illuminates my vision, I can't help but laugh. Step by step I walk at an exaggeratedly slow pace to the security door which leads to the elevator through another clownishly orange lit room. Each time my shoe touches the cold hard floor the sound reverberates equally through the vacuous space of the parking garage and the surprisingly calm, stoned, and tired space between my ears.

Elevator doors open and I step in, ready to rise. Eyes closed, leaning against the wall, trying to rest for the few moments of solitary elevator ascent.

Ping.

Doors open.

Now the search for Sarah's door. To the end of the first hall, left or right, right, end of this hall, left, and two doors down to the entrance I hope will lead to some much needed rest.

The door is open, I step inside and Sarah is nowhere to be seen. I check her room. In her bed the unmistakable form of a body outlines the sheets from underneath.

"Sarah, I'm back." The desire to make some stupid stoned joke occurs to me, but I realize just in time that saying *'Oh, hey, sorry, I crashed into your neighbors car,'* would not be well received.

"Okay," she says. "Sleep on the couch."

"Okay," I reply, with great relief.

I can't tell if she's serious or not, but I sure am. I'm tired, I don't feel like fucking, and that couch sounds super inviting right now. I turn and exit her bedroom, gently closing the door behind me in order to leave her room protected from the noise of the Joe Rogan podcast that I will predictably listen to as I fall asleep.

I can hear Sarah's voice in the back of my head, *'Do you really have to listen to that every time you go to bed? I'm trying to sleep too, ya know.'* Maybe on the couch is where

I belong? Not bothering her, not really part of her life in any meaningful way, no danger of having my life seep into hers and poisoning it with the chaotic instability that surrounds me.

As my eyes fall heavy, the sound of Joe Rogan's voice penetrates my ears, and in my last moment of consciousness before sleep I hear, *'Trying to stay comfortable is one of the worst decisions you could ever make as a man. Trying to stay comfortable is a terrible, terrible path. Because you're going to stay soft and weak and you're never going to figure out anything, you're never going to accomplish shit.'*

Sleep.

A warm hand gently caresses my neck and back, the smell of her skin fills my being and I'm awake, Sarah is here. But, where am I? Ah, that's right, her couch, that's where I am. She's talking but I'm still in a state of half consciousness, her words seem like a meaningless cloud while my mind takes a few moments to become fully alert.

"One second, I have to pee," are the first words out of my mouth.

Sarah leans back allowing me to be free; her hand falls down the muscles of my back as I stand up from the couch and stretch my arms into the air while releasing a lengthy yawn.

In the bathroom I pee, wash my hands and face and enjoy the soft sensations of a quiet, fall morning in Seattle. The air wafting off the Puget Sound gives this area of the city a unique ocean like essence.

I walk back into the living room and fall onto the couch, she resumes her gentle caresses, this time fondling my hair and playing with the features of my face. The truth is, I hate it when she, or anyone, touches my face, but I'm aware enough of the moment not to deny her this loving gesture. She seems to rather enjoy exploring my skin with her fingers, and I'll let her do it, at least for now I will.

"Why didn't you come to bed last night?" she asks.

"Really, don't you remember saying *'Hey, fuck you, go to the couch'*?"

Her eyes roll playfully as she adds, "I didn't say it like that. And besides, I didn't *actually* want you to sleep on the couch. If I'm ever mad at you like that again I don't want you to listen to me, okay? Just throw me on the bed, hold me down and do whatever you please with me, okay?"

"Alright..." I say, drawing out the sound to show that I'm not really on board with what she's suggesting.

She straightens herself a bit, flips her hair out of her face and looks at me earnestly before stating in no uncertain terms. "For you 'No' means 'Yes', understand?"

"Hmm, but how will I know if no actually means no, or if you really do want me to stop?"

"Just trust me," she says. "This is what I want. Don't ever take no for an answer from me. Just make do whatever you want, okay? It's what I want."

"Okay, if you're sure," I say, feeling as if I've just signed a contract that I barely read, let alone understand.

"I'm sure," she says. "I promise."

She lays her head on my chest and closes her eyes as we both drift back to sleep.

Chapter. 13 Time to Work

Intensified by the window glass, the shining sun illuminates the room, forcing my eyes to uncomfortably adjust while searching for my phone to check the time. It's almost noon and Sarah is snoring next to me. I carefully slide out from under the covers and tiptoe around the apartment while dressing myself and gathering my things, being careful not to wake her. Sure, it's rude to slip away without saying goodbye, and yes, I know this, and I'm doing it anyway. The overwhelming desire to get a move on with the day overpowers the quiet voice whispering for me to stay, to spend all afternoon cuddling and watching movies and then maybe even go meet Sarah's brother this evening when he returns from north of the border. But no, I'll sneak away now and explain myself later. Only one issue remains, I can't take her garage clicker with me because I don't know if she has a spare. There's always a button near the door to open it from the inside, right? I hope my intuition serves me, because if not, I'm going to be trapped in the garage with no building key and no way out to the street. I've gathered all my stuff and give a last look over my shoulder at Sarah as I stand by the door; her snoring confirms I can sneak away unnoticed.

The elevator is empty as I go down, shit. This is the one time that I wish this wasn't the case. If there was someone else going down then maybe they would be going out of the garage too and I'd at least have a backup option in the event that I can't find a button to open the door. I exit the elevator, pass through the security door and trap myself inside the garage. The search is on. I haven't smoked any weed yet today so my mind is sharp and focused. I head to the most likely option, the area immediately surrounding the garage door. I start scanning the edge of the retractable garage door, nothing. I search around the small pedestrian door off to the side, nothing. On the ground I see there's a foot sensor but no button anywhere. I look up and follow the mechanical workings of the garage door as they extend along the ceiling. About fifteen feet back there is a break from the main structure and some electrical cords turn at a ninety degree angle leading to the wall, here lays my only option of escape; one round white button encased in a thumb sized grey box that possibly holds the power to my freedom. I press it. The unmistakable sound of a garage door rolling up is as sweet as the sweetest music to have ever touched my ears, I'm free.

I run to my car and race to pull out before the door closes back again.

I'm out and alone in the world, and I have things to do. I might want to completely wash my hands of this whole marijuana business, but before I can do that I have to sell the remaining six pounds that are currently stashed away in the spare tire compartment of my car.

It's funny how life works, last week I was hoping that after this weekend I would be selling a lot more weed through the newly named Juan. And wow, things seemed to have played out exactly how I'd hoped, in an unfortunate and abstract kind of way. The essence of what was communicated was that he wants me selling four pounds a week. That would be a good goal for me; but currently, I can in no way, shape, or form move four pounds a week, each and every week. Maybe, *maybe*, I could sell fifteen pounds in a month, but the following month all my contacts would be filled to the fucking ears with weed and wouldn't be buying more anytime soon. I'd be lucky to be able to sell five pounds total over the next month with my personal market place so flooded with product. And selling pounds isn't like selling dime bags at school or on the street. The people who buy it are looking to resell it, and these people are hard to find and even harder to create. I've exploited my connections to their fullest extent. Four pounds a week is fucking impossible, and even if this guy was open to dialogue, discussion and negotiation, I still wouldn't give a fuck. I never want to see Juan again in my fucking life, no matter how much money I could stand to make.

Okay, so what now? First thing first. I need to sell what I have. I got it as cheap as ever, but now that I'm confident it will be my last shipment I'm not too eager to let it go at rock bottom prices. I'll go to the pot shop first. I told the guy it would likely be for sale at two thousand a pound, but that I needed to check first. I'll tell him two.five, no three. No, no way he'll do three. I don't need to be a greedy fuck, just ask for two.five and if he refuses I'll come back the next day and say my buddy got desperate and agreed to let it go for two grand. I'm getting ahead of myself; first he needs to see the weed. It's in no way top shelf shit, but not the worst either; I mean, it's more than smokeable. Okay, stop beating the side of your head with thoughts and scenarios. Let's go to Lake City and see the guy, then I'll catch Adam at work if he's not too busy, I'm pretty sure he won't be.

I guess the good thing about sleeping in until noon is that at this hour there's barely any traffic. I get onto I-99, the on-ramp is just around the corner from Sarah's place.

It's a beautiful, sunny, fall day in Seattle. The water and the mountains paint a picture of an oasis city nestled between two great forces of nature. Looking at the natural beauty seems to momentarily slow my racing thoughts.

But before five minutes have passed on the road my phone vibrates, forcing me to look down at it as I drive, *"Bye..."* reads the text message from Sarah.

Well, it's not the worst way she could have responded, and I didn't expect her to be thrilled that I snuck away without saying anything.

Another vibration sucks my attention back to the screen. *"Drinks at 6 with my brother at the Dillard Room, See you there :)"*

Shit, well fuck. I do not want to have to deal with this right fucking now and I can't leave it be because it will eat at my mind and fuck up everything I have to do today, I won't be able to focus on anything else. Jesus fuck Christ!

I jerk the wheel violently to turn off of 99 as soon as I exit the battery street tunnel. My breathing is hard and I feel pressure building in my head. Why the fuck couldn't she just wait until after I did all the shit I have to focus on today? I can't concentrate when someone is giving me ultimatums or making demands or whatever the fuck this is. I have never once told her, *'be here at this time, like it or not,'* I mean, fuck. Why can't she just let me be. Okay, breath motherfucker, deal with this.

Looking down at my phone I construct a quick response. *"I really can't tonight. I have to focus on figuring out what to do now that I don't have a job. I'm going to be busy for the next few hrs. I'll text you when I'm free."* Send.

Alright, that wasn't too bad. I wasn't a dick, but the message is clear, I cannot go hang out and have drinks and put on a phony smile and act like I'm having a good time engaging in small talk with your brother, sorry. No can do. I pray to fucking God that she doesn't respond. I wait parked with the engine running to see if she issues a quick reply. My eyes are glued to the screen of my phone like followers awaiting a profound teaching from a gifted master. Fuck these phones that hold our attention captive and give us nothing in return but increased anxiety and bad eyesight. After two minutes I can no longer keep waiting. I put my phone on Do Not Disturb and merge back into traffic.

Beth's Café is coming into sight on my left and I suddenly realize that I'm starving. It's still early enough, I can eat, relax man, you can eat, it's not like you have to go to work tomorrow and you just pulled a total prick move and canceled plans before they even got off the ground with the woman of your dreams due to irrational social anxieties, so now the whole night is free, too; free to sit and stew, alone in my apartment while smoking copious amounts of chronic and trying to avoid disaster while spiraling out of control in my own mind.

At Beth's Café I order a six egg chili omelet with jalapenos, and coffee, black. It arrives and it's big. Within minutes it's gone. I attack it with everything I have. I think I eat like this because it allows my mind a brief respite. While I'm totally and completely engulfed in the act of stuffing my stomach there is no room to be lost in thought. My thought is focused on the carnal act of rapid gluttonous eating. I devour food. Like many things in my life it feels like a compulsion. I guess I'm just lucky that my eating habits are accompanied by an equally insatiable appetite for movement. I burn the calories I consume without even thinking about it. Sweating and breathing hard with a heart that feels like it's about to burst is a daily practice that when neglected leaves me ramped up to ten with unspent energy and the sudden onset of insomnia. The food is gone, the last bite consumed while still steaming hot. What's next? Pot shop, Adam, workout; after these three things are complete I can switch my focus onto other matters, mainly Sarah.

I feel like a stretched balloon leaving Beth's. It's a short journey through the Green Lake neighborhood before arriving at my first stop.

There are a few cars parked on the street in front, but at this point it makes no difference, I'll wait it out for as long as I have to for some privacy to try and make this deal go through. I park and cross the lawn that separates the front door from the street. There's a nervous looking dude in the waiting area, which indicates that someone is already inside the sales room, I'm third up. I sit and flip though a magazine. After a few minutes, a woman leaves. The nervous man enters, takes an extraordinary amount of time inside, and finally exits with a look of relief and a brown paper bag containing his purchase. I'm up, time to sell.

I let a moment pass once the nervous guy has left the building. Calmly walking to the buzzer I take a deep breath. I press the button. Buzz.

"I.D. and medical license." Comes the order from behind the window.

I pass my drivers' license and medical marijuana card to the gentleman on the other side. The window closes and then the door slides open.

"Hey, you again. So is your friend still looking to sell his stuff or did you just stop by for your usual joints?"

"Yeah, he wants to sell. I've got it here with me. Want to check it out?"

"Yeah, let me see it."

"Well, it's out in the car..."

"Right, so, go get it and bring it in here," he says, irritably.

"Okay, cool. I'll be right back."

What a fucking idiot I am! How could I not think to bring some in with me? Ah well, maybe this is actually good, maybe this makes me look more the part of a concerned friend helping out a buddy and less like a part time drug runner punk.

Okay, okay, just open the weed up and make sure no one is around to see, grab a piece and bring it in for this guy to check out.

I lean suspiciously into the back of my car, darting my eyes up down and all around, ensuring that there are no witnesses.

Opening the hatch releases an odor of pot that could travel a full city block. I snap off a piece and cover it back up, hoping to tamp down the aroma, not that anyone would be surprised, I am standing in front of a fucking pot shop for Christ's sake. But, thus is life living as a trained human, only giving the reactions which society expects me to deliver. Weed smell?! Quick cover it up!

I walk back with a small nug gently wrapped inside my palm. Passing through the main entrance of the shack, I see that the secondary security door has been left open for me, that was considerate of him, or maybe just lazy, or maybe I should stop assuming I know the motives of others when I have no fucking clue.

"Hey, man, here it is," I say, as I place the gram sized sample on the particle board countertop.

He lifts it up to give a closer look. Sniff. Investing with his nose causes another pause for analysis.

"Doesn't look like nothing I sell here, does it?" he says condescendingly, as if I'm some fucking jackoff undeserving of basic respect.

"I mean it's solid when you smoke it. But no, it's not the designer weed like a lot of what you have here. But I bet it's a lot cheaper."

"Two thousand you said? Hum. Yeah, kid, I don't think so, not for that price."

What the fuck! Ten minutes ago I was fantasizing about getting two.five, even three for these pounds and now this hill-billy-red-neck-fuck says he won't even do two?! You've got to be shitting me.

Knowing that I must remain cool I bite the inside of my cheek, then casually state, "Okay, man. I was just hoping to help out a friend. Two is pretty cheap if you ask me, even for this stuff."

I wait and let him consider his decision.

Inside I'm freaking out, but I know I need to stay calm and act like he's the one losing out on a good deal, not me.

He stands there staring curiously at the sample of weed.

Finally I break the silence, "I guess I'll just take two of those full gram indica pre-rolls."

"Do you have the pound with you now?" he asks, ignoring my previous comment about the joints.

"Yeah, I do, but I really can't let it go for under two. It's not mine to decide the price on," I say, lying through my teeth.

I'm so full of shit and it makes me feel like a phony fucking loser, but it is what it is now. Honesty can take a back seat to getting rid of this product, putting some money in my pocket, and then walking away from this whole drug thing forever.

"Yeah, well, okay," he says, capitulating to my price after barely putting up a fight. "I'll give you two for it. But it better weigh out to a full pound. I don't want any light weight scam bullshit being pulled."

These pounds are always well over weight, I'm more than happy to put it on the scale and let it sell itself.

"I'll bring it in and we can weight it, cool?"

"Go ahead and bring it in. But be discreet about it, mk?"

"Alright, I'll be right back."

I'll bring the fattest pound in. I'll wait for him to buy it before mentioning that I have more than just the one. The way he's talking leads me to believe that he's forgotten that I offered more than a solitary pound. But whatever, for now let's get one sold before thinking about the next.

Out at the car I look at the stuffed Ziploc bags and determine that they are each equally filled to the brim. I grab one at random and head back in.

Entering the shop for the third time in fifteen minutes with a pound tucked under my shirt, I see that he has once again left the waiting room door open, and in addition has prepared a scale to weigh the product.

"Okay, let's have a look," he says, as soon as I reenter the shop.

I remove the pound from under my shirt and hand it to him. He places it onto the scale.

We wait with anticipation as the numbers on the digital scale race upwards.

'1.08lbs.' Reads the digital display.

"All there," I say, and instantly regret my comment of confidence. I should've just kept quiet.

"Sure is. Well, okay, kid, it looks like you got yourself a deal."

"Great, you want it now, yeah?"

The man reaches into his pocket and pulls out a wad of cash. He counts off twenty hundreds and hands them to me.

"Thanks," I say, feeling genuinely grateful for his business.

"What's your name anyway?" he asks.

"I'm Xavier. I don't think I've got yours either?"

"Rob. Good doing business with you, Xavier. You're a straight shooter," he says, behind a sly smile that makes me think he's just as unauthentic a motherfucker as Tommy and Juan.

How could this guy be any more wrong? A 'straight shooter,' I just lied at every turn. I mean, in general I agree with him, but in this particular circumstance, man, he is way off. I lied my way through this entire thing. But maybe I didn't have to. Maybe I was lying to make myself feel better, to separate part of myself from the experience and thus not take full responsibility for it. I mean, is this me, or if I'm lying, is this me acting?

Before leaving I blurt out, "My friend has a few more of these, so just let me know if you're interested."

"How long do you expect they'll last?"

"Maybe until the end of the week, there's only a few."

"Right, well give me your phone number and I'll let you know if I can buy another."

"My phone broke this weekend and I haven't gotten another one yet." Another lie. "But I'll swing by this week for sure."

"Yeah, do that, because if I can sell this, I'll definitely want more. Suppliers have been dried up for weeks. This is unreal timing for you to show up with this right when I could use it."

"Oh, really?" I say, trying to sound interested, and I would be if I hadn't already decided to leave the marijuana trade entirely and forever as soon as I get rid of these last few pounds.

Trying to appear relaxed, I ask, "Hmm, I wonder why they're all dry? Anyway, I guess that's good timing for both of us. I'll come by soon, maybe tomorrow."

One down five to go. I want to sell these by the end of the week and be able to place my attention on how to deal with my crumbling life; getting one sold quickly is a good start.

I walk outside feeling like a new man. Two grand in my pocket and I'm taking care of business and getting shit done. I feel good, like really good, like man, I need to do this all the time just as a fucking form of therapy.

Chapter. 14 Juggling

Back in the car I take out the evil smart phone and it informs me that I have three missed calls from Fred. I'll call him back, but first I need to get a hold of Adam. More selling, more success, more money.
Ring. Ring. Ring. Answer, you fuck.
"Hey, what's up?" he says.
"Yo, I just got back from Pullman. Wanna check the weed out?"
"Yeah for sure, I'm finishing up my lunch at Magnuson. Where are you?"
"On Lake City."
"Can you meet at Matthews Beach in 15 minutes?" he asks.
"Yes, I'll be there," I say, before hanging up unceremoniously.
Okay, deal number two is scheduled. I pray to God that he buys all five and I can finish this shit tonight.
Now to call Fred, and man do we have a lot to talk about.
Ring.
"FMP," answers Fred, as usual.
"Wow, man."
"Wow what? What happened?" asks Fred, with a touch of humor in his voice that tells me he has no idea how far south this whole situation has gone in the last day.
I want to reveal everything, but first I want to know exactly what he knows. I ask a jumble of questions. "First, tell me what you think happened? Have to talked to Juan and Tommy? Do you remember what I said when I left and you were half asleep in your car?"
Fred, again sounding as if there is some comedy to be found in all this, says, "All I know is that Tommy and Juan are acting suspect."
"What does 'acting suspect' mean exactly?" I inquire.
"Suspect, X, they're not talking, acting shady n' shit."
"Well, yeah, that would make sense, because first off...
They. Are. Fucking each other!"

"Wait, wait, wait, what are you saying, X? How do you know this?" Fred asks, his voice finally beginning to match the seriousness of my own.

"Yeah, man, Tommy and Juan are fucking each other. And Juan is threatening me with a fucking gun if I don't become his personal sales bitch. I'm out, dude. He's your friend, you've got to deal with him. I'm never going back to Pullman or buying any of that shit again, not from him, not from you, not from anybody."

In confused disbelief Fred tries to hold onto his ideas of how things were a mere twenty-four hours ago. "He's not fucking Tommy. What are you talking about? They're fucking with you, Xavier. Trust me, they must be messing with you."

"Man, Fred, I am as fucking serious as can be. I guarantee, 99 percent, that they're fucking each other, but that's not what matters right now. He's trying to extort me, make me his work bitch. I'm not sticking around to find out if they're just fucking around or not. To me there is no question about the seriousness of what they're saying. He pulled a gun out on me, Fredrick."

I never say 100% because I don't believe that it's possible to be 100% sure of anything, Fred knows this, and also knows that I wouldn't say I'm 99% certain about something if I wasn't God damn sure about it.

"I don't know about that," Fred says, sounding as if he's been inflated with hot air that forces the words to fly out of his mouth like paper planes at high velocity with little to no weight behind them.

"I am absolutely-fucking-sure, Fredrick. I saw them doing gay shit and the whole thing, but that's secondary right now. They're trying, or at least Juan is trying, to intimidate and threaten me. He's saying I have to sell pounds every week for him or else he's going to come looking for me with his goons and new AK."

"He won't do shit. I'll talk to him. I'll be back in Seattle soon," he says, sounding more and more concerned and confused with each exchange of the conversation.

"Like how soon? Don't you have practice all week? I thought you were going to be in Utah or somewhere for a game this weekend?"

"I'm off the team," he replies.

"What?!"

"Yeah, some of the new coaches want to use the guys they recruited, bunch of jack-offs."

"Dude, what the fuck, man. That sucks."

"Fuck 'em. But yeah, anyway, I've got a meeting with one of the coaches to drop off my playbooks tomorrow morning and then I'll be back in the city."

"Okay, I'll see you tomorrow then. But don't say shit about me to Juan, other than that I've disappeared and you have no idea where I am, okay? If he asks, just say I've been out of contact. Do not tell him anything about me. Not a fucking word! I want to disappear from his mind as soon as possible. I do not exist as far as he's concerned, got it? You have no idea where I live or where to find me, yeah?"

"X, you know I've got your back. I'll hit you when I get there."

"Okay, one more thing so that I can start to put this shit behind me. Can you get the four grand and leave it for Juan before you take off? I'll just pay you when you get here. I don't want him to have any legitimate gripe about money owed. I sold one of the pounds already, so I figure I'll pay for this last one before disappearing."

"I don't have it."

"What if I send it? Can you pick it up at Western Union?"

"Yeah, dude, don't worry, just tell me once it's sent and I'll drop it off."

"Okay, thanks, man. I'll text you later after I've sent it, but how are you going to get it to him? Are you gonna go see him or can you just leave it for him without actually meeting up?"

The panic inside me is making itself known as I speak; my words are punctuated with a frantic energy.

Fred can tell I'm freaking out and says, "X, I'll handle this, alright? I can leave it for him in his locker, just chill. I won't say anything about you to him or anyone else."

"Alright, act like you don't know anything if he asks. I'll talk to you in a few hours. Keep your phone with you and charged."

Time to forget about Juan and focus on the task at hand. Down 95th St NE, to Matthews Beach Park, where potential customer number two awaits me. Adam is sitting, reading in his green city parks truck when I pull into the parking lot.
I see him and begin to wonder about how I would like to work for the city, doing nothing, making a good living with full benefits; but I know that's not the life for me, and after a brief moment of consideration I write it off as unimaginable, too boring, and the people, man, some of these people.
I like Adam, he's still young and hasn't been beaten down by years of monotony, but I've found it's exceedingly rare to find enthusiastic, interesting people who work unenthusiastic, uninteresting jobs.
I'm not saying that every shitty job requires a shitty person, I mean, I think driving a taxi must be one of the most interesting jobs around, especially depending on when and where you work. How much craziness must a taxi driver see working the 2am shift downtown? But, anyway, no, no way, working for the city doing next to nothing is not going to satisfy my need for productivity or stimulation.
"You ready to make some money?" I ask, while popping my head through the open window.
"Oh, shit, man, you scared me. I didn't see you walking up."
"Is today one of those lunch-break-all-day kinda days?" I ask.
"Even better," Adam says between chuckles. "Guess what? We had our group meeting this morning; it was a two hour breakfast on the clock paid for by the city!"
"Wow, you guys really don't do shit, do you?"
"Nope," he says, grinning. "Anyway, let's check out what you got."

"Yeah, come over to my car. I got you five pounds. Two five each, but if you buy all five I'll do it for twelve k, knock off five hundred bucks."

"What? Seriously? Where am I gonna get that kind of cash?"

"I don't know, but I mean, you stand to more than double your money, so there's got to be a way."

"Is the quality as good as the last one?" he asks.

This question gives me a moment's pause because the last one was not so good. I mean, quality can be more of a subjective thing. The quality of this weed is nothing like the lab grown medical pot we're accustomed to here in Seattle, but I guess down in Florida where Adam plans to sell it, and spent his recently ended college years, this stuff is top shelf, A1, quality chronic.

"Yeah, it's good," I say, feeling completely disingenuous.

I walk with Adam to the back of my car. Open the hatch. Remove the carpeting and lift the covering of the spare tire.

"Here it is," I state, as I lift the large brown paper bags out of the darkness.

"Damn, that's a lot of weed," Adam says, giggling through his excitement.

"Yeah, man, you wanna smoke a little piece?"

"Yes, sure, but is it cool if we smoke in your car? I don't want my boss to come around and see."

"Yeah, get in."

I take out a piece of the weed from one of the Ziploc bags and begin to roll a shittily constructed joint, using the center console of the car as a not so perfectly flat rolling surface.

Yes, I've seen people roll practically perfect joints using nothing but a paper, weed, and a dollar bill, or using one hand while driving, rolling in midair seemingly able to will the rolling paper into formation around the product, but my skills are greatly lacking and I'm just pleased that it appears to be strong enough to hold its shape and stay together.

I light it and begin to puff before passing it to Adam and resuming the sale.

"I sold one pound this morning and we weighed it out. It was damn near one point one. There'll be some extra in there for you, too. Feel free to get high on your own supply and still give complete pounds to satisfied customers," I say, and instantly realize I'm sounding too much like a pushy salesman douche.

"Yeah, I know I'll make a bunch of money, but I've got to figure out how to get the cash first."

I can feel Adam ramping up to ask for a loan, or in this case, just five pounds of free weed until he sells it and has the funds to pay for it.

"Talk to your frat buddies down in Florida," I say. "Have them pay upfront before you drive it down there."

"Bro, it's not like they just have ten grand sitting around for weed," he says, sounding a bit exasperated, which makes me think he's been over this subject in his own mind too many times and is starting to tire of it.

"Maybe not one individual, but get a few together to pool their money... I don't know, man. Rob a bank, I don't know. But, fuck, man, this stuff is going to sell, if not to you then someone else, but I would rather you make a profit than some dickhead I barely know. Try to find a way. It's pretty good, yeah?" I ask, as I reach my hand out to receive the joint back.

An eruption of dry coughs redden Adam's face as he passes me the joint. "Yeah, it's good, it's good," he says, struggling to stifle his cough.

"So, I guess I'll give you a few days to try and get the money together and let me know," I say, as Adam continues to cough away.

"Why don't you just front it to me? I'm not going to rip you off."

Here are the words I've been waiting for, their tone exposing a anxious impatience just below the surface as if he's been waiting his whole life to ask this.

I must put an end to this now or it will become a sticking point and ruin, or at least drastically change, my vision of how this sale is supposed to proceed.

"I want this to go down," I say, my eyes staring intensely, intentionally into him as I want to be taken seriously and be sure that I'm heard. "But, I never have, and never will, do that. Just imagine that something happens and the weed disappears, or you can't sell it, or whatever. What am I supposed to do? We're friends, I'm not going to come find you and hold you hostage until you pay, so I'd be fucked. Listen, man, there is no way I can do that."

"How would it just 'disappear'?" he asks, his words now dripping with condescension as if I've insulted him or made some rude out of place suggestion that he must respond to while showing his distaste.

"How could it disappear?" I retort, adding a bit of drama to my own voice, making it sound as if his question is literally unbelievable. "The cops pull you over and take *it* and *you* to jail, and they're not going to be worried about reimbursing me for my loss, I'd be fucked. Or maybe you go to sell it and your buyer pulls a gun and robs you. It's in your car while you're getting gas and someone breaks..."

Adam's face changes from friendly conversation to 'fuck you man what do you know,' before he says, "Yeah, dude, I get it, but none of that is going to happen!"

"Well, all of that could happen and I'm not going to put myself in a position to be totally fucked if it does. Listen, Adam, if you can get the money, then do it, and make a big profit, and if not, then I'll find someone else, no big deal."

I reach into the back seat and grab a bottle of water. "Here," I say, as I hand it to him.

"Thanks, I've got to get back to my truck. Thanks for the smoke and we'll talk more about the pounds later," he says, before stepping out.

"Yeah, man, sounds good. Just try to talk to some friends, use connections. I know there's a way for you to make this happen," I say, as a last ditch attempt to motivate him into getting the cash by any means necessary.

And with that I wait for Adam to exit my vehicle and enter his own before I begin screaming profanities at myself. Adam is not going to buy it. I can feel it. His futile attempt to convince me to give him the weed upfront was his only play.

He seemed wholly defeated at the idea of raising ten grand in a few short days. I guess I'll go back to Rob at the pot shop and hope to sell the rest to him, or I could just wait for some miracle to appear and carry me out of his ever deepening pit of problems, I don't even know anymore. Keeping busy helps prevent negative thoughts from capturing my consciousness, and lucky for me I've got a lot of busy shit to do. I need to take this two grand to the bank and then Western Union four thousand to Fred so that he can drop it off to Juan and I can wash my hands of this whole mess. If I pay what I owe then that's that, I don't need any more business with this shitty Tony Montana imitation. I might as well start checking things off the list. To the bank I go.

Chapter. 15 The Meeting

I find myself sitting on the couch, pleased with what I've gotten done today; I've sold a pound, done my banking and sent the money I owed to Fred in Pullman, even got a short workout in that left me feeling satisfied, and although Adam now seems an unlikely buyer for the remaining five pounds, my mind decides not to dwell too much on the negative, not for now at least. I think I also might have saved my life by finally selling those two guns that were screaming out for me to use them against myself the other night. Another old friend who goes as far back as Fred, Miles, is a bit of a gun-nut and had offered to buy them a few months ago. I rang him today and he was happy to swing by the apartment and give me five hundred bucks for the both of 'em. He seemed ecstatic, so I assume I got a little ripped off, but whatever, I was never going to use them for anything productive anyway. Doing all these things has really changed my perspective, I'm feeling pretty good, accomplished, and busy, and I want to keep it up. I know I shouldn't just sit here stewing in my own worries; I've got to keep moving.

It's still early enough to go meet Sarah and her brother for drinks. She hasn't responded to my last text in which I declined her plea for my presence at the Dillard Room this evening. At first, I was grateful that she didn't bother me by continuing to text and pester me with her desires to control my life, but now I wish I had the comforting assurance that she cared, cared so much that she would push hard for what she wanted, and what she wanted or what she wants, seems to be me...I guess. And I like being wanted, at least by her I do.

I need to try. I must be better with how I handle my relationship with Sarah. What kind of lunatic-lying-to-myself-piece-of-shit am I if I'm going to declare that I would gladly be thrown to the torture chamber in perpetuity just to spare Sarah an instant of suffering if I'm not even willing to spend an uncomfortable hour over drinks having small talk? Am I not causing her to suffer by denying her my time and attention and the appearance that I care? Can I really not endure just one boring evening amongst the idiot masses in an uninteresting, crowded, overpriced pub to satisfy the wishes of the woman who I see as the embodiment of loveliness, sensuality, and companionship? Why do I totally and completely fuck myself by continuing to make irrational decisions?

Okay, that's it! I'm going to tell her I want to go tonight. I'll go and have one, maybe two drinks. Perhaps I can think of an excuse about why I have to leave at a certain time, get out early. No, no more lying to her. Just be honest. She knows I don't really want to go, so she'll understand that I'm not staying very long. She'll be happy that I made the effort and showed up. Okay, I'll do it.

I'll text her. *"Hey, sorry about earlier. I was just stressed and in the middle of something. Anyway, I'm done with all my stuff for the day. Should we meet at the bar or your place?"* Send.

If I'm really going to do this then I better get my mind right so that I don't blow it.

I most certainly need coffee, but just a little, I want to be alert but not energetic, it's a bar not a track meet. Weed, just a few hits right now and then no more, too much and I'll panic and call the whole thing off. Alcohol, yes, with the coffee some baileys and then at least one more and then one in the car; it's a bar; I don't want to be sober.

I light the joint between my lips with one hand and flip to some music on my personal tracking device (phone) with the other. I hit it hard, hit it hard again and then stamp it out in the ashtray, but it keeps burning so I suck in the last bits of smoke before giving it another tap tap tap on the glass dish to finish extinguishing the smoking embers.

There's old coffee in the coffeepot and no signs of mold or unhealthy aging. I pour a cup, add a dash of Bailey's, and why not, a larger dash of whiskey. Into the microwave for ninety seconds. Ding. Ready.

The aroma of all three liquids are exaggerated by the heat, each of their distinct smells touch my nose at different points. The first sip is the perfect temperature. A little weed, coffee and whiskey and we're in business. I drink the steaming beverage quickly and then head to the shower. Drying myself I hear my phone buzzing and upon stepping out of the tub and onto the hard, damp bathroom floor I see my phone's screen and the text from Sarah that awaits me.

"Hey, that's great! You can come here or meet us at the bar, you pick."

I'll meet them at the bar. In and out and over with.

"I'll meet you at the bar. Text me when you get there and let me know where you're sitting." Send.

Text from Sarah. *"See you at the bar."*

I towel off and commence selecting clothes. Jeans, slip on vans, three button t-shirt thing. Clothed, check.

One more drink and I'll hit the road.

Whiskey and some sugar free coke, lots of ice; I may not have inherited any wisdom, skills, or value system from my mostly absent family, but by the time I was twelve I knew the great importance of filling your cocktail glass with ice before adding the liquids, worth something I suppose.

I've never shot gunned a beer in my life, but I do tend to pound mixed drinks like water. In a matter of second it's gone. I make another and head for the door.

The air is brisk and the sun has already set. Into the elevator I go, down to the lobby and out the back of the building into the parking lot. Most of the people who live here are fairly professional, but at times there are issues with guests or riffraff from the neighborhood using the parking lot as some type of meeting ground for their clandestine activities; most often teenagers getting high.

As I approach my car I see a group of rough looking youths standing around an unfamiliar Honda parked in the loading zone. Walking by I capture their attention and they begin to act as if they need to hide whatever it is they're up to. I shoot them an accusatory stare that hopefully communicates my displeasure with their presence. I enter my car without taking my eyes off them. I keep watching the group as I pullout of the parking lot. Part of me wants to yell, *'Hey get lost,'* but I decide to mind my own business and focus instead on what I'll say when meeting Sarah's brother.

I'm feeling care free, confident and a bit buzzed as I merge onto I-5 and head for downtown.

A Curtis Mayfield CD further sets my mood as I observe the Seattle skyline while crossing over the ship canal bridge that elevates cars and their passengers into the air with day time views of the city, water, tress, and mountains that make up the Pacific Northwest landscape, but at this hour all I can see is the outline of a city dotted with lights in the darkness of an autumn night.

Downtown is a maze of tall buildings, cars, and lights that illuminate the otherwise dark streets. Normally I would park at Sarah's and walk to the bar, but not this time. I have no plans of heading back to her place at the end of the night. One drink and I'm out. Besides my desire to minimize this experience, there is the additional incentive of avoiding a DUI after indulging in more and more drinks. One and done. I park a block from the bar in a paid lot. I pay only for an hour, another good reason to keep this visit short.

"Are you here?" Send.

She answers right away. *"All the way in the back at the last booth."*

Okay, let's go. Wallet, check. Doors locked, check.

As I walk on the crowded street approaching the bar, sounds of the idiot masses assault my ears.

Only the most recent and in vogue turns of phrase are used in this part of town, only the safest, most mainstream and acceptable opinions will be shared here, the clothes must all identify the individual as part of a group, most choosing to remain part of the main mass of sheep although a few stray from the flock but not far, only far enough to re-identify as a member of smaller more clearly defined sub-group. Everyone here will say they want individuality, but deep down that's bullshit, they want the group to give them identity, give them purpose, give them thoughts, politics, friends, lovers, enemies, ideas, fears, passions. An individual is a rare breed and rarely, if ever, found where the masses are instructed to go. This place is virtually void of individuality and I hate it.

"ID," says the doorman.

I silently pass him my driver's license.

He puts a stamp on my hand.

It's loud, very loud, but not due to blaring music, instead it's from the seeming inability of anyone in this place to use a normal speaking voice. I nearly pass by the bar without stopping for a drink, big mistake, who knows how long it will take to get table service in here.

Hand, elbow, shoulder slide between two bar patrons who glance up rudely, then quickly return to their drinks when they see the six foot two man with eyes that scream *'don't fucking look at me'* standing between them. I catch the bartender's attention and signal service with a wave of my hand. He approaches and I have to shout in order to be heard over the ambient noise. "Whiskey on the rocks, please."

"Any particular whiskey you want?" he asks.

"Whatever the house is," I reply.

"This is the house." He holds up an unfamiliar bottle. "It's shit," he says.

"Yeah, I'll take it."

"Alright, don't say I didn't warn you."

"Thanks."

"Twelve bucks."

I hand him a twenty. He gives me change. Then I add a dollar to his top jar.

Light seems to be dissipating the deeper into the bar I travel. Darkness is good. It will make any unintentional off putting faces I make less recognizable.

I've spotted them.

Here we go!

Sarah looks beautiful; it's amazing that she and her brother are related. Shrek with a tan would be a fairly accurate description of Rayan's physical appearance. Sarah promises that he and I will be besties because we both practice jiujitsu and are interested in marital arts in general, I guess we're about to find out if she's right.

"Hey," I say, as I approach their table trying to look excited and not too drunk or high.

Sarah half stands up from the edge of the booth and leans in for a kiss on the cheek. I bend down to meet her and signal with my body language that she need not stand. Before sliding into the booth my hand extends across the table to Rayan, who has not made any motion towards standing or delivering a greeting of his own.

Eventually, after an exceptionally long pause in which I stand like an idiot statue with an outreached arm, he reaches his hand for mine while staring off into the distance. His grip is overly strong. I tighten my own grip slightly, not to initiate some sort of hand strength pissing match, which I'm sure I would win, but just to make sure that my hand doesn't fold and crunch under the pressure of his insecurity. My arm pulling away signals the end of this uncomfortable and aggressive first interaction.

Sarah slides deeper into the booth and I sit next to her. Her brother, Rayan, sits awkwardly in the center of the booth, leaving the far end unoccupied and the three of us appearing to be some sort of trio literally attached at the hips, scrunched into one half of the available space. I slide to the far edge allowing for a bit of breathing room.

Sarah's eyes catch mine the moment we sit and I want to kiss her passionately, but I settle for a firm squeeze of her thigh under the table, out of sight from her brother's already agitated eyes.

Rayan looks at his watch, a watch whose sole purpose is to inflate the perception of its wearer in the eyes of the easily impressed flock that ooh and ahh at the sight of shiny glittering overpriced objects. "Only twenty minutes late." Are the first words out of his mouth.

What a weak ass bitch,' I think to myself. If I wasn't drunk, and thus fairly relaxed and care free, I would probably stand up and leave after these bizarre, uncomfortable opening moments. But instead of leaving I just say, "Oh, yeah, I thought it was just drinks, do we have somewhere to be after this?"

"No, no, it's fine," says Sarah, as she directs a threatening look in the direction of her brother, and then pats me on the arm and asks, "Oh, you already got a drink? I just ordered us another round and got one for you too. Oh well, now you'll have two."

Before I can think *'fucking-shit-God-damnit-let-me-order-my-own-fucking-drinks-I-only-wanted-one-fuck!'* the waitress appears at the table with a tray of two cocktails and a beer.

"Who had the Manny's?" she asks, politely, but with a slight touch of urgency, surely due to the frantic pace of work in the crowded bar.

Rayan raises a hand without looking at or acknowledging the waitress's presence in any humanistic way.

"For you?" she asks, looking at Rayan while removing the beer from the serving tray with her free hand.

"Yeah, babe who else," he says, his mouth spewing arrogance with each utterance.

Holy fuck, man, this guy is a douche bag. How can he be her brother? How can she tolerate him even though he is her brother? In the three short minutes that I have known this guy in the flesh he strikes me as an overwhelming tool bag; a steady stream of insecurity masked by manufactured machinations of masculinity that could only fool fools. Is Sarah a fool? Or is blood blinding her to the reality of him? Or am I drunk, high and judging this guy prematurely? I'm unsure about all of this so I opt to continuing observing and analyzing before making any serious judgments that could lead to unfortunate comments or regrettable actions.

The waitress hands him the beer and her face tells me that she is in complete agreement with my sentiments about this guy.

Painting a bogus smile on her face she twists her attention to Sarah and I. "And the Martini?"

Sarah elegantly lifts two hands towards the waitress to receive her cocktail. "That's for me, thank you."

"And you must have the bourbon and seven?"

"Indeed, thank you very much," I say, as she sets the drink down in front of me.

"Can I get you anything else?" she asks Sarah and I without giving a glance towards rude Rayan.

"No, thank you".

As the waitress turns and leaves us I feel the desire to stand and follow her further and further away from this table and the impending conversations that will undoubtedly be as uncomfortable as an adult circumcision. Anxiety strikes and it's magnified by several long moments of silence between the three of us. I don't know where to look. I glance at Rayan and see that he's staring into his beer looking rather pathetic.

I don't want to talk to Rayan, but I don't want to seem like I'm ignoring him either. I say nothing.

Finally, Sarah tries to break the tension by asking me. "So what did you do today?"

Jesus fuck, what do I say here? I have to lie, I must lie, I cannot tell the truth that I've been selling drugs all day trying to dig myself out of a tight spot between a violent narco connected football player and being jobless without any other options.

"Oh, nothing that interesting," I say, smiling, trying to appear normal; I lie straight to her face.

"So Rayan, how have you liked Seattle?" I ask in order to change topics and appear friendly and interested in our visitor.

"It's alright, I guess. Vancouver is better though, not so white." The added racial comment at the end is, I assume, a continued display of his distaste with my presence. In today's political climate, especially in this bar full of mindless progressive flunkies who regurgitate rehearsed talking points about race and society without ever having deeply considered their nature, let alone having lived anything that would provide some perspective, it seems that my best course of action is to bite my lip and respond as if I'm just an agreeable guy who follows the flock like all the rest.

"Ah yea, Vancouver is a great city, lots of diversity. I haven't spent too much time up there, but I always think I should make a point of going more often," I say, somewhat holding my breath just in order to get the disingenuous words out.

Clearly showing his disinterest in conversing with me, he
wholly ignores my last comment and directs his attention
to Sarah, "What time is my flight on Friday?"
She begins to answer him but all I hear is my mind
beginning to spin out of control. I realize that I'm basically
chugging my first drink, only a sip remains. I guess I'll
pound the second one and drive home before it has time to
hit me.
Gulp. Swap. Drink number one is now a mostly empty
glass, forgiving the remaining ice, and drink number two
inherits its position in the curve of my right hand. I lift it for
a sip and, damn, it's a lot stronger than the first one and
that is not good. I don't want to be drunk drunk, just
comfortably socially buzzed.
"You drank that so fast, slow down," says Sarah, in a
loving, caring sort of way.
"Thirsty," I respond, pointing my eyes upward and
shrugging my shoulders.
Rayan begins to drink his beer faster after realizing that he
was lagging behind. Between gulps he adds, "I hear you
think you're pretty good at fighting?"
"I wouldn't say I'm pretty good, I mean, compared to who,
ya know, that's all relative. But, yes I enjoying training."
"Too bad we can't roll. I'd tap you so easily, you're so
skinny that I'd be worried I'd break you," he says,
snickering and shaking his head over-dramatically as he
returns to gulping his beer like an out of place high school
freshman at his first party of the year.
My body straightens up a bit and I ask curiously, "Oh yeah,
well, why can't we roll? Come to the gym tomorrow. Don't
worry, I'm sure you won't break me."
Still refusing to look in my direction he adds, "I haven't
been able to train in over a year for this damn back injury.
If it weren't for that then I would for sure tap you out."
Only an idiot and a coward would sit across the table from
someone and confidently proclaim their fighting supremacy
only to immediately follow up with their chambered excuse
of an injury.
"Oh, what a bummer. Maybe next time," I say, flashing a
grin the size of the Grand Canyon while staring at him

between his averted eyes as I imagine bending Sarah over the table and pounding her while she screams *'Daddy harder! More, please'*.

The alcohol is saving me from being controlled by anger at this rude cocky douchebag that I would handily defeat in any battle of wits or will.

Unknowingly, Sarah comes to my defense by asking him, "I thought you did jiujitsu when you were in Vancouver?"

"That was light," he snaps at her defensively. "I mean I can do some things but anything more and I could have a serious problem, really. I can't really roll right now; I mean not really, not with this injury, it's an intense injury."

By now I'm struggling to contain the laughter that wants to erupt right into this fools face. Straining my posture in order to maintain composure, I say, "Come tomorrow, we'll go light."

"No, tomorrow I can't. I have an important call back to Egypt."

Hmm, a call back home at an unnamed hour is preventing you from training at another yet to be named hour. Should I bring this fact to the surface and question him about his schedule, further pressing that we train? *'Anytime, we can go anytime, you make your call and we can go after, or before, whenever you want, Mr. I'd tap you so easily'*. No, I'll let it go. Besides, the last thing I want is more time with this guy. I mean, before I met him I didn't have any interest in spending time with him, and now that I see what kind of person he is I am even less interested than before. I'm here simply because he's related to Her, she's the one, not him, and now that I see what he's like I couldn't be more reassured of my decision to keep my distance.

"Ah too bad," I say. "Well, next time. Or maybe if I come to Egypt someday."

As I mention a possible visit to her home country I see Sarah's eyes light up. I imagine she's picturing our trip there together, showing me her favorite places, telling me stories of her childhood.

"Wouldn't that be fabulous," she exclaims.

Her idiot bother chimes in to ruin the moment. "Ahh hah, that's funny. I don't think you'd like Egypt every much. No offense, but it's not really for soft, American boys like you."
"Hmm yeah, okay. I don't know, I've never been, maybe someday," I say, as casually as I can.
I wish this guy would just disappear.
I begin emptying drink number two down my throat and notice prickly glances being exchanged between Sarah and her brother. She seems to be telling him to shut up and stop being an asshole with her eyes.
The conversation mellows and we discuss food that Sarah misses from home and what she will miss most from Seattle when she inevitably, someday, hopefully no day soon, leaves the U.S., and me, and returns to Egypt. She has been gently rubbing my leg under the table as we trudge through this small talk and I'm becoming slightly aroused. I don't want to arrive at a full erection, requiring action to conceal it. Holding the top of her hand I slowly remove it from my inner thigh.
One medium sized gulp and my second drink is finished. I feel okay to drive, and I also feel that I've completed my duty by coming here, having not one but two drinks.
Mission accomplished. I'm prepared to make my exit.
I wait for a pause. The two of them are discussing something; I'm not really sure what, as my mind has briefly wondered.
"The flowers there are gorgeous. We should all three go to Pike Place in the morning," says Sarah, as I mentally rejoin the conversation.
"Actually I have a job interview in the morning," I nervously blurt out, another lie, fuck.
"Really? You didn't mention it," replies Sarah, with a touch of surprise in her voice.
"Just today I started calling places and applying. Anyway it's a thing with a friend of a friend. I probably won't even take it if they offer, but I feel like I need to do something to be productive."
"Oh, okay," she says. "I guess Rayan and I will go. It would have been nice to spend the day with you. I was really

hoping that since neither of us is really working right now we would be able to spend more time together."

"I know, I wish I could." Another lie. As long as Rayan is around, I surely won't be.

"Anyway, I've got to get going. I don't want to be hungover and sleep deprived for the interview," I say.

"You just got here," Sarah whines, in that sexy way that only she can.

"We'll see each other soon," I say, as I stand, making clear my decision to leave.

As I stand at the edge of the table she holds onto my wrist, drawing me back down closer to her. I lean in for an unassuming goodbye kiss, but at the last moment I open my mouth and bite into her lip. She squeezes my arm because she can't scream out or grab my quasi erect member firmly in her hand to force my teeth to loosen from her lip, like she normally would. I relent playfully, then retract briefly before moving back in for another kiss, this one momentary and obvious in its message, *'Goodbye, for real this time'*. I stand up straight, smiling because I can't help it; she just does that to me. Once again I extend my hand for Rayan's, he cedes and extends his in return, another overly aggressive handshake commences.

"It was nice meeting you," I say. I would have said something else had I enjoyed even one speck of his personality, but I didn't, so I said *nice* because it seems like the only word phony enough to match the moment.

"Same," he says, while simultaneously shifting his attention to his phone.

I turn once again towards Sarah and move in for one last kiss on the cheek while whispering into her ear, "I can't wait to be alone with you."

She's like a magnet that draws me into her no matter how hard I resist.

"Text me when you're home," she says loudly over the bar noise as I walk away.

I nod in recognition.

It's over. I did it. I met her brother. The one thing she has been asking for more than anything. It's over with and done. He leaves in a few days and I won't have to see him or think about meeting him ever again. A weight has been lifted off my chest. What a relief.

I feel relaxed and light and slightly drunk as I walk somewhat uncoordinatedly back to my car.

Driving after this many drinks is maybe not such a good idea. I'm not drunk, but not sober either.

I'll focus hard, drive slow and be sure to follow the traffic laws like my life depends on it.

Different scenarios are running through my head, different analyses of the recently ended events. Something like editing a movie is playing out in my mind, going back and trying new lines, new looks, new moods. I run through the night's conversations over and over again.

The drive goes well, didn't even see a cop despite traveling past many heavily populated areas, thanks Seattle Police Department for your shitty job of policing the city streets. I exit onto Lake City Way and feel like I've dissected every word of the conversation, every telling eye contact, each shift of body language. I believe I have a full understanding of the night's happenings securely stored in my memory, ready to be drawn on whenever needed.

I pull into the parking lot, the young hooligans from earlier are nowhere to be seen. I park and head up to my apartment, ready to turn in for the night and enjoy a well-deserved rest. Exiting the elevator and walking the fifteen or so yards on the outdoor walkway to my apartment door, I notice something out of place. What's that on my door? Did the land lord leave another note about rescheduling with the painters? I walk closer, unconcerned and feeling confident in how I stepped up and did the right thing tonight. I think I handled myself pretty well in the face of an unwanted, uncomfortable interaction with a world class dickhead. What's this fucking note on my door that won't leave my attention alone? Finally I'm close enough to make it out. My eyes focus to read the scribbled letters on the front of the paper. 'whit bitch.' Hmm? What is this about? My intoxicated mind is searching through the cloud of weed smoke and puddles of whiskey for some point of reference that will make this note make sense. Then it hits me. Holy fuck, no! No! NO! NONONONO! Please tell me this is not

what I think it is. Fred and Cam are fucking with me, right? My heart races as my hands shoot up to snatch the note from the front of the door. I can barely bring myself to examine it. I want to throw it over the balcony, make it disappear, ignore it. However, the note itself is insignificant, I can destroy it a thousand times, but its meaning will not change. My body is so tense that the paper nearly rips in two while I'm holding it. I begin to unfold it. Inside on a lineless white sheet of paper it reads, *'next 4 pounds under your bed have the $ sunday.'* NoNoNo! I swear to God this better be a joke. Fred and Cam think it's funny. You know what, Fred and Cam probably set this whole thing up. Like all of it. The whole meeting with Juan and Tommy, the gay shit, the threats, they're fucking with me. There will be no weed under my bed. I'll call Fred and he'll be uncontrollably laughing, knowing that he got me good. I need to go inside and prove to myself that there is no weed under the bed. Open the door. Go in. What if Juan is in there? Fuck man, I don't know what to do. I check the door handle, it's unlocked. Damn, someone is inside, or at least was inside and didn't lock the door when they left. This is real. I release the door handle and remain outside breathing hard, wondering who was, or is, inside my apartment. I look into my bedroom window that borders the open-air walkway. The lights are off, I knock on the glass. No response. I knock on the door. No response. I crack the door open just an inch and peek inside, "Hello...?" I say into the void like a stranger in my own home. No response.
I push the door fully open. The kitchen light is on, but the hallway, bedroom, bathroom and living room remain in semi-darkness.
"Hello, is anyone here?"
It's silent. I flip the hallway light on. The apartment seems undisturbed despite my sense that something is very, very off. I stand in the entry way, the bathroom on my right, bedroom on my left. I peer into the bathroom first, no one and no signs that anyone was here. I take a step across the hall and flip the bedroom light on as I step in, no one. I open the closet, no one. I can't decide what to do first,

check under the bed for the supposedly left behind weed or check the living room for intruders. Safety first, the weed, if it is there, isn't going to go anywhere. I decide to clear the rest of the apartment. I step back into the entryway to make my way to the living room. I flip the light on, no one. I walk to the deck, no one. I check the dishwasher; it's full with the five pounds of weed that I put there earlier. Well, at least I didn't get robbed. I walk back into the bedroom and get down on my hands and knees. I take a breath and hope to God that there isn't anything under the bed. I lower my head down to the ground. I look, and there it is. From my position it appears to be a round shadow in the limited space and light between the bed and floor. I reach for it and pull it towards me, but before I have a chance to investigate it with my eyes the smell hits me like a knockout blow. I continue pulling the bag from under the bed while inhaling what is now a stench so powerful that I wonder if I'll get high just from the fumes. It's one large tightly wrapped ball of marijuana.

Well, there's no doubt any longer; a Mexican drug cartel has broken into my home and left me with drugs to sell for them under the threat of violence. I am completely fucked and have no idea what to do. I have no options. Sitting on the floor I rip my shoes from my feet and begin stripping my clothes off in a frenzied craze. I'm naked and panicking on the bedroom floor. I grab my phone and hammer the buttons with my thumbs to initiate a call to Fred. The line rings, rings again, I let out an animalistic scream as I hang up and slam the phone to the ground. It wouldn't matter if he had answered, I can't hold a conversation in this state; I'll sound like a raving lunatic not making any sense. Once again I grab my phone with rage and punch into the screen the buttons to contact Fred, this time via text message.

"They broke into my apt. and left more of it in here. I am fucked. Call me as soon as you can." Send.

Using my arms, as if my lower body had been crippled and left unable to assist, I pull my naked body off the floor and into bed. I lay alone, panicking, not knowing what to do. My nose is clogged with fear and mucus, forcing me to breathe heavily in and out of my mouth. A sort of hyperventilation is taking place and it's not helpful. Despite the ever deepening hole I find myself in, I feel no desire to end my life, in fact, I feel alive. Even though I'm totally fucked and out of options I do not feel depressed and defeated. I don't feel like I did a week ago on the night before I got fired and my life took a turn for the worst and began spinning out of control. I feel like I need to wake up early and make shit happen. I need to wipe these tears from my face and put my big boy pants on. I have problems that need to be fixed, real problems, not problems like how many shoes can I sell next pay period or do I really have to go out for drinks with my girlfriend's brother. Trouble and I have once again found each other. Hello old friend, I've missed you.

Chapter. 16 A Call for Help

Raindrops are falling, and according to the morning newscast they will continue to fall for the next ten days without rest. Ah Seattle, you wet sloppy wench. I make a fresh pot of coffee, clean the dirty dishes in the sink and begin to run through possible scenarios in my head. I don't need *a* plan I need *plans*, for every conceivable contingency. As my mind draws escape routes, rehearses dramatic conversations, and tries to predict the motivations and actions of others, I hear my phone ring from the bedroom. I leap to my feet and run like a possessed feen for the vibrating device. It's Fred. Thank God.

"Fred, where are you at?" My words are charged with urgency and sound sharp, almost accusatory.

"I'm in Cle Elum. Left Pullman last night then stopped here for a beer, ended up having ten and slept in the car," he says, his voice sounding like two pieces of sandpaper rubbing together, barely audible.

"Okay, great. Well, you saw my message, yeah? I'm fucked dude, totally fucked. Did he say anything to you? Did you pay him?"

"Alright, all I know is that I put the money in his locker when I was leaving. Cam said he's trippin' and rambling on about how he better keep his mouth shut n' shit like that, but Cam doesn't even know what he's talking about. He's trippin' dude, for real trippin'. You might want to get out of that apartment, I'm just sayin...'"

"Fuck man! Fuck! Come right fucking here when you get to the city or I can meet you at your place, but we've got to figure out what to do. Should you try to call him?"

"Yeah, let me hit him up. I'll call you back."

"Okay. Call me as soon as you talk to him."

"Alright, bro."

I hang up and am immediately informed that I have a text message.

"Good luck with your interview this morning;)." From Sarah.

"Thanks." Send.

She deserves more than a '*Thanks*' for her kind gesture, but I can't afford to burn even an ounce of mental energy on anything other than saving my own ass right now.

I want, no I *need,* to leave this apartment and not just for a few hours or even a few days, but for good. Fred says he thinks I should leave and that's not a good sign. If he wasn't worried that some real bad shit might go down he wouldn't have say that; he'd have said, *'Hey, man, don't be a bitch.'*

The month just started, but I've already paid the rent so if I need to I can pack my stuff right now and leave without notice. I'll dump my furniture at Fred's or give it to Goodwill and stay in a motel somewhere. I'll rent a U-Haul and move a few states over. Montana, Idaho, these seem like nice places. Maybe I'll go to Nevada or Arizona, warm and no winter, and not so much rain and drab grey skies. I should wait until Fred gets me more information before I make any snap decisions. But I can't just sit here. What can I do now? I can sell the remaining five pounds. Okay, I'll go to see Rob at the weed shop. It's early but he should be there.

In the kitchen I load the five pounds from the dishwasher into a large backpack and head for the door. The clouded sky makes the morning light weak and the rain dampens the usual sounds of the quiet but active neighborhood. My mood is brought down by the dim scenery as I play through the forthcoming sale in my mind. I step cautiously halfway out my front door before giving a glance around the corners, the coast is clear. I walk down the outdoor corridor towards the elevator. Down the shaft, out the lobby, and into the parking lot. I begin to run for my car to avoid the drops of rain.

As I approach my parking spot I'm forced to slow my pace and turn my body sideways in order to fit between my car and a black Honda Accord that is parked annoyingly close to my driver's side door. I twist to the side and squeeze between the two vehicles. Suddenly, in the moment before I grasp the handle and begin to climb in, the two passenger side doors of the Honda are violently flung open and I'm pinned between the cars, watching two eerily familiar figures emerge.

Maybe the events of the past day, past week, have emptied my adrenaline reserves, maybe it's too early, but whatever the reason is I don't feel anything, no fear, no panic, no flight or fight. I press my back against the door behind me and stare at the two faces that slipped out from the car beside mine and are now glaring at me as if they're actors in a bank robbery scene waiting impatiently for the teller to deliver his line. "Yes, can I help you?" I finally say, after several tension filled seconds of silence.

"You got the package, yeah? Is this it in your bag?" the oddly familiar stranger says, aggressively, as he reaches for my backpack, trying to get a look inside. I pull it back just before his hand has a chance to take control of it.

"No, I don't know what you're talking about. These are my books. Who are you and what do you want?" I ask. While saying this it dawns on me that these are the same hooligans who were hanging around the parking lot last night when I left to go meet Sarah. Are they with Juan? Are these the same fucks that broke into my apartment and left the bundle of dope under the bed? They must be, obviously.

The one doing the talking continues and leaves no doubt as to their identity. "Ay bitch, you know who da fuck we is. Don't play dumb," he mutters, leaning in and putting his face disturbingly close to my own. He looks like he could be as young as seventeen, he looks like a teenager, but he has a look in his eyes that could only belong to a hardened psychopath.

"Are you guys looking for Xavier?" I ask them, as innocently as a concerned citizen returning a missing wallet.

"Yeah and who da fuck are you? This your car, or nah?" he asks, sounding both angry and confused.

"I'm Brad," I say. "I'm house sitting for Xavier and I need to borrow his car to return these books to the library. He told me I could use it."

"Da fuck?" he mumbles, looking right, towards his accomplice, searching for some guidance before leaning even closer into me, shifting his eyes fiercely onto the bridge of my nose like he's examining the microscopic details of face, searching for the truth or a lie somewhere between my eyes. I stare back into him; this unexpected action on my part causes him to break eye contact almost immediately. He shifts his glare and begins looking down as if he's peeing into a urinal that isn't there. I have no idea what this is about so I instinctually follow the path of his eyes with my own, and it quickly becomes clear what it is that he's staring at so intently. He's holding a knife at waist level, pointed towards my abdomen, maybe all of an inch away from scratching the first layer of my clothing, not that some soft cloth fabric would provide any real protection against such a weapon were its possessor determined to use it for more than fear tactics. A shiver of existential fear tingles through me from the tip of my brainstem down to the clenched point of my asshole that suddenly feels autonomous from the rest of my body.

"We'll be back to see your friend," he says, while I gaze mystified downwards at the threat aimed squarely at my inner organs.

I can't take my eyes off the knife. Instinct suddenly takes over, the last remaining drops of adrenaline in my body pulse out, hitting my system and causing my hands to reach for his left wrist, just above the knife. With all my strength I violently thrust his arm across his body, causing him to go crashing into his silent friend- caught off guard by the unanticipated commotion. There is barely any space between us and our bodies bump and press against each other as he goes falling; thrown to the side he stumbles to the wet ground before steadying himself and coming to a stop on all fours at the feet of his companion. A moment is all I have to escape. My feet move me out from between the cars without a thought. I'm free and my body breaks into a full sprint across the parking lot and out into the street.

I run across 35th, lucky that there was no cross traffic as I didn't even bother to stop and look. Lucky that a drug dealing, do-nothing loser, is spared while somewhere on earth an unlucky child is punished terminally for not looking both ways before stepping off the curb.

I make it to the other side of the street and duck into a small coffee shop located in the strip mall that I make a habit of watching from my kitchen window, but have rarely visited. I'm maybe a hundred and fifty yards from the scene of the crime, the distance seems insufficient to provide any meaningful barrier of protection, but there's nowhere else to go. As far as I can tell no one gave chase, but the feeling of being pursued is still palpable. Predator and prey.

They won't come in here looking for me, will they? I order a coffee that I have no intention of drinking and sit two tables back from the window, hoping to go undetected from outside viewers while still maintaining a clear view of the street and café entrance. I'm staring fiercely out the window, trying to monitor the cars coming from the direction of my building. There! There it is! They're leaving. I strain my eyes and try to see how many occupants are in the car. Could they have left one to wait for me inside the apartment? As soon as I see the car turn onto and continue down 35th and out of sight I leave my coffee on the table, take out my keys and begin to jog across the street, back to the apartment building. As soon as my car comes into sight I break into a run, desperately pressing the unlock button just before I reach the door. I get in, throw my bag into the passenger seat and turn the ignition. I drive out of the parking lot as if I'm trying to outrun a fire. Pulling out onto the street, I tilt my head to try and get a look up at my apartment door. It appears to be closed and normal, but who knows, I only see it in passing and at a bad angle. While I drive the adrenaline begins to dissipate and my mind finally starts to process what just happened.

Inside a steel and glass cage, alone, and moving at 35 MPH I feel untouchable, but I know that this feeling is fleeting as I can't just keep driving forever, eventually I'll have to stop, get out, and expose myself to world again.

Fred's Seattle apartment is coming up on my right. I realize that I've been driving without even knowing it. I have no idea what route I took to arrive here, and there's really no reason for me to be at Fred's, seeing that he won't arrive for at least another hour. My mind has been racing and my normal decision making processes have been hijacked and forced into autopilot. Without consciously deciding to, my hand has turned off the engine and removed the key from the ignition. My head is resting lazily against the seat and my overall posture resembles that of a seated suicide victim whose skull was blown back by the force of a self-inflicted blast to the forehead. I am lost and alone and without a home.

Time has ceased to have any meaning and when I feel the sweet relief of my vibrating cellphone I have no idea how long I've been sitting here, dazed and confused. At this point, I'll welcome anything that will steal my attention away from the hamster wheel of doom and negativity spinning at warp speed in my head. It's Fred. I pray to fucking God that he has some good news.

I answer and immediately spring into action, "Fred! Did you talk to him?"

"Yeah, I talked to him."

"And?! What did he say?"

"He thinks he's some... I told him that I left the money you owed for what you agreed to pick up and that that was gonna be the last one. That he was freakin' you out and you were gonna be gone after this."

"Yeah, and?"

"And he said I owe him for what he left at your apartment and that if we don't sell the rest of his new shipment he's gonna send his boys for us."

"I can't do that, dude! I'm not going deeper into this hole. I'm leaving! I'm in front of your house right now. I can give you the stuff they left under my bed and then I'm out. For real, I'm packing my shit and leaving. He sent goons to my apartment and they pulled a knife on me, this happened like ten minutes ago when I was getting in my car. I don't want to deal with shit like this, man. I just ran the fuck out. Fred, I am not doing this anymore! Where are you at?! Almost back?!"

"He sent goons to your house? Wait, wait, man, hold up, what happened? They came back again after last night?"

asks Fred, trying to keep track of the constantly changing details.

"When will you be back? I'll explain everything then," I say. "Give me an hour."

"Alright, where can we meet? It shouldn't be at either of our places."

"Meet me at the Third Place Books Café in an hour," Fred says.

"Okay, man, I'll see you there."

Chapter. 17 Five Pounds to Freedom

I throw the phone onto the floor as soon as the conversation ends; following the fitful phone toss, I sit idly in front of Fred's empty apartment contemplating my next move. A nervous twitch forces my right eye to spaz out every minute or two, but I ignore the part of me suggesting I do something to subdue these involuntary muscle movements as I feel so helpless and feeble over my entire situation that even trying to control my own body seems pointless at this point.

Sitting idle, gripped by fear, I know I just need to take step one and start digging myself out of this hole. Currently, I have five pounds that I actually did purchase, of my own free will, and I need to sell them before I can decide what to do next. I don't know what to do with the other stuff that was forced on me, but I'll deal with that later. Okay, just take a deep breath and settle down, I've got an hour until meeting with Fred. Let's just go to Lake City and pray that I can sell the rest of what I have in the car to Rob at the weed store. It's a short drive from Fred's apartment on the edge of the U-district to the pot shop. I crawl to the back of the car and yank the bags of weed up to the front so that they can sit safely beside me. I'm so out of patience and fucks to give that I just want to march in there, throw the bags of weed on the table, and say, *'gimme eight grand and it's yours.'*

Despite my lack of patience and grandiose fantasies of a dramatic be-all-end-all sale, I know that I can't do it that way. What I can do is just stay calm and walk in there like everything is alright, perfectly normal. If he sees I'm freaking out, he's bound to freak out too, and then he surely won't buy any of it. Okay, okay, stop thinking, leave the weed in the car and go in there and sell.

Since departing Fred's I've changed my mind at least ten times about what the lowest possible price I could let these last five pounds go for, and as of now know, I've decided that eight thousand is the magic number.

I open the car door and run for the entrance of the pot shop, under the cold harsh rain. I arrive with muddy shoes from the unkempt lawn that customers are forced to walk through because no one has bothered to install a footpath. I do my best to kick off the mud, but enter without really giving a damn about tracking in a little dirt; we've got much bigger fish to fry. Inside, the waiting area is empty. I press the button beside the window.

"ID and medical card," says the voice from behind the door, apparently unaware of who is on the other side.

I hand him the requested items.

"I was hoping you'd be back soon," he says, as he opens the door.

"Hey, man, how's it going?" I say.

"Fine. How are you doing? You look a little shook up. Long night?"

"Oh, yeah, something like that," I reply, just now realizing that my eyes are probably bloodshot red and my general presentation rather disheveled.

"I sold the pound to a customer like that," he says, snapping his fingers to demonstrate.

Rob is in an oddly jolly mood, in a way I've never seen before.

"How much more of that can you get, my friend?" he asks. I'm suddenly convinced his jolly good mood is entirely phony by the disingenuous smile that engulfs his face. He looks like an ice-cream truck driving pervert trying to talk some kid into coming along for a ride.

This shift in personality and authenticity is difficult to interpret. Why is he feeding me this act? Is it an act or I am misreading this? At this point, all my internal warning lights are flashing red, but it doesn't really matter anymore. I came here with one purpose, and no matter what kind of shady shit this Rob guy has up his sleeve I won't let it derail my plan.

"Hey, man," I say, rather curtly, wanting to assert a serious, no nonsense tone. "Here is what's going on. He has five more pounds and he has to sell them ASAP, 'cause he's leaving town. He said if you can offer eight K you can have the remaining five." And I open my hands as if to say, *'Here it is, take it or leave it.'*

"Really? Wow, kid, that's a good deal. You sure he has five more pounds? This isn't some kind of set up, is it? This all seems a little too good to be true."

"Listen, man, I'm not with the police, obviously, and I live right down the block. I just want to help out a friend and get rid of this stuff for him. You want it? 8K and the five pounds that are just like the one you bought the other day, identical really, are yours."

"If you can get five more, identical to the last one, then yea, I'll take it."

"Great, can you get the money today?"

"Kid, whenever the fuck you get the weed I'll have the money," he says, trying to match my rude seriousness; having completely dropped the smiley best friend act.

"Like right now?" I ask.

"You have it with you?"

"Yeah, get the money and I'll bring it today."

"I already told you, kid, I have the money. How many fucking times are we gonna go over this?"

"Right now? Should I get it and bring it in, right now?" I ask, wanting to confirm that he does in fact have the cash on him, right now, no bank runs, no waiting for someone to bring it, but now.

"Go," he says, gesturing me towards the door like a bug being wafted out an open window.

Okay, this guy is an old asshole, great, now I know. But, it looks like this old asshole is about to do exactly what I want him to do and that is great fucking news.

I exit the waiting room door and do the Seattle-rain-jog to the car. The bags are too big to stuff under my shirt so I just hug them in front of me, hunched over the top to give as much cover as I can, and shuffle from the car to back inside the shack. I take refuge from the rain in the waiting room and notice the door to the back room has been shut. I place one of the bags on the ground and try the handle, locked. What a prick. I forgo the buzzer and give a knock on the door.

"Yeah, yeah, hold your horses," he says, from behind the flimsy wall.

The door opens and I hoist the bag from the floor and enter.

"Here it is," I say, as I place the individually packed pounds onto the countertop.

"Okay, here's the money, go ahead and count it." He hands over a stack of hundreds then says, "I'm going into the back to weigh this. Gimme a minute."

I begin to count the money. One two three four five six seven eight nine ten, that's one pile. I continue this process until there are eight even stacks of ten hundred dollar bills lined in front of me. The sight of this money fills me with positivity, the sense of powerlessness fades as the rush of possibilities built on greenbacks begins to fill me with new hope. Now that their count is confirmed, I pile each stack on top of the next and bend the bills over before shoving the oversized wad of cash into my pocket. Standing here, waiting for Rob to return, I nervously check my phone, then check it again thirty seconds later, then again, and then Rob returns, empty handed.

"It looks good to me," he says.

"Okay cool, the money looks good, too," I say, sticking out my hand to confirm a deal well done with a gentlemanly shake.

"The fuck is that?" he says, looking down at my outstretched gesture of goodwill. "I don't know where you stole this shit from or what you're up to, but I know a piece of shit when I see one. You shouldn't come back around here, understand?"

"What?" I say, as I retract my hand feeling wounded, like we often do after someone intentionally tries to degrade us.

"Yeah, kid, get the fuck out. Thanks for the weed, no one sells stuff that cheap. Now get lost."

My gaze remains on him only for a second before bowing my head and making haste for the door. I run through the rain and nearly slip on the wet grass before reaching the sidewalk. Put a fucking walkway in would ya, you lazy fuck.

In my car I recount the money and try to figure out what that guy's problem is. I guess he thinks I'm a thief who stole this stuff. Who knows, but, man, he was a fuckin' jerkoff just now.

I look at the phone once again and see that no one has contacted me and there are still thirty minutes before my scheduled meeting with Fred, when we'll scheme and plot and try to stop the world from coming to an end, at least for us.

I might as well just head there now and wait for him. They have good coffee and I can wonder through the book aisles of the store until he arrives.

The idea of stopping at the bank and depositing a portion of the cash crosses my mind, but, nah, fuck it, I'll do it later.

I park in the lot at Third Place Books and walk inside. The bookstore is in front and the restaurant/café is in the back. This place has special spot in my memory. Years ago, Fred and I were at a party and an unknown drunk girl had left her purse open and unattended while partially passed out on the floor. Fred and I were drinking on a bench or couch or whatever it was when I spotted the open bag. I asked Fred whose it was and this prompted him to give it a closer look. He picked up the purse and gave a quick shuffle with his fingers, rummaging around its contents. Spotting, amongst many other, more valuable, items, a Third Place Books gift card, he promptly lifted it from the purse, inspected it to confirm its identify and then tucked it into his breast pocket.

'Really?' I asked, believing that this was rather unjustified, unfair and unbecoming. 'Hey,' he told me. 'I've got a thirst for knowledge that only Third Place Books can quench.' I'll never forget that line, 'I have a thirst for knowledge that only Third Place Books can quench.' After he said this I burst into laughter and suddenly it seemed totally fine what he was doing. As if the immorality of it was washed away with a few poetic, comical words that made him appear the desperate beggar only making off with necessary bread and water for his survival. I imagine this is how many revolutionaries or cult leaders go about justifying their uncouth actions. They wax poetic and cast themselves as the oppressed, taking action to liberate their people from unfortunate circumstances, all the while reassuring followers that one must crack a few eggs to make an omelet, or something like that. But anyway, yeah, this place shares some history with Fred and me so it's only fitting that we should meet here during the low point in each of our respective lives. It dawns on me in this moment that Fred may very well be more fucked than I am. I mean, if Juan is threatening him in the same manner as me *and* he just lost his football and college career down the drain all in a day, well, then, man, I guess I should just feel lucky that I'm not him.

Walking through the rows of books is unavoidable in order to arrive at the café, so I figure I'll take my time, browse a little and maybe find something interesting to read. I stop to examine a book on mediation and the power of the mind, Waking Up by Sam Harris. It seems interesting enough, and I could probably use some strategies related to calming the mind, so I decide to buy it and bring it with me to a table in the back corner of the café. To my great surprise Fred is already sitting there, at the exact table I would have chosen. He hears my footsteps approaching and twists in his chair to get a look behind him and see who it is. Despite his black skin his face looks pale; his eyes are wide but somehow droopy at the same time. He doesn't look like his normal self, he looks like he's sleep deprived, or like he's just seen a ghost, or maybe like he drank ten beers and slept in his car last night. He doesn't look well at all.

Chapter. 18 Third Place Books

"X, man," he says, letting his head slump and shake slowly from side to side. "This isn't good."
"Yeah, no fucking shit this isn't good," I say, as I sit down. "What did he say to you?"
Fred takes a deep breath before answering. "He's saying that if we don't ..."
And just then an attractive bubbly blonde appears at the table and interrupts our barely off the ground conversation.
"Hi! Can I get you two started with any beverages or are you ready to go ahead and place a food order."
"I'll just take a coffee for now. Black. Thanks," I say.
"And for you?" she says, turning to Fred.
"I'll take a water and an orange juice. Five eggs scrambled hard. Whole wheat toast. The oatmeal. And the corned beef hash."
"Wow, hungry I see."
"I'll help him out with it," I add.
"Okie-dokie, I'll be right back with your drinks and the food should be out shortly," she says, before turning away and giving us back the necessary seclusion that allows a return to our feverish discussion.
Fred picks up where he left off.
"He says he's going to make us sell the next truck load whether we want to or not." His voice, although tense, is droning and sounds wounded. If I've ever seen Fred look so wholly crushed I can't remember when it was.
"Yeah, that's pretty much what he said to me in Pullman," I reply. "I can't go back to my apartment. He had some group of thugs wait by my fucking car and pull a knife on me. We have to leave. Like really leave, out of Seattle." My creaking, stressed voice gives me notice that I likely don't appear much better than Fred at this moment. We both must be coming off like junkies, desperately debating where to get a much needed fix like our lives depend on it. As kids, Fred and I had made plans to ditch town at least half a dozen times. Shit would hit the fan and inevitably

one of us would say, *'Hey man, let's just pack a bag and get the fuck out of here.'* Then, the less desperate of us would talk the other one out of it. Today there is no 'less desperate', we both are in dire need of a serious change in scenery. Maybe our childhood fantasy will finally come to fruition.

"We can't leave, X. Where would we go anyway? Why can't we just sell this one..." I cut him off before he can finish.

"Ain't no fucking way I'm going to stick around, Fredrick! I am not selling any more of this shit. Not a fucking chance. Not one fucking ounce," I say, now intentionally shushing my voice even though the waitress is out of earshot and the rest of the café sits empty.

Fred stares at me without words. He doesn't look like he's going to cry, but I wouldn't be surprised if he passed out this very instant.

I can't take the silence and I can't leave any room for misinterpretation. "Take the four pounds that he left under my bed and do whatever the fuck you want with them. I'm leaving, you can deal with Juan or whatever the fuck his name is, but I'm not sticking around to see what happens."

"I'll take the four pounds!" croaks Fred, over eagerly.

"Okay, but make sure you tell him that *you* have it! I don't want him to have any more reason to think about me, let him be your problem, he's your fucking friend, isn't he?" I say, now feeling my blood beginning to warm.

"I know I fucked up by getting you involved in this, but let's not make a rushed decision."

"The only decision left to make is where to buy a fuckin' plane ticket to, man," I say, sensing that he's trying to turn this conversation into *'Let's just sell a little more and then get out'*.

"So what, you're just going to move and never look back? Get real, Xavier."

"Yes! That's exactly what I'm going to do. I have no job, and now that the homeboys found it, I have to leave my apartment. What fuckin' reason do I have to stay?" I respond, my voice screeching with stress, the volume once again rising to a near shout.

"What about that girl Sarah you've been seeing? What's she gonna say?"

With this my heart drops out of my chest and comes to rest on the café floor.

Why did he have to go there? I was angry, pissed off, but thinking clearly about what has to be done and doing a pretty good job of working out a way to save my own ass while maintaining a least a sliver of emotional control. Now I'm biting my lip and trying not to burst into tears at the table. It wouldn't be the first time I've spontaneously erupted into crying hysterics in front of Fred, but the experience of breaking down and weeping in public is an uncomfortable one that I'd rather avoid.

"I'm sure she'll be thrilled," I say, sarcastically, the words barely making it out past the frog in my throat. "I'd be doing her a fucking favor! Why would she want to be with a fucking loser like me anyway!" I shout, with a quivering lip and dampening eyes. I snatch my phone, wallet and keys from the table, stand up and march for the door.

I know that Fred understands my anger is directed inward and not a reflection of my feelings about him, but I still feel doubly shitty now for having exploded like that. Instant regret slaps me in the face as I reach the bookstore door. I nearly stop and turn around to return to the table. That would be the wise, rational thing to do in this moment, what someone with a shred of emotional control and stability would do, but I can't. I feel too far gone, too embarrassed, too upset; the right thing, the wise thing, the logical thing is the only thing I cannot do. All I can hope for now is to curl into a shell and emerge with a new perspective and not too much self-inflicted damage, or damage inflicted on others due to my selfish, compulsive, shortsighted behavior.

Chapter. 19 Cocaine Confidence

Nihilism seems an appropriate word to describe my current cloud. I decide to return to my apartment to pack my things. The idea of bringing a crew of people with me to protect against the return of the homeboys in the Honda seems unnecessary; I've accepted my fate as a loser beyond measure and begin to re-welcome thoughts of my own demise. If they're waiting for me I'll just walk up and say, *'Shoot me in the fuckin' head why don't ya? You'd be doing me a fuckin' favor.'*

I pull into the parking lot and survey the area for any potential signs that they've returned, but everything looks normal.

After about three hours of lugging garbage bags full of clothes and other items from the apartment, my car is filled to the brim. I've had to leave several things behind because I'm unwilling to make two trips. I head to the Value Village on Lake City Way and drop off a load of shit that I don't expect I'll be needing any longer.

It's mid-afternoon and hunger is starting to overpower the caffeine. I head to Dick's drive-in and place a relatively reasonable order, considering my normal eating habits. Two deluxe burgers, one fry, one vanilla shake, two ketchup, and two tartar. Oh, and a cup of water. Fred had called about an hour ago and now seems like a good time to ring him back.

"Hey, X," Fred says, rather solemnly when he answers.

"FMP," I respond, with a total lack of emotion. Neither of us laugh, but we both understand that my statement is a half-apology for storming out of the café earlier.

"You're right, dude, we gotta get the fuck out of town. Four guys were waiting for me when I went back to the house," he says, after a brief pause in which neither of us wanted to take the lead.

"Were they like nineteen or twenty and in a Honda Accord?"

"Yes, dude, same ones," he replies matter-of-factly.

"Well, fuck, where are we gonna go?"

"Shit, I might just head to Cali and stay with my aunt Valerie for a while."

Aunt Valerie is a savage woman who writes porno scripts in the LA valley and comes to visit Fred's family every Summer, bearing gifts of whiskey, vodka, weed and porn for Fred, and by proxy, me, ever since we were the ripe old age of thirteen.

"That sounds like a good plan," I say, but what I want to say is, *'Hey, what about me? Can I go to Aunt Valerie's too?'*

"What about you?" Fred asks, as if reading my mind.

"I have no idea. I'm in my car right now and it's filled with all my shit. I left a note for the land lord that I'm out. I'm not going back. Where are you at now?"

"I'm at the house, come through."

"What makes you think those guys aren't coming back?" I ask.

"Who the fuck knows, but I doubt it, come through. Don't be a bitch."

"Yeah, okay, I'll be over there in about fifteen."

I make my way to Fred's U-district apartment and park in front. I realize that I've packed the four pounds that the homeboys forced on me beneath all the shit that fills my car to the point of having shirts and pillows flap out the window as I drive. I was going to bring them in and officially pass them to Fred, washing my hands of this whole damn thing, but I guess they'll just have to remain trapped under all my junk for the time being.

I walk to the front door and twist the knob, to my surprise, it's locked. I've never known Fred to lock any door, for any reason, at any time. The man shits with the bathroom door wide open while engaging in conversation with whoever happens to be near. I knock and hear from the other side, "Who is it?"

"It's me, Xavier."

Click, clack, the lock is undone and the door swings open.

"Locking the door and asking who it is, I see. Who's the pussy ass bitch now?" I ask, trying to lighten the mood.

Fred is in deep need of sleep, his eyes are starting to look cartoonish and his skin appears to have a sheen of cold sweat painted over it.

"I can't go to Cali, it's not far enough," he says, looking at me intently with a strangely erratic stare.

"These guys really have you that freaked out?" I ask. "I mean I'm spooked too, but what would be far enough? What are you thinking?"

My question launches Fred into a lengthy response spoken with urgency. "Out of the country! I'm thinking Asia, somewhere cheap where we can go for a while and not be seen or heard from back here. Somewhere Juan isn't gonna have any cousins or way of getting to us. We've got to leave the country and not for a week, but for a month, maybe a year, I don' know. Where do you want to go? Asia? Does Asia seem cool with you?"

He's talking a million miles an hour and it suddenly begins to dawn on me that...

And as the clues continue to present themselves the reality of Fred's hyperactive state comes to the surface as he reaches into his front shirt pocket to produce a small bag containing white powder.

"Do you want some?" he asks.

"Yeah, sure, why not," I say, although I doubt that I will actually partake.

He throws the tiny bag towards me, it lands on my lap. I opt to let it sit there, keeping it from Fred for the time being and preserving a somewhat sober head space while we work through this potentially life altering decision.

"Asia?" I ask. "Like where in Asia?"

"I don't know, X. Thailand, India, they say you can live in these places for five hundred bucks a month, live like a king, X."

"Okay, but who are *they* who are saying this? Do you know anything more or is this just the cocaine talking?"

"I did some research and we can go to Asia or South America, and live for a year, X. Juan will be gone by then, I can feel it," he says, his words bouncing like they're coming from a preacher reaching peak prophet status, bellowing to an eager congregation.

As calmly as I can, I say, "Okay, so when would we leave? And what are we going to do about those last four pounds? I say we drop them off at Juan's house when he's not there."

Fred's lip is involuntarily twitching and his eyes are so wide that he would make the perfect extra for a movie scene in a mental hospital.

"No! We can't do that. He'll kill us if he sees us. Besides, he doesn't give a shit about those four pounds, and we're gonna need the money."

"Why do you think he'd kill us if he saw us?" I ask, with a renewed round of nervousness smashing into me.

"That's what he said. After his boys were waiting for me here I called him and you know a lot of, *'Fuck you. No fuck you. No fuck you.'* And by the end of it all he said was, *'It's death on sight.'* That we're disrespecting him in the eyes of his crew because he can't keep up his sell rate without us, he's desperate, dude. He's gonna come looking for us. Toss me back the baggy if you don't want any."

I throw him back the bag and watch as he inserts the end of his car key into the oval opening, removing it with a peanut size pile of powder on the tip, then up and into the nose. He snorts, snorts again, swallows, then repeats this process two more times in short succession.

"Okay, well I just sold the last of the six pounds I actually bought and I can't go back to the dickhead on Lake City, so I don't know. I guess I could check with Adam, but he didn't seem that into it. Can you move part through your connections or is it all on me again?" I say, somewhat accusingly.

"Don't worry about it, X," Fred says, now approaching a state of frenzied insanity that if I had not known him my whole life would surely send me running from the room. "I'll sell it. Just let me get 'em and I'll sell it all."

"Okay, they're in the car, but who are you going to sell them to?"

"Man, I'll find a way, Xavier, just let me have 'em. I need to get some cash before getting on the plane."

"What plane? We don't even know when or where we're going. But okay, you can have them. I don't even want

them, but who the fuck are you gonna sell them to?
They're pounds, not grams, Fredrick."
"X, it doesn't fuckin' matter who I sell them to. I'll take
them to the Ave if I need to and get them off there. Give
me an hour and I'll make those bitches disappear," he
says, with cocaine confidence.
Fred is clearly delusional right now, but there's nothing I
can do to combat it so I just go with it.
"Okay, man. They're all yours but I wouldn't go to the Ave
and try to sell them to random fuckos on the street. You're
going to get yourself killed or end up in jail. They're in the
car buried under all my shit. Come help me dig them out."
We walk outside and I open the rear door, several items
fall out onto the pavement and Fred scrambles to gather
them in his arms before throwing them into the front seat,
short term fix I suppose.
"Okay, where are they at?" Fred asks, excitedly, while
rubbing his hands together and sniffling the last remaining
remnants of his last bump deeper into his system.
I move in front of Fred who's crowding the open door and
begin to carefully move items around and peek in to get an
idea of the best way to go about retrieving the weed from
beneath the rubble.
I see where I think they are, but it's going to be impossible
to pull them out without emptying nearly the entire
contents of the car. "Okay, I see the bag they're in. It's at
the very bottom," I say. "Under the desk, in a blue duffle
bag."
"Move back," says Fred. And I do so, taking a half step
backwards and allowing Fred to get in close. He peers into
the apartment packed into a car and then begins grabbing,
moving, removing, and setting everything that was packed
onto the sidewalk.
"Fred! Fred! What the fuck are you doing?"
"I'll put it all back, just chill, I'll handle it, everything will go
back in, I swear. I'll do it," he says, talking a mile a
minute.
"Yeah sure, whatever, man."
I know Fred will put everything back, but I also know it will
be carelessly stuffed inside, in no way resembling its

original form, not that it really matters, all this shit is just going to end up in a closet somewhere in the next few days anyway.

"Got it," he says, after several minutes of high paced disorderly unpacking.

"Okay, hand it to me and I'll take it inside while you put all this shit back in the car."

Fred tosses the duffle bag containing the weed out onto the side walk. I pick it up and walk into his apartment.

Fred's computer is open and I sit down to do some research of my own about where might be a reasonable place for us to flee to. His browser has several windows open. I close out of the tab titled *'throat pie'* and begin to read the other pages he has left open. Lists of cheapest countries to live in, best places to retire, least expensive cities in the world. Fred was right; Asia is cheap, at least according to the internet, but God damn that's a long flight. I keep reading.

Fred is taking an unusually long time to get back inside. Eventually, I decide to go out there and check on him. No Fred, no car. What the fuck. Panic has become my friend these last few days and it makes a return just now.

Did my best friend just steal my car and all my belongings? No way, and why would he let me take the weed if he was going to take the money and run? I check for my keys in my pocket, not there; no shit, it's not like Fred hot-wired the car; he must have grabbed my keys and I didn't notice. I call Fred, no answer. What the fuck is going on. I decide to go back inside to wait and just as I do I see my car come driving down the street. I walk to the curb and throw my arms up in the air in a gesture that hopefully states, *'What the hell, man?'*

Fred parks and exits the vehicle, returning my *'What the hell, man'* gesture before reaching into his pocket, retrieving a can of chewing tobacco and shouting from the other side of the car. "I needed a can, and you needed gas. I filled 'er up, you're welcome," as he tosses me the keys and we head back inside.

"I was looking at your computer and those articles about where we could go," I say.

"Yeah, and what'd you think," Fred says, before spitting chewing tobacco residue into a clear plastic water bottle. "I think Asia is far as fuck and we would need to apply for visas for damn near all of those countries."
"Yeah, okay. What other ideas do you have?" he asks.
"South America," I say. "I found another article; I left it pulled up on the computer if you want to take a look. It's about a little beach town in Ecuador called Montanita. They say it's like the little Amsterdam of South America, but on the beach. Weed, surf, bikinis, and a burger and fries cost all of two American dollars, and they use U.S. dollars down there as strange as that sounds, so we could bring all the cash we have with us and not have to worry about exchanging it."
"Yeah?!" Fred says, excitedly. "Pass me the computer."
I hand the computer to Fred and excuse myself to the restroom.
I piss and wash my face and hands. I need to touch base with Sarah and find a way to minimize the dishonestly while I break the news to her. I decide to send her a text.
"Hey, can we get together tonight? I have some news for you."
I can hear Fred frantically punching keys on the laptop from the other room. I need to clear my head a little so I stare into the mirror and just think.
I don't know how I'm going to broach this subject with Sarah. Maybe I should just leave and not say anything. I mean, that would for sure be easiest for me, and I think it would probably be best for her, too. There's no fucking way I'm telling her the truth about this whole fucked up situation and she doesn't deserve to be lied to, so what? Do I just leave? Yes, just leave and she'll forget all about me before the end of the year, maybe before the end of the week. Fuck, why did I just text her. I should just smash my phone right now and get on the next flight to anywhere. I've got more than enough cash and savings to last a year in any of those places Fred and I are talking about. Part of me has always wanted to just disappear and now the opportunity to do so is here and I'm terrified. I want to leave and leave Sarah in the process, but I can't

imagine the pain I'll feel when I realize that I'll never see her again and I didn't even say good bye.

Buzz. From Sarah. *"I'd love to see you tonight. What's the news about?"*

The sudden urge to smash the phone and run is real. I can see it happening in my mind. Throw it on the ground, stomp on it and then throw it into the trash. Run away. Disappear.

"Okay, great. Can we meet at a bar? Somewhere near your house is fine, 7?" Send to Sarah.

"Pioneer Brewing at 7 then;) Can't wait to hear your news, babe."

Reality sets in and forces my head to tilt forward and my neck to bend into a posture that undoubtedly states 'defeated.'

"X, X, quit shitting and get in here," Fred yells from the other room.

"Yeah, what it is?" I ask, as I make my way back to Fred, who looks like a mad man possessed by the computer screen, white powder now staining the edge of his left nostril.

"Medellin! X, we're going to Medellin," exclaims Fred, sounding less like a soon to be murder victim and more like a recent lottery winner.

"Oh yeah, why is that?" I inquire.

"No visa, cheap flights, low cost of living, and I found a place for us to stay! X, we're going to Medellin!"

With this Fred leaps to his feet, knocking his computer to the ground. He begins to celebrate with fist bumps and bump bumps. I stare at the scene unfolding in front of me with disbelief. My entire life has unraveled before my very eyes. In this moment all my senses become strangely clear, I smell the familiar scent of Fred's living room, I see the baggy pinched between his pressing fingers and the computer spilled onto the floor, I hear Fred continuing to ramble about getting on the first flight possible, I can feel my feet on the ground and my breath entering and exiting my body, it's as if every sense is separated and elevated. With this sudden onset of sensation my worries seem to slowly evaporate as consciousness takes center stage. It's a relief really, and I decide to try and enjoy it for as long as it lasts. Just breath, breath and forget about the past and the future, presently all I have to do is breath. I wish I could remain in this state forever, but Fred's voice needs a response and this impinges upon my blissful tranquility and sends me crashing back to my normal state of being lost in panicked thought.

"We can leave tomorrow," says Fred. "For four hundred-n-something, we can fly out tomorrow night and be there the next day. Seattle to Miami to Medellin. I'm gonna buy the tickets. X, give me your passport number."

Luckily, just six months earlier we took a trip to Canada, the first time out of the country for either of us, and the annoying process of getting a passport for just a weekend trip now seems serendipitous.

"Dude, I don't know my passport number. Hold off on buying the tickets, I have to try and comprehend all this shit."

"I'm booking mine now, then I'll email the guy down there who has the rooms we can rent."

"Okay, Fred, well I have to go and see if I can dump all my shit and leave my car at my mom's house while we're gone. You don't think Juan and his boys would track my car down and do some dumb shit over there, do you?"

"X, I don't know what those animals are capable of, but I wouldn't take any chances. Leave it at Sarah's," he says, as if her being harassed would be an acceptable alternative.

"I'll see, man, but anyway, I've got to get out of here."

"Hold up, let me book my flight then I'll give you the info so you can get on the same one and we'll fly together," he says.

"Man, are you sure you really want to do this? I mean, we could drive to Oregon and stay there for a while. Do you really think fleeing the country is necessary?" I ask.

"Yes, we can't establish ourselves anywhere with jobs or anything legit that would allow us to be found. And anyway, we would blow all our money in a few short months staying here in the states. Let's get out and go fucking enjoy this a little bit, dude! We have money, nothing tying us down, so let's just live a little. Spirit quest," says Fred, before reaching for the little baggy laying on the table and jabbing his key inside for yet another pick me up.

I wonder how much that baggy has influenced Fred's spur of the moment decision about where we should escape to. We must be the only two people in the history of the world who have fled *to* Medellin in order to get *away* from drug violence, oh well, our lives have always been rather unique and against the grain.

"Fred, book your ticket and I'll book mine after I get my passport and unload the car. But we both know you don't have the balls to do this," I say.

Fred, who is mid bump, sniffs in like he's trying to inhale the key along with the treasure on top as he stares at me with eyes that say *'oh yea, pussy, watch this'*; and he places the computer on his lap and begins to work. After about five minutes he says, "Done, we leave tomorrow at ten thirty pm. Now you don't be a bitch and make sure you get on that flight."

He grabs a pen from the table and jots down the flight information. "Here," he says, and passes me the paper.

"Jesus fuck Christ, man, are we really doing this?"

Once again Fred is brought to his feet by a combination of cocaine and excitement over our newly confirmed journey to the other side of the world.

"Yeah, X. Don't be a bitch! We're going," he screams, before embracing me in a bear hug that feels like it's about to pop a rib.

"Great, man, well in that case I've got some shit to do. I'm going by my mom's to see if I can leave some of my stuff there and then I have to go see Sarah and tell her the news. We should meet up after to go over everything, yeah? Nine or ten cool with you?" I ask.

"Yeah, man, I'll see you then," he says.

Chapter. 20 Going Home

The drive to my mom's house should only take a few minutes. I don't bother calling first to check and see if she's home.

Approaching the house on a quiet, hillside, residential Seattle street, it is clear that not only is she home, but there are guests as well; my sister Bridget's car is parked in the driveway. Great. I don't want to see anyone or explain anything, and my sister will certainly dig deeper than I would like in order to figure out what's really going on. I better cheer the fuck up and not break down and confess everything.

I have to cook up a story to explain my sudden departure. I'll blame it on Fred, as I used to do as a youth whenever my hidden porn collection was unexpectedly discovered. *'Oh those, those are Fred's. He found them in the woods and gave them to me. I don't even want them; really, honestly, they're not even really mine.'* I would say, while feeling overwhelmingly embarrassed. Today it will be, *'Fred got kicked off the football team and oh, yeah, by the way, I got fired a week ago, so since we're both basically bums now we've decided to take our little bit of money and run to South America.'* Well, we'll see how this goes.

I walk to the front door, the sounds of my nephew and niece playing inside are audible from the front yard. The door is slightly ajar so I let myself in without notice. Immediately, Kevin and Melanie go running by barely noticing my presence. "What are you doing here?" asks my nephew, before continuing to chase his sister without waiting for my answer.

My mom and sister are sitting in the living room, conversing in casual tones as I pass through the entryway and interrupt their chatter.

"Hello." My voice catches them off guard as I enter the room and sit myself on a chair across from them.

"Well, what are you doing here?" asks my mom, sounding surprised to see me, but in a good way.

"Oh, I came by because I have some news..."

"Oh no, what is it this time?" asks Bridget, trying to add a touch of humor to her voice, although we all know she's asking this with upmost sincerity due to the troubled happenings of my past.

"Oh, well, actually, Fred and I are going to travel," I say.

"Travel?" my mom and sister ask simultaneously, seeming confused about what in the world I could mean by 'travel'.

I sit staring at them and repeat, "Yes, travel. We're going to go to South America."

As shocked as they seem to be at this revelation, I feel as if no one in the room is more shocked than I am. I can barely contain myself and my discomfort shows in a large smile breaking out across my face. I begin to chuckle to myself uncontrollably, like someone who has just witnessed a gruesome accident and reacts inappropriately by laughing at upsetting scenes.

"Really, well that's great news!" says my mom. "Where exactly will you be going? And when are you leaving?

I continue to chuckle and then add, "I actually got fired, and Fred got kicked off the football team and doesn't really want to continue in college so we just bought one way tickets. We're flying into Medellin. We leave tomorrow night."

"You're kidding!" says my mother, as Bridget sits silently with a look of puzzled skepticism.

"Nope, I'm dead ass serious," I say.

"Well, that sure is short notice, but it sounds wonderful. I'm sure you two will have a great time. Please be careful and don't let Fred drink too much and get you two into any trouble, okay?"

"I promise," I say.

I get to the point of why I'm here. "I was wondering if I could stash some of my stuff here while I'm gone? I moved out of the apartment kind of last minute."

"Of course."

"And what about your car?" inquires my sister.

"I was actually thinking the same thing. I'm not sure. I need to find a place to leave it, hopefully with someone who will drive it once in a while just to keep the fluids moving and all that."

"I can help you with that," my sister adds.

"Really? That would be great."

"Well, Gary just sold his truck and is using his Dad's car, so it would help us too to use yours while he looks for a new one."

As nice as this sounds, and as convenient as it is for me, I know that she would in no way offer to help if it wasn't in some way benefiting her. I'm sure she'll dump it in an abandoned parking lot as soon as her husband buys a new car and mine converts into nothing more than an inconvenience, but for the time being this solution serves both of us and I agree.

"Okay, great. I'll drop it by here before leaving tomorrow for the airport," I say.

"Will you need a ride to SeaTac?" asks my mother.

"I don't know yet," I respond.

"Bridget, maybe you can take him in his car and then just drive it home. Wouldn't that be nice?" my mother suggests.

"Oh no, I don't think so," says Bridget. "I don't like driving at night. Maybe I could drop you off at the bus stop though."

"Oh no, I'll be fine. Fred will probably set up a ride for us or I can ask another friend or something. Don't worry about it. But hey, I'm going to start to move some of my stuff out of the car and into the basement," I say, as I excuse myself.

My nephew and niece go running by once more as I walk towards the front door.

"Hey fart-machine," I say, as Kevin passes by. "Want to build some muscles?"

"Sure!" replies my nephew.

"Great, come help me move a few boxes from my car to the basement."

Unlike his mother, Kevin is always willing to lend a helping hand and although he's only eight he works his ass off for thirty minutes carrying boxes that often dwarf his small frame.

The list of things to do is seemingly never ending; next up on the list is getting a ticket for the flight that Fred is booked on. I buy the ticket and can't believe that in just over twenty four hours I'll be leaving this world behind for a land I know next to nothing about, besides the tales of violence and corruption that its most famous son, Pablo, left in his wake.

I shower, and then take Kevin to Kidd Valley for a burger as a thank you for unloading the car and as a proper goodbye, one of the few I plan on making.

I need a nap and decide I can afford to close my eyes for a few minutes. I set my alarm for half an hour and lay down in the spare bedroom at my mother's house for some much needed rest.

Waking up, I see that Fred and Sarah have both called and sent texts.

"X! No sleep til Brooklyn," is all Fred's message reads.

"I'm really busy reviewing my new trainings for work. Can we do tomorrow instead?" reads Sarah's text.

Fuck. Well, I suppose I could go see her tomorrow, but I won't have much time. Fuck it, I can't go tomorrow. Tell her it has to be today.

"I'm actually going out of town tomorrow. That's what I wanted to talk about. Any chance I could just come by your place tonight to explain?" Send to Sarah.

I lay in bed staring at the screen waiting for her response. A few seconds pass and... *buzz.*

"Yes, but it would it have to be past your bed time. After reviewing my trainings I'm going to meet my new boss for a drink in Bellevue. Could you do 9 at my place?"

"Yes, just text me when you're headed home and I'll come by." Send.

What kind of fuckin' boss meets their new employee for drinks at night before they have even worked a single day?! This guy is clearly going to try and fuck her. And good, she'll need a new guy and I would rather write her off than spend the next several months agonizing about our separation, clinging onto hope that when I return, whenever the fuck that may be, that she'll be waiting for me. No, that would be too painful and slow, better she fall in love with her new boss tonight. I hope that when I get to her place she breaks down and confesses that she just fucked him in the bar bathroom, that she couldn't control herself, that she just doesn't want me anymore, that he is the one for her, that she's already forgotten me and that I will be better off the sooner I forget her because she's not going to take me back, not ever.

I roll out of bed and see a note has been slid under the door. It's from my sister. It says, *"Have a nice trip."*

I walk out of the bedroom and into the living room to find my mother still seated there.

"I'm gonna hit the road. I've got to go see Fred and go over some details about the trip. Can I sleep here tonight?"

"Of course," she says. "Oh, and Gary came by while you were napping and took the car. You can use mine though; I won't need it between now and tomorrow."

"Oh, okay, I'm glad Bridget checked with me first. Thank God I took that dead body out of the back," I say, sarcastically, while actually thinking, *'holy fuck, thank God I gave those four pounds to Fred and didn't leave them hidden in the car somewhere."*

"My keys are in my purse on the kitchen table," she says, before returning to her book.

"Thanks," I shout down the hallway as I head for the door.

Chapter. 21 A Night to be Forgotten

I might as well go see Fred again while I wait for Sarah.
Ring. Ring. Ring.
"FMP," answers Fred.
"Where you at? I'm comin' by."
"X, I'm at Coopers, come here," he says, the frantic joyous
tone of his voice tells me that the little baggy he had has
been fully funneled into his nose and he has likely already
headed back to Cap Hill for another.
I arrive at Cooper's and my suspicions are confirmed. Fred
is high as a kite and drinking heavily. I sit down to join him
at the bar and without delay he palms me a new, nearly full
baggy, filled with white powder.
"Take it easy, Pablo," I say, placing my hand face down on
his leg, immediately returning the bag before consuming
any.
I order a Rainer tall-boy and allow my eyes to wonder to
the television as I settle into the familiar bar stool.
"What are you going to do with your apartment?" I ask.
"I paid that fuckin' land lord for six months, cash," he
replies.
"How'd you get that kind of money? Are you gonna be
broke when we get down there?" I ask, knowing Fred's
history with money and not wanting to become his personal
bank while we're away.
"Nah, I sold those four pounds right after you left to the
guy who sells me the blow on The Hill," he states casually,
as if this were some everyday transaction.
"No shit? How much did you get for them?"
"Not a ton, but it had to go, five k. And I've got a plan for a
come-up before we leave tomorrow night."
"Oh really? What's that?" I ask, expecting a half cooked,
cocaine fueled idea that would place him up against nearly
impossible odds.
His reply is rather grounded and reasonable compared to
my initial assumption.

"I'm gonna go in through the roof of that pot shop where you sold your stuff," he says calmly, as if he's simply recounting what he had for breakfast and not detailing a cat burglar style heist.

"Man, don't get caught and don't get killed. When are you hoping to do this?" I stupidly ask, momentarily misremembering that we leave tomorrow and thus there is only one plausible answer.

"Tonight," he says.

"Well, good luck. Don't ask me to go with you."

I want to change the subject, so I inquire, "Did you get us that place to stay that you were talking about, the place run by the Jew from the states?"

"Yeah, we each got a room there for the first month. I paid for us both already. You buy the second month, deal?"

"Yeah, sounds good, round one on you, round two one me. How much was it?" I ask.

"Dirt fuckin' cheap," he says. "Three hundred each for the month. The place is called Casita del Mundo. You're gona have to run through some backpacker pussy while we're down there."

"Why me? You're the one for that, man. But thanks for taking care of finding the flights and rooms. How are you getting to the airport?"

"Fuck if I know, man. You gonna have Sarah give you a ride? Leave her with a good fuckin' in the airport parking lot before taking off?"

"Sure, something like that."

"Slide me that baggy," I bark. Fred's face lights up with excitement as he passes it stealthily underneath the bar-top.

I Know the usual protocol is to get up and go to the bathroom, as to not be so fuckin' obvious about it, but at this point the old rules and customs of life seem to be a thing of the past. I give a quick glance around the mostly empty bar, and then stick my key into the baggy and partake while sitting on the stool. I set the key and bag on the bar top and look at Fred. "Don't be a bitch," is all that needs to be said. Fred appears ready to repeat the outlandish behavior, but then hesitates, surveys the area, and proceeds to empty a small pile onto the bar itself, quickly maneuvering it into two long white lines before snorting them up his nostril. The sound of his powerful sniff and the odd placement of his head directly above the bar would make it pretty damn obvious what we were doing to anyone who happened to be paying attention; luckily it seems no one is, they're probably all staring at their phones, too distracted to notice the scene unfolding in front of them.

"Baa'tenda!" Fred shouts, to one of the usual staff who recognize our faces and whose own face now seems a tad annoyed at the overzealous hollers emanating from Fred. "Two shots of Jack Daniels and two stouts," he says, staring at the bartender with a cocaine glaze covering his entire essence. Fred is beginning to smack his lips and grab at various body parts and pieces of clothing as we speak. That last bar-top-dose seems to have hit him hard.

"Fred, I am not taking shots. I have to go see Sarah in a few hours."

Fred stares at me with a mix of bravado and knowingness that comes from a brotherhood reinforced over years of follies, fuck-ups, and outright disasters; these are the things that build bonds, not picnics and good times. He doesn't have to say anything, the message is clear; we're leaving our lives behind and setting out for an adventure of unknown length in an unknown place, under dire circumstances. This might be the last shot we take in our old neighborhood bar for who knows how long; now don't be a bitch and let's get drunk on our last night in Seattle. "Fuck it, I'll drink the stupid fuckin' shot," I say. "And pass me the baggy back again, too."

I briefly hesitate with the bag of powder in my hand. If I show up at Sarah's all drunk and coked out she won't be happy, but fuck it, I don't want to be sober when I break the news to her anyway. Maybe she'll be so disgusted with how fucked up I am and the way I'm leaving that she'll just throw me out and tell me to never call her again. In a way that would be nice, it would free me from the unknown, the dreams, hopes and expectations of a nice happy life with a beautiful wife, something I know that I'm not destined for.

Fuck it, I'm gonna get fucked up with my best friend on our last night here. I jam the key into the bag then and into my nose.

"We'll take two more shots," I shout to the bartender.

This cycle continues until Fred seems on the verge of a complete mental breakdown, his eyes darting crazily all over the room and his hands moving, moving, and moving some more.

Buzz, my phones alerts me that I have a text message from Sarah. *"I'm going home now. See you there soon."*

"Fuck, Fred, man, I have to hit the road."

"Okay, but can you help me load a ladder... ah never mind, I can do it myself. Hit me up in the morning," he says.

"I'll see you before that. I'm going to come by after Sarah's. I want to see what you get from your heist."

"Alright man, just hit me up." And with this Fred stands and embraces me in hug, a rare occurrence that doesn't often happen without the involvement of powder, but in this moment it feels like the right way to say goodbye.

I start walking to my car in the cold damp darkness and it's clear as day that I should not be driving right now. Walking is a bit difficult and I'm feeling sick in my head. Every few seconds the world starts to spin and I have to steady myself before taking another step.

I stop midstride and try to recover my nerves. I take a deep breath, then another; I nod my head forward and continue walking towards the car. I retrieve my keys from my jacket pocket and unlock the doors.

I stand at the edge of the car and take some more deep breaths. I can do this, stay calm, stay focused.

It's a ten minute drive straight down the freeway. I get into the car and turn the ignition. Time is a blur, the past minutes don't seem real and the future is too far off to contemplate; all I can do is work through the drive moment by moment. Okay, drive. Blinker. Steering wheel. Let's go.

I make it out of the spot I was parallel parked in, what a miracle. It's only a few blocks to the freeway. I make it one block, then another, then, damn it, I need to pullover. I maneuver to the side or the road and throw open the door. I'm struggling to unbuckle my seatbelt and get out before

it gets here. '*Hurry*', I think, as I frantically jab at the
seatbelt button!
Click.
I lean out over the edge of the seat and begin vomiting
violently onto the street below. In the time it takes me to
fully empty my stomach it feels like I've been stopped here
for an hour, although I know it's likely only been a few
painful minutes. I'm paranoid that in the next second I'm
going to spot flashing lights pulling up behind me. I reach
for a bottle of water and start rinsing out my mouth. Okay,
I can do this. More deep breaths. I pull back onto the road
feeling much better. No music, phone out of sight, I'm
completely focused on the task at hand. I turn off for
Sarah's exit and feel as though I've done the impossible.
I'm just relieved to have arrived, alive, but now the hard
part starts. I still haven't developed a good script of what
to say. I mean, I know what I have to say, and I know
what I absolutely cannot fucking say, but how I'm going to
say it is still a mystery. And in this moment I can only hope
not to puke, cry or do anything else that I'll regret in the
morning.
Elevator, empty, thank God.
Miraculously I arrive at her door, in what is undoubtedly
the worst state she has ever seen me in.
"Are you okay?" she asks, with a startled look on her face
as she opens the door.
"Yeah, yeah," I blurt out, allowing too much of the
stimulants in my body to express themself in my speech.
"I'm fine. I just had a bit too much to drink, I think. Fred
wrestled me to the bar and made me take shots with him."
"Just come lie down and let me make you feel better," she
says, as she grabs me by the crotch and begins to lead me
towards the bedroom.
"No, wait. I have to tell you something. Can we sit down on
for a second?"
"Yes, okay. Is something wrong?" she asks.
She can most definitely tell that something is up.
It could be the mix of drugs and alcohol pulsing through
me that she detects, or it could be she has a sense of the

forthcoming news. I'm not really sure, but her eyes give away her concerns.

"I need some water," I say, while getting up and heading into the kitchen to chug one glassful before refilling it and walking back into the living room, joining Sarah on the couch.

"Well," I say, before pausing for much too long while I search for the right words. I can't say it. I take a breath.

"Well," she says, taking my hand in hers and looking reassuringly into my bloodshot eyes.

I can feel her warmth and loving affection even through the fog of cocaine, alcohol, and marijuana that are dampening my ability to stand straight, let alone explain away a last minute move to another continent without rhyme or reason.

"I... ah, well, Fred and I are moving to Medellin, tomorrow," I say, trying to look her in the eyes but unable to. I stare at the ground like a coward as I break the news.

"You're what?" she says calmly, unable to understand the news that seems so out of place it might as well have come from another planet.

"Fred and I are going to Medellin tomorrow. I'm really drunk right now, but I'm sure I'll be better at explaining it in the morning."

"For how long? When did you decide to do this? Why are you telling me now the day before you leave? Xavier, this is really.... surprising," she says, while her face twists and turns along with her mutating understanding and analysis of what I've just said. She appears to be, well, sad. Her eyes are staring down at her crossed legs on the couch; she reaches out her hand and takes hold of my arm, pulling herself closer to me.

For a moment, having her next to me makes me feel safe and secure and happy and loved and without worry, but the next moment these feelings flee and I'm left imagining the total absence of it all and the one and only person who can give it to me.

Somehow, when I'm away from her I can, for the most part, put her out of my mind and this allows me to constantly fuck things up between us when we're apart, but when we're together I can't think of anything besides her and the way she makes me feel.

It's like her touch, no, her very presence has some magical power over me. I need her like I need air when she's in my arms, but I know this feeling will fade when I leave her and will eventually die all together if left unattended for too long.

After a long silence filled with gentle caresses she finally speaks, "What's going to happen between us?"

"I'm not going to forget you when I leave. No one has ever made me feel the way you do," I say with slurred speech.

She lets out a little laugh, "That doesn't really answer my question."

More silence, then.

"I love you," she says.

The sober me would surely have a better response to her opened hearted confession of love, but in this moment I can feel the spins creeping back and the best I manage is to kiss her head and whisper, "I don't want you to leave."

Her head jerks back and she looks at me like I'm a total fucking idiot. "I'm not leaving, you are," she says, with her head swaying in disbelief. "Wow, you must really have had too much. Move, I'm going to get some tea from the kitchen."

She heads into the kitchen shaking her head at the stupidity that's just fallen from my mouth. I need a moment to steady myself, so I stand up slowly and waddle into the bathroom to try and focus my brain. The stream of piss springing from me at unusually high speed seems to last several minutes. I try to scrub my mouth clean using the finger brush technique. I look at myself in the mirror, and what looks back is barely recognizable. My eyes are fucked, pupils dilated, raccoon circles but with a reddish tint, I look like hell. I wash my face hoping that the effects of the booze and blow will wash away with water, no luck. I walk out and find Sarah still in the kitchen, preparing her cup of tea. She's wearing a bathrobe and slippers. I drink another large glass of water in an attempt to flush my system. I set the glass on the countertop and put my arms around Sarah's waist. I'm standing behind her, resting my chin on her shoulder, kissing her neck and softly grinding into her backside. My hands move from her waist to her wrists, I press her hands harshly onto the countertop in front of us.

Crash!

My water glass breaks on the floor. Her body tries to bend down towards the broken shards to clean them up. I lift her up firmly and press her against the counter.

"I'll take care of it in the morning," I whisper into her ear from behind, like some kind of drunken bar patron attempting to seduce the waitress after hours in an unwanted advance.

"Let's go into the bedroom," I say, and before waiting for a response I pick her up, carrying her in front of me; with one arm under her legs and the other under her torso.

I carry her out of the kitchen, past the living room and into the bedroom where I unceremoniously drop her like a sack of potatoes onto the bed.

"Owe, my head," she says, after being dumped onto the mattress.

She looks up at me as I struggle out of my clothes. Her expression tells me she is not impressed with anything that is happening right now. I throw myself on top of her. She lays there, uninterested. This has never happened before. Usually she's the one badgering me for more sex. My mind is jumbled. I'm trying to think of a way to snap her out of her near comatose state of disinterest when the words briefly float into my consciousness, *'If I'm ever mad at you again I don't want you to listen to me, okay? Just throw me on the bed, hold me down and do whatever you please with me, okay?'* and then, *'For you no means yes, okay?'* I keep kissing her neck and mouth, playfully biting her lower lip and, nothing. What does she want right now? Despite the drinks and drugs my member is somehow up and ready to go. I grind it against her to demonstrate that I'm prepared. She lays there, motionless.

"Do you want to me to be rough with you?" I say, looking down into her eyes.

She looks away.

I grab her by the jaw and turn her face towards mine. I ask again, "Do you want me to rough with you tonight?" She gives me a blank look before once again turning her face away.

I grab her jaw and force her face towards mine, "Yes or no?" I ask.

She violently trashes her head free of my grip before stating, somewhat angrily, "No. And you can't make me."

I bury my head next to hers while pulling one of her legs up and pressing into her, she moans, however it's unlike her normal moans of pleasure.

My hand slides down her body until it reaches the edge of her panties; it goes under and finds a warm, inviting home. I rub her with increasing speed and pressure as she arches her back and presses into me, moaning, now with what I interrupt as a bit more normalcy, and suddenly she grabs the back of my head with one hand, holding tightly across my shoulders with the other. I think she's into it, but I can't really tell.

She lets go of my back and reaches for my arm that is at work her between her legs.

At first, she rests her hand above mine, but then she takes my wrist firmly and tries to pull my hand away from her.

I lift my head and look into her face trying to find some clue as to what to do next. She smiles before her blank stare of disinterest returns.

She's playing with me. She wants me to show her that I want her as much as she wants me, that I will do anything to have her in any and every way. I lift myself up so that I'm in a sort of plank position hovering above her. Using one hand to reach down and pull my boxers part way down my leg, my opposite foot retracts up, the big toe hooking the waistband and helping to remove them. Next, I grab her panties with a hand on either side and yank them down, she stirs from side to side struggling to fully free them from her feet. I slide back between her legs and tap her with my erection that is now full with anticipation.

"No!" she says, pushing my penis away with her hand. Next thing I know my knees are by her ears and my shins are pressing over her arms. She is pinned, my body towering over her as she lies on the bed. I'm positioned on my knees, trapping her arms under my legs so that I if were to sit back I would come to rest on her torso. My hands are free; hers are uselessly attached to her arms trapped beneath the weight of my pressing shins. My cock bumps her face, neck and hair as she lightly struggles under my weight. I grab it with one hand and start to slap her in the face with it. "Open your mouth," I instruct her. Again she says, "You can't make me," and turns her head from side to side.

I stick a finger into her mouth without much resistance. From here I pull her head slightly up and off the mattress and thrust it into her mouth. She capitulates and allows it to slide in and out while I have her mounted.

Looking at her nothing is clear, my vision, her mood, my intentions, her desires; I have not a clue, but at this point little matters. I pull my cock from her mouth and flip her over onto her stomach. Without delay I start pounding her from behind. She lays there continuing to look into the mattress, away from me, uninterested.

By the end of it I'm sweating and starting to feel the spins again. I finish on her stomach and as soon as I roll off of her she stands up, walks quickly to the bathroom and slams the door behind her. I can hear the shower. I want to sleep, but there's no way that will be possible, not for at least another few hours, the stimulants need to fade before I can even think about real rest.

That was unquestionably the worst sex Sarah and I have ever had. I wish I was sober so that I could clearly process what just happened, because what I'm feeling now is that I just violated the person I care most about in this life.

And I did it right after telling her a half truth, half cooked story about why I have to leave, and leave her, as if she was the most unimportant, insignificant person in the world, although the opposite couldn't be more true; but somehow my actions betray my true intentions and I end up feeling sick with myself, not just from the time at the bar, but with what just transpired here.

The sound of the shower turning off directs my attention to the bathroom door. I'm still lying in the bed trying to think of what to say when she comes out. Should I apologize? The bathroom door opens and Sarah steps out from a backlit frame towards the darkness of the bedroom.

She pauses in the doorway. I think I can see a tear rolling down her cheek, although I suppose it could just be water dripping from her still wet hair. I start to sit up and move towards her.

"Stop," she says. "You should leave."

"I.. I.. I'm, I thought... why didn't you say something?"

"Go," she manages to say over choked down tears.

I know I should think of something to say, explain myself, tell her I believed her back when she told me, *'For you, no means yes'*. Why didn't we discuss this more before it blew up in our faces? How does she see me now? As Xavier, the guy she's been tumbling through love and lust with? Or as something new, a piece of shit who is just using her and leaving her with no notice or reasonable explanation?

I shouldn't have come here tonight. I'm too fucked up. The best thing I can do now is leave before I dig myself into a deeper hole. But there's so much I want to say to her, to explain, to pour out my soul on the ground in front of her so that she can finally, for once, see it, see me for who I really am.

She sees me more clearly than anyone, including myself, she sees every part of me except the one part that I want to show her, the part of me that can't live without her, that feels that she is the missing piece in my life, the piece that makes me feel more alive and carefree than I ever experienced before knowing her, the part of me that loves her but can't show itself outside the hidden confines of my own mind. Get out and show yourself, *love*; show her that you're inside beating the sides of my head and screaming to get out and be recognized.

I stand up and Sarah takes a nervous step backwards, retreating from the piece of shit in front of her. I gather my clothes and step out of the bedroom and into the living room to dress myself. I leave embarrassed, without saying another word.

The drive back to the north end is a blur.

Once again, I luck out and don't kill anyone, nor do I get pulled over and given the long overdue DUI that I've somehow managed to avoid for the last couple years. Having no home of my own, I'm unsure where to go next; being high, drunk and questioning the legitimacy of the sex I just had, sex isn't the right word, makes it difficult to decide anything. I just want to melt into the car and disappear. Whatever *that* was, it had nothing in common with the sex Sarah and I shared before. The spinning thoughts in my head reveal that there is only one destination available to me; I'll go by Fred's and crash there. I want to see how his night heist plan is going anyway; I just hope there won't be any more cocaine; all I want to do is sleep, to turn off my mind from this sickening reality.

"Hey!" I yell, as I slip my head into Fred's apartment through the front door that he has carelessly left unlocked. I cautiously take a step inside, suspecting that at any moment I'll spy a shadow, then hear, *'Ay, the white boy is here, kill him.'*

"Fred, are you in here?" I ask, into the seemingly empty apartment.

A noise from the bathroom startles me, someone is in there.

"Fred?" I say again, as I begin to approach what I hope is a harmless friend on the other side of the bathroom door. Before I make it across the kitchen to the bathroom the door swings open and out steps a man dressed in all black, wearing a ski mask, holding a rope in one hand and what appear to be a number of empty plastic bags in the other. I should be scared stiff at this sight, but my decade plus of friendship exposes this shadowy figure for what it really is; Fred, donned in cat-burglar attire preparing to go out and do one of the stupidest things he's ever proposed.

"Fred, man, what the fuck!"

"How do I look?" he says, and he rips the ski mask from his head before reaching into his breast pocket to withdraw the dwindling bag of blow. Key into bag, key out of bag, up nose, sniffles.

Fred rubs his nose and stares at me with intense wide
eyes. "How'd it go with Sarah?" He asks.
"I think I just raped her, I feel like fucking killing myself!" I
begin to cry like an infant. I collapse onto Fred's couch and
bury my face in the pillow.
"Ok...," says Fred, rather alarmed by the sight of his friend
curled up in the fettle position whimpering to himself.
A few moments later Fred returns and places a blanket
over me.
"X, I'm gonna go hit this lick. I'll be back in an hour,
hopefully less."
And with that, Fred leaves to go rob the pot shop and I
somehow find a sufficient calm that allows me to drift off to
sleep.

Chapter. 22 The Morning After

The morning air is fresh and crisp. The blinds have been left open and I look out to see piles of leaves and blue skies. I guess the weather man was wrong; Seattle has been blessed with a beautiful fall morning. The sound of Fred snoring in the next room is a relief; at least I know he didn't end up dead or in jail. I can smell something, too. Weed. The stench is overpowering. Well, I suppose Fred was successful last night, smells like it at least.
I stand up and stretch out. I can feel the effects of last night on every inch of my body. My mouth feels like an abandoned chemical factory, the sensation that a thin layer of filthy behavior and bad decisions covers my skin, my head aches with the pain of last night's drinks, and my soul feels crushed and empty and irreparable. I step into Fred's bedroom and view his naked body lying face down on the mattress. I grab his ankle and give it a shake. "Big score last night? Wake up. What'd you make out with last night? I can smell it. Where's it at?"
Fred's arms reach out as he arches, twists and turns in an attempt to snap out of a deep slumber. A self-satisfied smile spreads across his face even before he opens his eyes.
"Ahhh, yeah, man, it went pretty well. It's in the kitchen cupboard in a few plastic bags. Go check it out."
I rush out of the bedroom and into the kitchen. The first cupboard I check is empty but the smell is now so strong that I'm thinking Fred must have the whole goddamn store stashed somewhere in here. The second door I check reveals four overstuffed plastic bags filled with prepackaged, high quality, medical marijuana. There's everything; joints, ounces, oils, edibles. He must have gone into the sale's room and unloaded the entire contents of the display case. What a score. I grab one of the joints and head back into the bedroom.
Lighting the joint and casually leaning against the door, I say, to a once again mostly sleeping Fred, "Jesus fuck

Christ, man, you did good. But now what? You're not going try to sell all that before we leave tonight, are you?"

"Cus' I am. You think I'm leaving that shit here for Juan and the boys to come steal while I'm gone? Fuck that. I'll take it back to The Hill and get it off for the cheap, better than nothing."

As glad as I am that Fred seems to be making magic happen and filling his coffers before we leave, I'm also concerned that when he goes to sell this stuff to his cocaine supplier that he's going to buy another baggy and continue the circle of booze and blow right up until we arrive at the airport; I just hope they let him on the plane.

"Back to The Hill, huh? You'll sell it and pick up another baggy, I assume?" I ask, with an accusatory tone.

"Fuck you, choirboy," says Fred, without lifting his head from the pillow.

"Best of luck selling that stuff. I'm going to shower and get changed at my mom's. How are you getting to the airport tonight?"

"Egghh," responds a half conscious Fred, maintaining his horizontal posture.

"Alright, man, just keep your phone with you today and answer it, okay?"

A nearly imperceptible lift of his hand signals that he heard me, and with that I leave.

My bags are packed, a backpack and a duffle bag, just two carry-ons are all I'm bringing. Clothes. What else am I going to need anyway? Sarah called, but I didn't answer. She sent a text right after asking if she could take me to the airport; that she doesn't want our last time seeing each other before I leave to be the horror of last night (my words, not hers). I know I need to see her, as hard as it will be to look at her through the shame and embarrassment, I need to see her and not leave her thinking that I am who I was last night. I have no plans to confess the variety of substances that contributed to my numbness and lack of humanity, I don't want to try and make excuses. The best thing I can do is forget last night and hope that she can do the same. I've got a few hours to kill so I figure I'll just lay here on the couch reading "Waking Up" and trying not to fret too much about the world I'm leaving behind and the uncertainty of what lays ahead.

I'm barely a page into the book and my already delicate attention is broken by the incessant buzzing of my cellphone. I try to ignore it once, twice, it stops. I open the book again, buzz, okay, fuck it, who is it? Incoming Call: Adam.

I answer, "Hey, what's up?"

"I got the money! I got it and I got a van! I'm going to drive to Florida. I'm doing it! You still have the weed, right?"

Adam is speaking with joyous excitement at the prospect of easy cash. I have to let him down and I feel the need to apologize for not informing him sooner that the stuff was already sold.

"Hey, man, I've got some bad news. It sold yesterday."

"No, you're joking, right? I got the money already!"

"I'm not joking, Adam. I've been in kind of a tight spot and had to get rid of it ASAP."

"Aww, no, this sucks," he says, having gone from speaking with over the top exuberance to barely making his words audible as they fight past the disappointment.

Just then it dawns on me; I might not have any more pounds to sell, but Fred has an entire weed store in his kitchen cabinet.

"Hold up, hold up, there might be something I can do. I'll call you back in 2 minutes, okay?"

"Okay, I'll be waiting," he says.

I call Fred and deliver the good news that I have a buyer with at least ten K ready to spend. It's a deal. Fred and Adam will meet and exchange green plant for green bills. Everyone's a winner.

Chapter. 23 Goodbye: From SeaTac to the Great Unknown

I wait in front of my mother's house for Sarah to arrive. It's dark and cold. I'm wearing a coat that I plan to leave with her, as I surely won't be needing it in sunny Medellin. My mom is at work so the house is empty. I choose to wait outside and enjoy the last moments of crisp, fresh Seattle air before leaving the only city I've ever known for an undetermined amount of time. The headlights of Sarah's Mercedes bounce as she turns into the uneven drive way. Her car is another symbol of the invisible distance that separates our lives, another clear indication that she is too good for me, that I don't belong with her.

I shuffle to the car carrying my overstuffed luggage. The trunk opens, I put my bags in the back and get into the passenger seat, I reach over for an embrace and kiss. She kisses me back more passionately than I would have expected. I want to tell her to drive to her apartment, that I'm moving in, that we're going to live together happily ever after; but I can't, I know the fairytale would only last until it didn't, until Juan and the boys found me and by proxy, Sarah. No, I can't drag her into that shit, not even a little, not even a chance. We begin to drive towards Sea-tac airport, words passing sparingly between us. A cloud of melancholy hangs over the car, dampening our spirits and making words, no matter what they are, seem useless. I hold her right hand as she drives with the left.

While we pass over the bridge with a view of the lit up city across the lake, she asks, "Do you know when you'll be back?"

"I hope in a few months."

"Really?" she says, sounding a bit annoyed.

"Yeah, just a few months, it's not that long. Time will fly with your new job and everything. I'll be back before you know it. You'll barely notice I left before I get back."

"That's not true. I'm going to miss you every second you're away," she says.

Silence.

We pass by Seattle, leaving it behind us on our way south. The airport directs us to stay right and follow the signs for 'Departures'.

"Is your friend, Fred, meeting you at the gate?"

"I don't know. Knowing him, I'll be sitting on the plane and he'll come running through the doors right before takeoff." She puts the car into park as we've arrived. She unbuckles her seatbelt and turns to face me. Before she can speak her voice breaks, for a moment her body trembles, she swallows and straightens her posture. She's trying to maintain composure, and I wish she would because I know that once she starts with the tears that I'll be helpless not to follow her down that path, and eventually that path will lead to me waddling through the airport like a big dumb crying idiot. I grip my knees with my hands and take an intentional breath. We look at each other. There are tears in her eyes and at the sight of this mine begin to well-up with emotion as well.

Again it is she who breaks the silence, her strength in difficult moments is something I adore about her, it reaffirms that she is the strong partner that I need.

"You're not a piece of shit. I don't know why you think that you are. I, I, I think you're actually ..." And she breaks. The tears flow and she reaches out for me, head bowed, both arms extended like she's looking for a light in the dark. I take her into my arms and try to comfort her with my touch. I need to speak but the only words that seem appropriate are 'I love you.' I say it. "I love you, Sarah. I hope you know that I do. And I know my actions don't always show that I do, but I do. I want to try to be better for you. You deserve someone better than me, but I don't want to live without you. I'll be better, I'll never be the person you deserve, but I'll try."

She pushes back, out of my embrace and stares into my eyes. Her mouth moves but no words come out. Her body softens and once again I am holding her in my arms awkwardly as she leans across the seat. "I love you, too," she whispers softly.

"We can't stay here," I say, trying to laugh a little as I speak to shake us out of the sadness.

"I know, I know. I just don't want you to leave."

"I'll be back. I won't be long. I'll be back and we'll be together. Really together, not like it has been; I want to share my life with you."

"Come back soon, okay. And don't have any fun down there," she says, adding some lighthearted laughter of her own.

We step out of the car and I pull my bags from the trunk. We kiss, stare at each other and kiss for a second time, longer and more erotic than I would normally be comfortable with in public, but in this moment I feel as if we are the only two people in the world.

Her eyes and face have turned from sadness to acceptance; again she shows a strength superior to my own.

I turn and enter the airport, alone, but feeling full and reassured that I won't ever be truly alone as long as she is part of my life, no matter the physical space between us.

The one nice thing about being in a totally fucked-up situation is that there's always something to do, something to occupy your time and your mind. My next step is finding Fred. I step to the side of the walkway and whip out my phone. There's no time for texts so I call him up. It rings, rings, and rings some more. No answer. I hang up and call him right back. Ring and more ringing until the voicemail gives me a chance to leave a message, I forego this outdated option and opt for a text.

"Im at the departures. In front of Delta. Where are you?"
Send.

I stand by the ticketing machines, waiting for Fred to appear out of thin air. I decide to keep moving along with the process while I wait with increasing anxiousness for the missing man. I check in and print my boarding passes. Seattle to Miami to Medellin. We're scheduled to arrive tomorrow around lunch time. A few minutes have passed since I called him, maybe ten. I'll wait another ten and then start slowly making my way to the security line. There's so many people coming and going, each with their own unique story of which I know nothing, but somehow the gravity of my own situation has been inflated in my head to make me think that my trip, my flight, my journey, is far and away the most important, dramatic and exhilarating in the airport. It's a kind of high knowing that I'm taking drastic action, jumping off a cliff and not knowing how far the fall is or what awaits me at the bottom.

Once again the words from Joe Rogan's podcast pass through my head and confirm that I'm making the right decision. *'Trying to stay comfortable is one of the worst decisions you could ever make as a man. Trying to stay comfortable is a terrible, terrible path. Because you're going to stay soft and weak and you're never going to figure out anything, you're never going to accomplish shit."* Joe Rogan, Adam Carolla and other talk radio hosts and podcasters raised me in a strange kind of way. Having never had a mentor or anyone to teach me about being a man when I was growing up left me looking for guidance, and I found it in the voices being pumped into my ears over the airwaves. I've felt profound connections with certain statements made by these men over the years, but none has struck me with the meaning and timeliness as when I heard Rogan talk about comfort and how it can ruin someone.

Well, right now I'm about as uncomfortable as I ever have been; I guess I'll either figure something out about life and grow as a result, or I'll... what..? Shrivel into dust and blow away? No. I just need to keep hammering down the path and eventually I'll figure a way out of this mess. This will all work out in the end if I just keep moving forward.

Still no Fred. It's time to move on without him and just hope that I see him on the other side of security. I pass through the check point without incident. Still no sign of him. I walk to the gate. No Fred. I call again. I wait. The nearly incomprehensible voice of the flight crew cackles over the speaker system to announce boarding is about to begin. I guess I'll be going to Medellin alone. Fred has once again done exactly what can be expected of Fred; to disappear without a trace only to reappear at his earliest convenience without an excuse because he doesn't feel he needs one. I doubt he got picked up by Juan and the boys, but I guess anything is possible; anyway there's nothing I can do about it now.

"Now boarding group three."

That's me. The one good part about all of this is that I had the middle seat and Fred the window. I'll take the window and enjoy the extra room in the vacant space to my right. Fuckin' Fred, man. I make it to my seat and place one last call to the missing man with little hope that it will be answered. Once again, voicemail.

I'm exhausted from the events of the past few weeks, but right now I feel fine allowing my mind to fantasize about a utopian future where Sarah and I will live in blissful peace without a worry in the world. The airplane doors close. Its official, I'm going alone. Fuckin' Fred, man. As we taxi onto the runway my eyelids become heavy and I feel myself drifting in and out of consciousness, trying to allow pleasant pictures to dance in my head, taking center stage and relieving me of the frightening reality that is my current situation.

Part II

Chapter. 24 Medellin

The soft hum of a blender, mixing who-knows-what in the kitchen, interrupts the singing birds outside my window. The sun is out and the house is warm despite the early hour. Glancing at the clock tells me it's not quite eight o'clock, and this seems as good a time as ever to roll out of bed and go see what Fred's concocting downstairs.

The first month in Medellin was a whirlwind. Seattle, and all of its troubles, disappeared the moment I got off the plane and was forced to adapt to a city that was as foreign to me as the language spoken throughout it. Love at first sight would aptly describe my relationship with this paradise city that's nestled into a green valley, with mountains protruding straight up all around it. It's like nothing I've ever seen before; a metropolis dropped into a jungle. The people are friendly and somehow seem to be more alive than those back home. I credit this to the fact that the smartphone and unlimited data plans haven't yet taken hold and begun to retard individuals, and thus society, as is the case in more developed parts of the world. The people here still look at each other in eye, and know all of their neighbors by name, and raise their children, and go to church, and have some flickering flame of life still burning inside them, unlike the spiritually dead idiot masses back in the states.
I can't speak for Fred, but I believe he would echo my fond feelings about this place, although in his case, it might be more lust than love. And his infatuation with the city might have less to do with its unique landscapes and culture, and more to do with the hordes of traveling young women passing through its center like a revolving door. I've never seen someone's sex life transform so radically as that of Fred's when he finally made it to Medellin, two days after his originally scheduled flight. His blow binge came to an abrupt end when he finally fell asleep riding the bus to the

airport, causing him to wake up confused in the abandoned bus terminal while I was soaring over land on my way south, wondering where the fuck he was. He ended up hiding out at a friend's house for a day while waiting to get the next available seat out of Seattle in route to Medellin. He made it, and ever since, the near daily rotation of Gringa or European backpacker pussy that he's been pulling would be impressive by any metric.

I slide into a pair of shorts and slip on Atletico Nacional chancals before heading downstairs. The bird song outside my window gives way to the boisterous singing of Fred as I move closer to the kitchen.

"My eyes are cryin' cryin' lonely tear drops, my heart won't ever stop."

Fred, despite all his faults, does have an impressively beautiful singing voice. Had his father not told him, 'theater is for faggots,' when he was entering the seventh grade, Fred might have become a successful showman; singing, acting, entertaining, Fred is a natural at all three.

To announce my presence I must yell in order to be heard over the orchestra of noise that accompanies Fred's breakfast preparation. "Fredrick!" I shout, trying to overpower the whirling mechanical buzz backing up Fred's musical performance.

"Buenos dias, Don Juan," responds Fred, as he clicks off the power to the blender so that we can hear each other without yelling.

My eyes begin to scan for last night's conquest. "Where is she?" I ask.

Fred turns and looks at me with a puzzled expression. "Where is who?"

"Whoever the gringa is who you ended up fucking last night? Did she already leave?"

Laughing as he searches the kitchen for his next ingredient, he says, "It's not every night, X. Last night was cien por ciento Colombiano, I just threw back some guaro with the fellas over in Itagui."

"Hmm, how strange, I hope you're not losing your powers. I've never seen someone who might actually have a pussy magnet hidden in their cock, but after this last month I believe it's possible. These traveling backpacker bitches just can't seem to control themselves around you. We need to call the Discovery Channel and have them send a film crew. This should be documented."

Fred's laugh grows louder and carries a touch of self-satisfaction as he tries to speak humbly on the topic of his recent sexual conquests.

"I mean, how many now, really? Maybe six, seven, eight if we count that guy's girlfriend who I fucked in the bar bathroom for maaayyybe thirty seconds but nah, that one doesn't count. It hasn't been that many, X."

"That doesn't count?!" I gasp. "Bullshit! That counts for two. She literally dragged you into the bathroom and dropped to her knees while her boyfriend was buying drinks at the bar."

I suspect that Fred's newfound success in this area is the result of several factors. First off, all the girls he's fucking are on vacation or 'traveling' and this gives them the freedom to act without the consequences that would normally accompany such behavior at home. None of their friends or family will ever find out about it. It's free casual sex in terms of societal repercussions; they come and go and don't have to pay the bill. Fred helps his cause by going out almost nightly. Naturally he's the life of the party, drawing attention to himself all the while lowering the inhibitions of those around him with his upbeat, *you only live once,* attitude. Add to this his penchant for pouring drinks like it's going out of style and you have the perfect combination to finish the festivities with a one night stand. The final factor is that all these girls are young, white, and from middle to upper class families going out into the world looking for adventure. Enter a big black eccentric athlete and you've found just what they're looking for to fulfill their exploratory sexual fantasy. Something that corporate daddy back home would likely roll his eyes at, if not downright freak out about.

"What are you mixing up in the blender?" I ask.

"We got some pina, manzana, lechuga, a little ajo for da health and...." Fred opens the cupboard above the sink and removes a fresh bottle of aguardiente, twists off the top and, snap, open. "And some guaro for dat ass," he says, as he proceeds to empty the entire bottle into the blender while I stare at him with shocked disbelief.

"Well. Great. Thanks, Fred. I'm not drinking that shit; it's not even eight in the fucking morning."

Fred pours the alcoholic smoothie into a glass and chugs it halfway down before lifting his brow slightly to make eye contact. I read his mind and at the same time we both say, "Don't be a bitch."

As much as I would like to rail against Fred and this unhealthy habit, there's not much I can say. Fred, even with his extreme amount of drinking, has been thriving. He's getting laid more than ever, learning Spanish, and hitting the gym one, two, sometimes three times a day, to the point where in just a month he's transformed from having the physique of an oversized bulky linebacker to being so shredded that he's looking more the part of a fitness model.

Fred refills his glass with the remaining breakfast-smoothie/mixed-drink, as I proceed to reheat an old cup of coffee from yesterday before we head out to the balcony to survey the street while we chat.

"Any word from the landlord back in Seattle?" I ask, as we sit down in our respective sillas.

"Nothing new. He'll for sure take my deposit, but if he tries to keep the six months' rent I paid before leaving I'm gonna go slap him across the face with my dick. And I told him as much," says Fred, as he opens wide, tilting back his glass at an exaggerated angle, allowing the thick mixture to slide slowly into his waiting mouth.

Shortly after we fled and cut off all contact with Juan, he sent a group of homeboys to Fred's apartment. They broke in, took the few valuables that were left behind and turned the place inside out. While the gang was leaving they apparently threatened a few of the neighbors and broke some windows, causing more than one of the buildings' tenants to call 911. All of this culminating in a distressed voicemail from Spike, the landlord, informing Fred of his immediate eviction from the building. Honestly, if that's the last of it, I'll say that we made it out fairly unscathed. So far I haven't had to confront any similarly disturbing news from back home, thank God.

"How about with you? Is Sarah still saying she's going to come down here for a visit?" Fred asks.

"That's what she's saying."

"She must be really into you, X."

"Yeah, maybe she's retarded," I utter, unable to understand her attraction to someone like myself.

Fred rolls his eyes and takes another sip from his drink before saying, "X, you could have her or damn near any girl you want. Half the chicas from Casita del Mundo were jocking your nuts, and you ignored all of them, the fuck man? It's like we were back in high school. You become a wall flower at the party and ten minutes later some artsy chick is ready to leave with you. I don't understand why you get into these moods and become a broke dick faggot. Live a little, dude."

"I just have to decide what I really want with Sarah. I don't want her to come down and then leave with gonorrhea because I've been dick slinging while we're apart. You of all people should understand. You've always been overly faithful to girlfriends; even the shitty ones like Andrea who made you wear a condom for the entirety of a yearlong relationship. I still don't know how you..." I pause, trying to remember the word in Spanish. "Agunataste eso. Agunataste, yeah? Am I saying that right?" I ask.

"Yeah, I think so. But anyway, X, she's not your girlfriend. She wasn't when you were in Seattle, so how are you gonna leave and suddenly get serious? You're not thinking, X," says Fred, as he taps the side of his head with two fingers to illustrate his point.

"Yeah, yeah, I know. It's just, I don't know. I'll figure it out, man. But, yeah, she says she wants to come visit next month, maybe for a week. We'll see. I'm not sure why, but in the days after the shit hit the fan with Juan I found myself needing her more than I've ever needed anyone in my life, like a gravitational pull was bringing us together. Maybe it's just my mind looking to distract itself, I don't know."

Fred, rolling his eyes and leaning towards me, continues, "You need to get some pussy. Your mind's not right. Shit, you think she's not back in Seattle with someone else? A girl like that with her bedroom needs? Yeah fuckin' right. Move on, X, you're in Colombia now."

Part of me wants to tell him to shut the fuck up, that he doesn't know shit and shouldn't talk about what he doesn't understand. I mean, Fred's only met Sarah once, and that was for all of twenty minutes; what does he know about her? But, another part of me feels like he's probably right. I left her and couldn't even say why I was leaving or when I'd be back. There's no way a girl like her, who could have anyone, is going to sit around sulking, plucking rose petals and patiently awaiting the return of her prince in shining shit, not a chance.

Maybe I should stray a bit and enjoy a night here tucked into something nice and warm besides a bed sheet, it's not like she'll ever find out. Fred's reasoning is resonating more and more with each word and I decide to give into his line of thinking. I slap his shoulder and say, "You're the man of the town. Where would a single, ready to mingle guy go if he were looking to meet a not so nice young lady for a night?"

Fred's eyes widen as he inquires, "Tonight? You want to do this tonight?"

"Yes, tonight. Let's go out and ruffle some feathers," I say, feeding off the excited energy suddenly present on Fred's face.

"Ah shit, Xavier is going to come out from under the rock. I'll see where the girls from Casita del Mundo are headed tonight, we'll follow them."

Fred doesn't get it. These backpacking broads aren't into me the way they are him, and furthermore, I don't want to spend my night with a bunch of gringos. If we're going out I want it to be somewhere authentically local, where there's no chance we even see another tourist.

"No, no, no, I don't want to go gallivanting around with the gringos in El Poblado or Laureles. Think of something else. Somewhere far away from Parque Lleras or La Setenta," I say.

"I got you, we'll figure it out. Are going to come hit the gym this morning?" he asks.

The gym, for Fred, are the pullup bars in the park down the street. I prefer trekking a bit further for the Unidad Deportiva de Belen, an outdoor rec-center of sorts. Pools, soccer fields, and a full outdoor gym with weights, bars, everything one could possibly need.

"You're headed down the street, right? I'm going to run the few miles to the Unidad and get it in there," I say, as Fred tilts his glass towards the heavens, extracting every last drop before responding. "Suit yourself, Forrest Gump. I'll catch you back here in a few hours."

Fred stands and heads into the kitchen, I follow as I make my way towards the stairs. He pauses by the kitchen sink, not turning on the water, but just standing suspiciously without purpose. I pass by, but before ascending the stairs I decide to wait by the corner and peer back into the kitchen. Fred reaches for another bottle of guaro in the cupboard, he cracks its seal and pours half of it into his glass. Placing the bottle back in the cupboard he's careful to shut the door quietly, in what appears to be an attempt at keeping his actions undiscovered from inquisitive ears. He lifts the glass then waits, his head turns quickly and he catches my prying eyes watching him from the hallway. Shame, or something close to it, forces him to turn back around before chugging what's in the glass. I consider chastising the man but deep down I know it will do no good; I head up the stairs without saying a word.

Chapter. 25 El Centro Plan

The gym, and the run to and from, seems to have recharged my battery; I arrive back at the house feeling confident and ready for the late night ahead. Fred beat me back and is napping on the couch. I change out of my sweaty clothes and head out to lunch, alone.
Bandeja Paisa.
Walking back to the apartment, I feel compelled by a stomach full of chicharron to follow Fred's lead and get a little shut-eye in anticipation of the night that awaits us. I go up the stairs to my bedroom and shut my eyes. While napping I have a dream. Check that, a nightmare. At some point during this 'dream,' the image of being hit by a car while running to Unidad Deportiva presents itself, but it wasn't really me who got hit. You know how dreams are; they don't make much sense a lot of the time. And in this dream it was me who was running in front of the car, but someone else was struck and died, someone who I feel must be a part of me or at least connected to my life in some way, but I just can't put my finger on who or what it was. Maybe it was just the memory of the woman in Pullman who narrowly missed being hit that has resurfaced and reimagined itself in this new subconscious form. Or maybe not. The drivers here can be beyond reckless so it's no surprise that the worry of an accident could be buried somewhere in my thoughts. Anyway, this dream has me sufficiently freaked out. Waking up, I feel the paranoid desire to check-in with everyone I'm close to and confirm their *alive and well* status. The feeling of the dream world followed me into the real world and left me with the strangest sensation of death being inside me. "Fredrick!" I yell out from the bedroom.
I know he's awake because it was his singing that broke my nap and thankfully ended the nightmare.
"X!," Fred yells in return.
"Come up here," I shout back down.

Lifting his voice several octaves Fred replies, impersonating a nervously astute maidservant, "Coming, your honor."
He enters the room with a curtsy and sly grin that may be more guaro than pure good hearted joy.
Fred takes a seat on the edge of the bed and I ask, "So what's the plan for tonight? Where we headed?"
"Strap your nuts on, hombre. We're going to El Centro."
"Jesus fuck Christ, Fred, most of the Colombians won't even go into El Centro after dark. Do you have a place in mind or are we just going to wander around until one of us gets stabbed?"
Fred looks straight through me as he predictably replies to my concerns with this usual turn of phrase, "Don't be a bitch."
El Centro during the day is a shady beehive of activity where one can't possibly watch their back from all angles. It's populated by business people, workers, homeless, prostitutes, drug dealers, drug addicts, and during sunlight hours, the police; but as it's been explained to me, the police turn the area over to the roving criminal gangs once the sun goes down below the valley walls. Fred frequents this area after hours with his local buddies from Itagui. As he tells it, no one fucks with him because they assume he's a massive Afro-Colombian who must have a reason to be there and likely business that the low level criminal elements would rather leave unbothered. I, on the other hand, am viewed as a walking ATM. There's no denying my gringo status and the poor, hungry, and addicted act as you would expect when they see a walking ATM stroll by. They jump up and try to extract as much as they can with whatever they have; sad stories, threats, polite requests, whatever they can muster to try and get theirs. I've been letting my darkly shaded beard grow, and this can, at times, give a moment's pause as to my true identity as a foreigner, but my height, white skin, and non-Colombian demeanor bring out the truth in a matter of seconds after encountering me. It's not that I want to me mistaken as a local in social situations, but as far as walking down the street unmolested, it would be nice not to be singled out and harassed every few blocks. It's a strange change of

normality here, where Fred, the black man, is given the freedom to roam unbothered, whereas I am stopped every few minutes and harangued for change or to buy a bit of bread and a soda for people living in dire circumstances. I imagine that I'm getting off easy with these street interactions, as it would certainly be a much more intrusive and uncomfortable series of events being, let's say, stopped and frisked on a weekly basis by the NYPD or whatever police department happens to make a habit out of harassing people who they view with constant suspicion based solely on their appearance.

I head into the kitchen and grab a beer from the fridge. If I'm going to go out, I want to go out a little buzzed and try to enjoy myself. I flip open one of the Spanish language books on the counter and brush up on some necessary vocabulary while I sip from a cold bottle of Pilsen and wait for Fred to come downstairs so we can head out and begin the night.

Chapter. 26 El Centro Punishment

The non-stop ringing of my phone brings me out of the dream world and into the painful reality of the morning, accompanied by one of the worst headaches of my life. It's Sarah calling, I can't answer, I can't talk to her or anyone right now. If I open my mouth I'm sure it will quickly be filled with projectile vomit as my body starts trying to cleanse itself of the garbage that was dumped into it last night. Why the fuck do I try to drink right alongside Fred? Beers, rum, aguardiente, and at the end of the night Fred had the brilliant idea of ordering a bottle of Baileys and drinking it over ice, no mixer, no nada, just straight, thick, sugar filled Baileys. One of the worst decisions of my life was to accept the full glass of this mud looking brew and slurping it down at three thirty in the morning. I can't take it, the thought of last night combined with the aftertaste on my tongue cause me to hurl. The sound of warm vomit crashing onto the floor combined with my violent heaving as I try to make sure it all gets out has alerted Fred to the scene unfolding a floor above him, here he comes, singing. "Ain't no mountain high, ain't no valley low, ain't no river wide enough, baby!"
"Hello, Fredrick," I say, as I manage to stand from the bed, tip toeing around the lake of fresh throw-up. The act of purging has brought short-term sweet relief from the pounding headache and painful knot in my stomach.
Fred puts an arm around me to help steady my balance and leads me into the bathroom. I sit on the toilet and try to press out the ball of fury that is slowly working its way from my stomach to my asshole. I want to empty myself of everything from last night. Alcohol never has been my friend and this morning she is putting an exclamation point on that fact. Sitting on the toilet, allowing all the excess liquid in my body to come pouring out, I begin to remember bits and pieces from the night before. Details are blurry, to say the least, but the overall message I came away with is that the people of Medellin are my people.

My worries about El Centro from the day before, about being knifed, constantly berated for money, or even drugged and robbed of all my belongings, now seem silly. The strangers we passed the night with couldn't have been warmer, friendlier or more welcoming.

Sure, we saw a bit of the ugly side, but overall I felt like I had walked into a family reunion after returning from some far off dangerous adventure.

These people didn't know Fred and I, but when they saw that two gringos were coming into their bar to drink and share in the experience, they welcomed us with open arms. I didn't get laid, but I didn't really try either. I was living in the moment and enjoying myself too much to try and impress some girl with false bravado and manufactured charm.

Fred swings open the bathroom door and hands me a glass of ice water.

"Fred, thank you, man. How are you feeling? No hangover?"

Standing in front of me, unbothered in a bathroom filled with the fumes of fresh shit, Fred replies, "I feel good. Are you gonna be ready for another one tonight?"

"Not a chance. I'm never drinking again," I say, before spitting between my legs into the toilet bowl. The sour taste of booze is unrelenting on my taste buds.

"Ah, you say that now. Get some rest and we'll see what happens tonight."

"Yeah, we will see. Thanks for the water. You think I can I get some privacy while I wipe my ass?"

"Yeah, sure thing, boss," Fred says, and turning to leave he shuts the door behind him. I can hear him doing something outside the door and I'm concerned about what could possibly be taking place in my room while I sit here suffering. After a moment or two it dawns on me that the noises I'm hearing are those of Fred cleaning up the bedside mess I made. Say what you will about Fred's erratic behavior, alcohol induced fucked ups, and general unpredictability, but he remains one of the only people in my life who would do this for me. I wish I was confident that I would do the same for him, but in the back of my mind I question whether or not I would. I need to be a better friend to him, to forget the bad and embrace the good.

I manage to get into the shower and stand leaning against the wall, letting the water crash over me. I could spend all day here letting the steady stream wash the pain of the hangover down the drain. I would stay here all day if my body wasn't telling me that it desperately needed at least four more hours of sleep. I exit the shower and brush my teeth over and over; brush then rinse then brush again. I want to remove every bit of wretched leftover booze that's hiding in my mouth. I refill my glass with water from the bathroom sink and take it with me to bed. The warm weather doesn't stop me from wrapping myself tightly in the covers. I look at my phone and see that Sarah called twice and there's a text that reads. *"If I'm going to visit you it would be nice if you acted like you cared."*

I toss my phone onto the other side of the bed, not wanting to deal with her right now, feeling rather disconnected from my old life in Seattle. I let my eyes close and drift back to sleep.

Chapter. 27 Intercom Fears Called Up

By the time I come to, the sun is setting and it sounds like Fred is downstairs entertaining a guest. I instinctively check my phone as is my habit; it's as if the phone has established itself as priority number one in my life; I wake up and move to check the phone, I feel social anxiety in a public area and I check my phone, I feel bored with my own thoughts and I check my phone. I'm always returning my attention to this stupid fucking square that feeds on my soul, sucking it out through my eyes and into the void of man-made technology. Part of me wants to throw it out the window and go on living without it, but we all know that society would punish me for that, but how? By 'disconnecting' me from others? These phones claim to connect us, but that's entirely bullshit, they do the opposite. They give us empty information sent from point to point while wholly cutting us off from the beauty of our current experience, our experience that doesn't rely on technology or society or the modern world.

My hand reaches for the damned thing, eyes immediately fixate on the glowing screen. Sarah has sent another message: *"Maybe I shouldn't come. It's obvious it doesn't matter to you if I do or don't."*

In my barely waking state I lack the energy to formulate a text and prefer to remain with eyes closed anyway, so I decide to call her.

Allowing my head to rest back on the pillow and my eyes to close gently I wait past two rings before hearing a disturbing sound on the other end of the line. A man answers and starts to say, "Hel--," before the rustle of a frantic hand grabs the phone away from the owner of the masculine voice.

"Hi" says Sarah, on the other end of the line.

This unexpected event has caused me to snap out of my subdued state and sit upright in bed, suddenly brought to attention by my worst fear of what may be transpiring back in Seattle while I'm away.

"Hello," I say. "Who was that?"

Sarah sounds startled and uncomfortable, but at the same time happy and joyous like someone on the receiving end of an unexpected but welcome tickle attack.

"Oh, I'm at my new job and my co-worker thought you were someone else from work calling. It's nothing really," she says, obviously aware of the suspicions rising inside of me.

"Oh, okay, how's it going with the new job?" I ask.

"I absolutely love it! I can't wait to bring you here and show you around when you get back. Do you still not know when you'll be coming home?"

"No idea, sometime after the New Year, I would guess. Are you still planning on coming down here to visit? Your texts kind of freaked me out. I'm not trying to ignore you, it's just I'm trying not to be so glued to my phone all the time, ya know. And when I don't have Wi-Fi down here I'm out of touch. But yes, obviously I care if you come. I've been missing you like crazy."

"Really? It doesn't seem like it, but I believe you; I've missed you too. Though honestly with the new job I'm not sure it's such a good idea that I take vacation right away. I'll have to think about it a little longer and talk it over with my boss."

"Hmm, okay, I wasn't expecting that. Just the other day you seemed excited and ready to come down for a week, but I guess I understand, having just started there and all. What else is new?" I ask, hoping to keep things light while probing for any clues about the mysterious man who answered.

"Hey, can I call you back? I don't have a lot of time right now," she says, in a rushed tone that makes me imagine the owner of the voice that answered the phone is now gently pulling her hand towards his crotch and she can't last any longer without one of them inadvertently making a sound that will reveal their unfaithful actions.

"Yeah, sure, just call me after work. I love you," I say, allowing my words to trail off at the end, unsure of what I'm saying and whether I really mean it.

"Uh, sorry, I really have to go. I'll call you later," she says in a hurry before terminating the call without returning my open hearted confession of love.

I throw my phone hard across the room. Instantaneous regret crashes into me, sending my body scrambling in a panicked search, desperate to confirm it's still intact and usable; because what would life be without this stupid fucking piece of technology that ties itself to us with a force more powerful than that felt between human beings. I find it lying on the floor of the bathroom, still alive and working; thank God for Steve Jobs, or the Chinese slave who constructed it, or the African child laborer who dug for the required minerals while living in abject poverty. I place it back on the bed and walk downstairs to share my sorrows with Fred and whoever his flavor of the night is.

Fred and one of his previous conquests, Emily from St. Louis, are dancing in the kitchen when I make my appearance.

"Ay, Xavier," he says. "You remember Emily?"

"Yes, nice to see you again," I say.

"Hi," she replies, barely taking her enchanted eyes off of Fred as she caresses his chest and they continue swaying to the sounds of vallenato.

I grab a fria from the fridge and head outside to sit on the balcony. My mind contemplates the phone call and the voice that initiated it. Am I really stupid enough to believe that that was just a co-worker? Am I really so distrustful that I can't believe the words that the love of my life is telling me? Either way, I feel a great angst building inside of me. The memory of this morning's hangover faded fast with rest and water and I now see no reason not to drown my worries in another round of excessive drinking.

The curtains part and Fred and Emily come to join me. Fred sits, then positions her on his lap. Our history extends deep enough that he has developed a sort of sixth sense that allows him to tap into my emotional state purely from proximity.

"What's up, X? Something happen with Sarah?"

"Ah man, yeah. How'd you know? You can see it that clearly on my face, huh?"

"What happened?" he asks.

I proceed to explain the phone call, my suspicions, analysis, everything that's passed through my mind in the last fifteen minutes since hanging up.

He looks at me with knowing, compassionate eyes before speaking, "Come to the hostel tonight. Emily's friends are there. Maybe they can help take your mind off all this."

Emily jumps into the conversation, adding, "Yeah, come, Xavier! Everyone keeps asking where you've been." Immediately after speaking she seems a touch embarrassed with her comment, as if she's spoken too soon and revealed some secret; she tucks her face into Fred's neck.

"Sure, I guess I'll do that. But Fredrick, let's take it easy on the booze tonight, okay?"

Fred doesn't speak, but his gaze communicates his usual catchphrase, and with this I go upstairs to shower and prepare myself for another long night of aguardiente, ron, and whatever else happens to be poured into my glass.

I'm washed and ready to go

Downstairs, Fred, Emily, and I take a shot of guaro before heading out in search of a cab to carry us to Belen, where we will pass the night drinking on the roof of the hostel, enjoying the incredible three hundred and sixty degree views of the city with whoever happens to be there.

Chapter. 28 Gringa Pussy Regret

It's six a.m. and the smell of cigarettes and booze
protruding from the body next to me are enough to drive
me out of bed, despite my own body crying out for more
sleep. Emily's friend, Luisa from California, left no doubt
about her intentions as soon as I arrived last night and
positioned myself on one of the rooftop beanbags. She
came right over and asked if she could sit, on my lap was
apparently what she had in mind, and I gave no protest. It
was a rather fun night back in the bedroom, but nothing
mind blowing and I don't feel any connection with her
besides the mutual pull of sexual gratification that we
apparently find in each other.
I've got to get out of here before the rest of the house
wakes up and entangles me in the hours of sitting around,
lounging through the awkward morning as inevitably will
happen after these types of nights. I head to the
downstairs bathroom instead of the one attached to my
bedroom to shit, shower, and brush the booze out of my
mouth, not wanting to not wake the sleeping beauty
snoring away in my bed.
I don my workout clothes, head outside, and begin to run
without a decided destination. My feet carry me towards
the Unidad Deportiva de Belen, but I've already decided
against going there. I need something different. In the
distance I see a familiar, but unvisited sight that calls out
to be explored. One of the mountains that engulf the city
appears to have a dirt path carved into the face of it. If I
focus my eyes I can barely make out tiny ant sized people
trekking up and down the path. I try to visualize how to
arrive at this far off place and let my feet and subconscious
do the rest. As I move towards my desired destination the
view of the mountain becomes blocked by buildings and a
city that is waking up and coming alive. I stop at Parque
Belen, already in a full sweat, and ask one of the vendors
working from a sidewalk cart selling coffee and empanadas,
"Como llegar a la montana? Donde subir?" And I point in

the direction where I believe it to be. After a long inquiring glance while contemplating the meaning my broken, heavily accented Spanish, the man replies, "Ahh, cerro de las tres cruces. Sigue por ahi."

I point with my arm to where I believe he is telling me to go, and he confirms the direction, saying, "Si, si pa' alla, parcero."

"Okay, gracias," I say, before resuming my sleep deprived run, hoping I'm headed for the now named Cerro de las Tres Cruces.

Emerging from the condensed center of Belen, I begin to see other people dressed in active wear; jogging, riding bikes, walking dogs and all heading in what appears to be the same direction. I follow this loose mass of people and luckily they lead me to what I'm looking for.

At the end of a long and quiet street lines of parked motorcycles leave no doubt that I have arrived. As I run, the street begins to thicken with activity; groups of people drinking water, juice, and eating fruit, smoking joints, either beginning or returning from their voyage up to the top of the little mountain on the edge of the city.

Without delay I start to make my way up the path. Passing by dozens people, dogs, and plants, I make it to the top after about thirty minutes of vigorous hiking, straight up hill, there are no switch backs here. At the top, the view of the city is breathtaking. I think of my life, mainly of Sarah and how badly I've fucked things up with her. I've abandoned the woman of my dreams and after yesterday's phone call I fear that I've driven her into the arms of another man. I can feel all of the fuck-ups, insecurities, and lost opportunities from the last few months come welling up to the surface. Sitting on a bench overlooking the city I begin to weep. I can't control my emotion even as I try to stifle my tears and slow my breath. As I sit with a trembling lip and tear streaked cheeks an older gentleman comes to sit beside me, reaches a hand out and pats my back before taking my hand in his for a few moments, a fatherly gesture of compassion, goodwill and understanding before he silently heads back down the path towards the city without ever saying a word, without needing to. The concern he felt for a crying stranger touched my heart, and I feel as if I'm home; that without Sarah waiting for me back in Seattle there is no reason to leave this place. I wipe my eyes and proceed to head back down the hill. The whole time my mind is questioning what to do. To try and forget Sarah even though I know I won't be able to? Or to go back to her, to do everything I can to make things work between us even though I sense it might already be too late? I don't know what I'll do. My mind changes every few steps. The apartment is coming into view and I just pray that it's empty.

Chapter. 29 The Dream Decision

Back in the living room my sleep deprived mind is playing tricks on me. It may be mid-afternoon, but I can't stay awake any longer. The few uncomfortable hours tossing, turning, and trying to force myself asleep beside Luisa after our fun but rather vanilla round of sex weren't sufficient to power me through the day. And the nonstop drip of tintos I've been funneling into my system are starting to make me twitch. My body is drained of energy from the run and my mind is barely hanging on. I need sleep, now.
Fred, Emily and Luisa still haven't left the house. They've ordered enough delivery to feed to whole damn neighborhood and Fred has already started drinking again. I'm trying to be polite, but I want to scream, *'Don't you fucks have anything better to do than lounge around the house all day! Leave!'* but I know that's just my tiredness getting the best of me, turning my friends into enemies. I've tried to subtlety signal to Luisa that I'd rather be left alone for the time being, but my hints have gone either unnoticed or ignored. She's holding my hand against my will as I sit slouched on the couch listening to Fred recount stories from our youth. I gently pull my hand away and give her a reassuring nod before stating to the group, "Guys I need to rest a little or I'm going to fall asleep here on the couch. Don't wake me up, okay." And with that I make haste for my bedroom, moving quickly as not to give Luisa a chance to follow.
Once in bed my body feels like it's going to fall apart. The run today was longer than any I'd done before and I wasn't prepared for it. The aches and pains of satisfaction from a job well done are a welcome prize for my efforts, and in a weird way I enjoy each little jab of sensation that shocks my feet, shins, quads and back.
I feel like my body is telling me I did a good job. As my eyes close and I begin to drift in and out of consciousness, my mind is filled with thoughts of her. Sarah. She's living inside of me. I can feel her spirit touch every part of me as

I fade into sleep. I dream vividly of Sarah, of her soft touch, her perfectly placed words, her inner strength during trying times, her eyes that I feel I've known my whole life regardless of the recent nature of our relationship.

I wake up with no question as to her meaning in my life; she's the one.

It feels as if the dream world has decided for me. I'll return to Seattle as soon as I can and never again leave her side. I'll confess everything, Juan, the drugs, all of it. I'll pour my soul out at her feet and profess my desire to spend the rest of my life with her. I now have a purpose, to ensure that I never risk losing her again. In the morning I'll arrange for a flight home.

Chapter. 30 I Loved and I Lost

I'm surrounded by darkness as I wake up from a much needed rest. The house is eerily silent. I walk barefoot across the hard cold floor into Fred's room, listening carefully for the breath of a sleeping being, nothing. I flip on the light, the bed is empty. I turn the light off before making my way downstairs. The glowing microwave clock tells me its four forty five in the morning. Fred must still be out drinking or have found a bed for the night with Emily or another nice visiting gringa who didn't want to sleep alone. Before going to the balcony to sit and plan out the words I intend to say to Sarah, I prepare a cup of instant coffee on the stovetop, huddling over the flame, lost in thought like a vagabond street person pondering a new day's unknown. I take my steaming beverage and head to the balcony to observe the predawn street below.

The emotion rolling over me immediately after waking up from the dream was strong, crushing me under it weight, but it's fading now with every passing minute. Doubts are creeping into my mind. I had sex with a girl I barely know just a night ago; how can I say I'm in love with Sarah when my actions tell such a different story? Was I just tired and thinking nonsensically, then dreamed up a fantasy that I couldn't possibly bring to fruition in the real world? Or can I do this? Can I go to her and be the man she deserves? I know she's the one person in this world that I need by my side, but I feel unworthy and thus unwilling to corrupt her perfect life with my poisonous presence. What if I go back and we live together and after a few months she hears a knock on the door while I'm away and standing there is Juan with his crew? Even without the threat of external forces interfering with her life, there's me. What kind of effect would I have on her, on her life of success, happiness and normality? I fear that I'll fuck it all up, but I know I have no other option. The pull to her is too strong to deny. I'm getting the goddamn plane ticket and going to her.

It's getting close to five a.m. here which means it's two in the morning back in Seattle. As lame as I feel sending a text to convey an emotion that a hundred of the most eloquently written pages couldn't portray, I know that calling and rambling on and on at this hour would be an even worse option. I'll send her a brief, to the point message that she'll wake up to in the morning.

To Sarah: *"I've been thinking about us and I realize I can't deny what I feel for you any longer. I want to be with you. I'm coming back to Seattle ASAP and I want to spend every day with you from here on out. Ps Im sober;) Just drunk on you."*

Now the hard part starts. Waiting. I might as well look at flights, but first I have to eat and get some more coffee. I doubt much is open at this hour but maybe I can find a bakery to get an empanada and some fresh bread. I throw on decent enough looking clothes and head for the door.

Stepping out into the hallway, I can hear people coming up the stairwell, the unmistakable voice of Fred the loudest in the group. In typical drunk, five a.m. fashion, it takes them an exceedingly long time to reach the top of the stairs, where I stand, waiting, arms crossed, painting the look on my face of a disapproving father. It's the same group from the night before, Fred, Emily and Luisa. And Luisa appears to be the drunkest of the three. She lunges at me with open arms as soon as she reaches the top step. I take her by the elbows to help steady her balance.

"Kiss me," she says, with barely open eyes and a posture that suggests her bones are made of rubber.

I direct my attention to the other two in the group, asking in jest, "So, looks like you guys decided not to drink tonight, huh?"

Fred is leaning on the door as Emily checks her phone with difficulty. For some unknown reason, none of them have entered the apartment. Luisa pulls her slouched-self straight, clinging to my shoulders as she hoists herself upward. Her mouth envelops my ear and I instinctively jerk back a bit and look down into her glazed over eyes. "Fuck me," she whispers, in the least sexy way imaginable. I turn to Fred, trying to contain my laughter and signaling for him to take over as Luisa's personal scaffolding. He reaches for her arm and helps her to the door. The three of them go inside. Luisa shoots me a dirty look as she passes through the doorway.

I'm happy to leave that scene behind.

I walk for a few blocks and eventually find a bakery that's open and bustling even before the sun has come up. I sit down and order a tinto, agua, dos bunuelos, y una empanada. Printed on the table is the Wi-Fi network and password. I know that Sarah must be asleep and won't have replied to my message, but the glint of hope that she woke up unexpectedly and has already responded causes me to connect and check my messages. To my great surprise I see the notification of one new message from, Sarah: *"Don't come back. Not for me. We need to talk, sorry."*

I can't believe this. What could this be about? Deep down I think I know what it's about, but I don't want to accept it. I type out rushed response. To Sarah: *"Tell me what this is about. Just be honest and don't worry about hurting me. I want the truth."*

The waitress serves me my order while I stare possessed at the screen in my hand that holds the incoming answer to my destiny.

Ping.

One new message. From Sarah: *"I'm seeing someone else and it's serious. I'm sorry I didn't tell you but you're gone and I didn't want to do it over the phone. It would be better if you didn't contact me again."*

I sit stunned, unable to comprehend what's happening. Rage suddenly takes control of me and I stand, phone clutched tightly between the crushing pressure of my spastic hand. Smash! I throw the phone to the ground with full force, causing it to shatter into a million pieces. I stare at the fragments of broken glass and cracked black case spread about my feet. For an instant I feel nothing. After a few long moments in which my mind races through hours of condensed thought, I look up and see all the faces in the bakery staring at me. They must think I'm some coked out gringo finally losing it after too many days pounding the powder. I can't speak, especially not in a foreign language, so I take out a twenty thousand peso bill and leave it on the table before turning and running at full speed down the empty early morning streets until I reach the apartment. Tears are streaming down my face when I arrive at the door. There's music inside and I tell myself to get it together before going in. I need to hurry past everyone inside and launch myself into bed without making a scene. Luckily, once I open the door I don't see anyone. It looks like the three of them have all passed out in Fred's room. I shut the music off. In the kitchen I go to Fred's stash of guaro in the cupboard. I pour out what remains of an already cracked bottle into a cup and drink it halfway down before gagging and needing to rinse with water. The tears have subsided and so has the panicked breath. Before having a chance to finish what remains in the glass, Fred appears.

"What's going on?" he asks, struggling to stay awake, but clearly concerned enough to leave himself no other option.

"Sarah told me to go fucking kill myself," I cry out, my voice cracking under the weight of heartbreak.

"What? What happened?" he asks, as he comes closer and takes the glass from my shaking hand.

Rubbing my eyes and sucking in a few deep breaths I manage to say, "She didn't tell me to kill myself. She would never say that. I told her I wanted to come back and be with her and she told me she's seeing someone else and that I shouldn't even fucking call her again. I don't know what to do, man. How did I fuck this up so bad? It took me all this time to finally realize how much she means to me and now that I do she leaves me for some fucking guy at work."

Fred pats my shoulder and takes a sip of the guaro. He walks with me to the couch and hands me back the glass, now only a quarter full. I drink it down. Fred sits with me on the couch, listening, while I manically pontificate on a lonely future.

Chapter. 31 Death in the Afternoon

The streets of Medellin are buzzing with activity this
afternoon. I convinced Fred to join me instead of taking off
on his regular routine; I think he's taking pity on me
following my emotional breakdown in the early hours of the
morning. Amazingly, I managed to fall back asleep and had
to be roughly shaken awake shortly after noon. We wasted
no time setting off on the five or so kilometer run in order
to reach the Unidad Deportiva for a workout together. We
chat as best we can while running, and I relive the pain of
first seeing her message while I recount the details from
the scene at the bakery. Fred continues to repeat that
he's *sure I'll get over it in no time'*, but I'm doubtful that
the memory of her will ever leave me.
Fighting against the crushing sensation of loss, feelings of
gratitude start to flicker in the distant darkness of my mind
like fireflies in the night sky. The gratitude I feel for having
someone like Fred in my life seems to be amplified by the
physical exercise of repeated motions carrying us to our
destination; using only our bodies, the way we were
designed to travel, the way we did so for thousands of
years before we began to forget and neglect our natural
instincts with the passage of time and the advent of
technology which continues to move us farther and farther
away from our true purpose. It's as if the running motions
of my body, the burning in my lungs, my racing pulse are
helping to open my heart and allowing it to feel the caring
love of true friendship. I try to verbalize this gratitude to
Fred but it comes out winded and broken as we run.
"Fred... thank you... for being a friend, a real friend... I
need you more than you know right now... thank you."
Fred just looks at me and laughs as he flicks beads of
sweat from his brow. I didn't need, or expect, any other
answer. His years of actions, caring for me in times of
need, have made it clear just how he feels. We reach the
Unidad Deportiva, sweaty and out of breath. I feel rather
spent and need a few minutes to recover, but Fred jumps

right into his workout, wasting no time. After a lengthy rest on one of the benches bordering the gym area I decide to join him on the pull up bars.

I've barely started, but Fred is already closing in on a hundred pull-ups for the day while I'm struggling to finish sets of five and still haven't made it to fifty. The emotional rollercoaster of the last few hours has taken a toll both mentally and physically. I can't remember the last time I felt so weak.

"What are you at, Fredrick?" I ask.

While working out, Fred has a tendency to lose all personality and charm, becoming robotic in his communications. "One hundred and seven," he responds, deadpan, before hoisting himself back onto the bar and proceeding to bust out a set of eleven before dropping down and plainly stating, "Ya termine. Vamos pa' agua."

"Listo," I say, not feeling any to need to further exert myself while in this emotionally weakened state.

We walk to one of the tiendas that sell drinks, snacks, fresh fruit, coffee, whatever you could need before, during or after a workout, and ask for dos bolsas de agua before finding a table to sit at.

The people here stare with curious eyes at the two out of place, oversized gringos who ventured out of the tourist district of El Poblado. A few strangers holler out familiar English words, "hey," "hello, mister," "motherfucker". We wave and respond with a simple "buenas", not wanting to be overly inviting and thus end up in a long, difficult to understand conversation bouncing between two languages that neither party has mastered fully.

Recovering our strength and sipping water, we fall into conversation and surprisingly Fred seems more interested than I would have expected in this whole Sarah thing. His advice that, *if I truly don't think I can forget her and let her go, then I should go back and make her mine,* shocks the shit out of me. He's never been a romantic, and in my view he's rather chauvinistic in his approach to female relations, but maybe he sees something that makes my need for her undeniable. However, it's his lack of knowledge about her that allows him to believe this to be possible. I, on the other hand, know Sarah well enough to know that if she says *'don't contact me again,'* then she means it. I've never known her to go back on anything she's said. One of the things I love about her is her dedication to her word; if she says it she means it and she will live it. I know that there's no getting her back. Regardless of my protests about it being a dead end, finished, for good, Fred gives an impassioned plea about love and destiny and ends it with, "If it's meant to be then go make it be. If it doesn't happen, then at least you know you tired."

"Fred, you don't know this girl. If go back and start a full court press she's going freak and file for a restraining order. If she says it's over then it's over."

"She really got to you, huh? I guess sometimes you just have to accept shit the way it is and move on. I know you can't just *'move on'* that easily, but in time, X. In time you'll meet someone else forget all about her."

I tuck my head into my hands and say through a covered mouth, "Not one like her I won't. I'll never find another Sarah."

Fred stands from the table and disappears behind one of the buildings. I'm left to contemplate my new place in the world, a place of loneliness and with little hope that I'll ever again find someone who connects with me the way she did.

Fred reappears quickly, poking his head from around the corner and giving a shout to get my attention. "Ay! X, come here," he mumbles, with a lit joint dangling from his mouth.

I walk over to him, asking, "Where did you get this?" while gesturing towards his mouth and the half smoked marijuana cigarette.

"I just asked that group over there smoking for, *'un poquito'* and they handed it to me."

"You probably scared the shit out of them," I say.

"Nah, they were cool," he says. "Ay, I've been thinking a lot lately and reading up on bad motherfuckers throughout history and how they fulfilled their destiny and all that shit. The type of motherfuckers who are getting shit done that most of us would think of as impossible. And, man, let me tell you, I don't think we've got anything to worry about.

We're young and dumb but we've fucked up so much already that we've got the experience of someone three times our age. As long as we stay alive and don't fuck up too bad, I know that shit will work out for us. We've just got to keep hammering."

Another of Fred's long, weed enhanced soliloquies is on the way and I close my mouth and prepare my ears to listen intently to try and soak up whatever wisdom may be coming my way.

"Look," he says, while inhaling deeply from the joint before passing it to me and continuing. "Most motherfuckers never take the first step because they're too embarrassed to start at step one, at the bottom. Look at all these dudes doing pull-ups and shit out here, most of them never do even one *real* fuckin' pull-up, and never will. Not even one. They bend their arms half way and never do the full range of motion because they're scared to look weak doing sets of one or two, but, fuck, man, that's what we all have to do if we ever want to truly move to the next level. Most these people will live and die at level one of life because of fear. But, man, as weak as you might look and feel in your own head you've got to start with only doing one, one correct is better than ten with bad form. Those motherfuckers are going to spend years wasting time doing half pull-ups because they're too prideful to take step one; committing to an honest practice with good form. But, X, I've seen it, man, you put yourself at step fucking one, in the basement, and that's why I know you'll be fine. You're not afraid to find the absolute fucking bottom and go from there."

"Thanks, man, I for sure feel at the bottom right now," I say, while letting out a good humored chuckle.

"You ready to run back?" asks Fred.

"You sure you don't want to grab the metro? I'm dead tired."

"Ay, without pain and discomfort there is no growth. Lace your shoes up and let's get ready to suffer," he says.

"Okay, fine, we'll run, but pass me the end of that joint first."

I take a few hits before passing it back to Fred. He hits it one last time then flips the butt into a trash receptacle and starts jogging slowly out of the park.

Even at this relaxed pace I'm having trouble keeping up with him. He glances back occasionally to make sure I'm still following, but proceeds to open up a gap of a few dozen yards between us. I slow at each intersection to check for cars and this careful approach further widens the gap as Fred chooses to throw caution to the wind and dash through the streets, narrowly slipping between traffic. Fred is drifting in and out of sight as he continues to lengthen his lead. I need to push it a little and catch up or he's going to lose me and damage my ego in the process. I start to increase my pace to a damn near sprint. Once again I see Fred up ahead, he's waiting on a corner for a break in the traffic in order to maneuver across. I arrive at his side out of breath, lungs burning, heart thumping, and my feet screaming to be set free from their shoes and dunked into a bucket of ice water.

I clap my hand onto Fred's shoulder and say with exasperation, "You've got to slow down a bit, man. Just a bit."

Fred's head swivels towards me and he feigns surprise at my appearance, then disgust at my request that he slow down. Head turned behind him and hand raised as if to wave goodbye, he launches himself back into a running motion without taking his eyes off me. One step, then another, he's now into the street moving recklessly forward. As he takes his third bounding leap into traffic I suddenly see what's coming.

The terror in my eyes registers with Fred and he begins to turn his gaze back in front of him, but it's too late. A bus traveling at high speed is on a collision course with the only true friend I've ever had. The sound and sight are sickening, louder and more violent than I could have imagined. His body goes flying. His shoes dislodge from his feet and are left lying at the point of impact. I run forward. I reach his body and instinctively drop my hands onto his chest, unmoving, as his lifeless body rests in the middle of the road.

His head is concaved from the impact with the front of the bus; one of his eyes appears to have liquefied. Everything is silent until the sound of my own screaming voice slowly returns me to my senses.

There are dozens of people standing around, everyone eagerly gathering to catch a close-up glimpse of the often feared, but rarely viewed, death scene. I get up and walk back to the sidewalk, allowing the paramedics space to discover what is already plainly obvious to everyone who has seen his contorted body, he's dead without a chance of coming back.

At least an hour goes by before I can summon the strength to begin the necessary responsibilities of informing people about the tragic death of a young person who touched the lives of everyone he came into contact with. Back at the apartment, I grab Fred's cellphone since I no longer have my own. I'll need his family's contact information and a way to reach people. Thank goodness Fred had nothing to hide and was nonchalant about giving out his pass code.

I thoroughly embarrass myself while breaking the news to his father. At first I didn't think I could do it at all. I'm a blubbering, crying, child on the phone, unable to offer any strength during this tragic moment of loss. His father takes the news stoically, surely unappreciative of the sloppy, emotional wreck blabbering without tact or grace on the other end of the line.

I can't stay in the apartment; the sense that Fred will be coming back any minute is beyond unsettling. I gather a few belongings and necessities, throw them into a bag and leave as quickly as I can. I have no decided destination, but I figure I'll eventually check into a hotel for the night. Wondering around aimlessly the tears continue to flow, not steadily, they stop for a few minutes but inevitably return. I've been loitering around the neighborhood trying to hide in plain sight for what seems like hours now, although I know it hasn't been nearly as long as it feels, time is crawling. I need to leave this area and go somewhere unknown, try to disconnect by distracting myself with new surroundings. I walk to the metro. In route I predictably begin balling my eyes out yet again and need to take several moments to calm myself before entering the station. I pull my Civica card from my wallet, pass through the turnstiles and walk down the stairs onto the platform of the Industriales metro station. Fearful that I'll once again begin weeping, I walk to the far end and stand with my back to the entrance, putting as much distance as I can between myself and the other soon to be passengers. Time has become an abstract idea that I'm no longer able to track in my head. I don't know how long I've been standing here, too close to the edge of the platform, allowing my mind to be filled with darkness, when I hear, "Senor, senor." The voice coming from someone behind me, speaking with urgency.

I turn to face the beckoning voice and discover it's a metro police officer, pointing to my feet as he speaks in not fully understood Spanish.

"No cruce la linea amarilla," he says.

"No entiendo," I reply, not understanding what he is trying to tell me.

The police officer pauses to think, then says in slow, heavily accented English. "Brother, no step in the yellow line."

"Ah, okay, entiendo, lo siento," I say, and step back from the edge of the platform that is painted with a wide yellow line, informing passengers to stand back to in order to avoid falling, intentionally or otherwise, in front of an oncoming train.

"I no want you to end hurt. Are you okay?" he says, looking into my eyes with a knowingness that shows he could tell what I was thinking in the back of my head as I stood dangerously close to the edge.

"Estoy bien. I'm okay, thank you." I say.

He gently takes me by the arm and leads me several additional steps back towards safety. Reaching into his pocket he removes something that at first appears to be a tissue, and I assume that I must have started crying again without even knowing it. My eyes focus as my hand reaches for what I now recognize as some sort of business card coming my way.

"For you, brother," he says, handing the card to my slightly quivering hand.

"Thanks," I say, without carefully examining what it is he's handed me. He smiles a concerned, kind smile before turning his back and resuming his walk; pacing up and down the platform. I bring what he handed me closer to my face so that my worn out eyes can make sense of it. 'Sacred Medicine' is all it says, and there's a phone number below and the logo for the messaging app, Whatsapp. I place the card into my pocket, noticing that the next train is arriving.

I get on and ride until the Acevedo station where I transfer to the metro-cable that carries passengers high up into the hills of the favela. From the hillside I continue ascending higher after transferring to the connected metro-cable from Santo Domingo to Parque Arvi, a nature reserve located on the crest of the Aburra Valley mountains that encompass the city below. Stepping out of the dangling cable car, after passing over several miles of uninhabited jungle, the air is cold, fresh and clean.

I begin walking with no sense of direction, not caring where I end up. I have enough clothes and supplies to last me a night or two, but eventually I'll need to return to the apartment to collect my things and make the terrible decision about what to do with all of Fred's stuff. I wonder long enough that I eventually end up in the town square of Santa Elena.

Sitting in a café, wanting to distract my mind, I decide to turn on Fred's phone and contact the number on the 'Sacred Medicine' business card. If anything, I hope it will be a way to get my mind off the last twenty four hours.

I receive a response almost instantaneously. I'm sent a document containing pages of information about sacred medicines and the group 'Sendero a la Luz'. As far as I can comprehend, the person on the other end of the whatsapp number is with a foundation that uses ancient plant medicines to heal traumas and impart knowledge to those who choose to explore the spirit world. They call the medicine Yage, something I've never heard of before, but after a quick Google search I realize that it is just another name for Ayahuasca. I've heard about Ayahuasca on the Rogan podcast as he regularly has on guests who are users of psychedelics and praise their experiences as being positive and transformational. If I ever needed healing and knowledge in my life, now would be the time. I ask if they have any availability in the coming days and he tells me that tonight they will begin a two day ceremony at their Santa Elena location. As it turns out, my ride up to the top of the valley has left me only a short walk from the retreat center. He asks if I would like to participate in the ceremony that is set to begin in a few hours. Without giving it much thought I agree, asking him to save me a spot. He offers a ride, but after seeing the location on the map I decline and tell him that I'll start walking and should be there in under an hour.

Chapter. 32 Yage: A Portal to the Spirit World

Arriving at what I hope is the retreat center, I see nothing from the driveway that would lead me to believe that this property is anything other than a large family home. It looks like all the other plots of land that I passed by on my walk here, no sign, no nothing. Making my way down the path and turning the corner, a long building that clearly isn't a house becomes visible. As I continue to walk farther down the path, more and more of the property shows itself. There is a large garden, tall trees, more yard than any one family could need and a round thatch structure that looks like something straight out of an ancient Amazonian village. It's clear I've found the place I'm looking for. I walk towards the home that is situated on the upper half of the sloping property; and as I approach, a man walks out through the front door. He has his hair cut razor short, he's wearing skate shoes, sweats and a hoodie. He looks at me and smiles and I can feel happiness radiating out of him.
"You must be Xavier," he says, in perfect English with barely any accent, although there is a slight twist to his speech, caused by an oversized ball of something placed squarely in his cheek that reminds me of chewing tobacco, but must be four times the size of any 'chew' I've ever seen planted in someone's lip.
"Yes, I'm Xavier," I say, as I extend my hand.
We shake and he says, "I'm Juan David, we spoke on whatsapp. Welcome to Sendero a la Luz. Did you have any problem finding the place?"
"No, not at all, I just followed the map."
"Okay, that's great. Since you came kind of last minute I need to go over some medical forms and ask you some questions, if that's okay?"
"Yeah, sure, no problem, should we do that now?"
"Sure, why don't you go put your bags in one of the upstairs bedrooms and then come back down and we'll go over everything," he says, casually, with a simple smile that somehow confirms his authentic desire to connect

beyond the surface of banal greetings. His presence is stoic but joyful and makes me feel welcomed and at home, even tranquil, despite my fragile emotion state.

"Great," I say, before heading up the wooden staircase and leaving my bag on one of the beds in the upstairs bunk room.

I head back down and find Juan David drinking agua-panella outside at the table that sits covered by an awning and overlooks the property, perched like a lookout post.

"Okay, Xavier, have a seat," he says, as he opens a notebook and begins to write notes on a fresh page.

He asks me all about my medical history, illnesses, injuries, and medications. I relay to him that I am healthy and feel physically and psychologically ready for whatever comes my way during the ceremony.

"What brings you here?" he asks, with a change of tone that suggests the required medical necessities are finished and it's time to start getting serious about this question and answer session.

I don't know what to say. Should I keep it simple? Or go into an hour's long explanation of the last few hours, days, weeks, months that have somehow resulted with me walking blindly into an ayahuasca retreat with less than half a day's notice? Without giving my mind a chance to formulate a decent response, I blurt out, "I want to heal some old wounds and I've heard people have really positive experiences with Ayahuasca, or sorry, Yage. So I wanted to try it."

He looks at me, contemplating my answer and I can feel his stare pushing me to continue, but I don't want to freak out and break down while recounting the tragedy of this morning or explaining the fresh wound on my heart left by Sarah.

"Anything else?" he asks.

Again, without much thought I begin talking, trying to tell him what I think he wants to hear and what will hopefully end the questions before I crack.

"I guess I would like to build some relationships with my family that I never had. My Mom and Dad, you know? I hope that maybe this experience can help me feel comfortable talking to them since we never really had a bond when I was growing up." I hope this will be a sufficient answer and stop his probing questions as to my motive for being here.

"Okay, thanks, but what about a wife or girlfriend?"

"I'm single with no kids," I say curtly.

"Any recent loss or hardship with friends that you're dealing with?" he asks.

I feel like he somehow knows what happened and is poking me to get it out in the open. I can't speak about Sarah or Fred without breaking down, so I just say, "Nope, not really," as I bite the inside of my cheek, trying to hold it together.

"Okay, thank you, Xavier. You're going to do fine," he says, as he shuts his notebook and stands to go back inside.

I pass the time strolling about the property and causally meeting the other shamans who are beginning to arrive for the ceremony. Each one of them seems to have stumbled upon the secret to happiness. They laugh and joke and bring a jovial energy that puts me at ease, and almost even makes me smile despite the deep pit of loss, angst and hopelessness that I currently sit at the bottom of.

Juan David, I've come to learn, is the lead shaman and owner of this retreat. One of the younger, apprentice shamans explains to me the origins of the foundation and how they are not all 'Indians,' but rather, individuals from all walks of life and parts of Colombia who have dedicated their lives to working with the scared plants in order to heal, attain knowledge, and connect with the spiritual world; at least that's the best I can understand it while being hit with mountains of information and also struggling to remain stable in the face of recent heartbreak and loss. Sitting on the couch in the living room of the guest house I see two men appear who, judging by their look, I assume must not be shamans. I stand up to introduce myself, feeling overly formal in the relaxed vibe of the place.

"Hi, I'm Xavier," I say, as I shake hands with the first to enter.

"I'm Levi," replies the one with glasses, disheveled hair and a traveler's backpack.

"Hey, brother," says the second, a bald man with short facial hair and a wide grin, as he declines the handshake and pulls me in for a rather unexpected embrace. "I'm Gamal."

We sit on the semi-circle couch and begin to chat while the shamans and their wives and children pass between the kitchen and living room, preparing for the night ahead. Gamal asks where I'm from, and my response of, "The U.S." seem insufficient. He stares at me blankly, waving his hands in a *'come on give me more'* motion.

"Seattle, I'm from Seattle. How about you two?" I ask, wanting to get the subject off of me and learn a little more about what brought these two apparently sane, normal looking guys to a hillside finca outside of Medellin in order to ingest a powerful psychedelic.

Gamal goes first. "I'm from Jordan, but I've been spending about half my time here in Colombia for the last six or seven years." As he says this a shaman dressed in all white enters the room from outside and wraps him in a bear hug from behind, while saying, "G man, you back, so good to see you, brother."

Gamal begins conversing with his old friend and Levi gives me a run down on where he comes from and what he's doing here. "I'm from Israel, yea. I came here for the first time, maybe it was three years ago. And after the last ceremony I received homework to go and help my family back home. So, I helped my family back in Israel, started a business and spent a year following the guidance from my last journey with the medicine. And now I am back here to ask God for more guidance. This is my home; I have been to Peru and Brazil to participate in ayahuasca ceremonies and there is nowhere else like here, at least none that I have known. You picked the right place, here they care for you, they support you, you'll never be left alone like you would at many other places. I just do not understand why here is not more popular. Colombia is the closest point of South America to your people, the North American's, and the community here is like the perfect family. People should be coming here; this place should be packed with people every week. I do not understand why it isn't. What they do here is something special."

When Levi speaks it's clear that he's sincere in his feeling of attachment to the community here. I get the feeling that these people have all known each other for some great length of time, although I know that is not necessarily the case, but the sense that they're one big family is apparent in both their words and actions.

The sun set hours ago and we finally hear the music being played from the ceremonial long-house down below that signals the start of the night's rituals. Many more participants have arrived. There are two friends who have traveled together from France, a young woman from New Jersey who makes regular trips to Colombia for the sole purpose of coming to this retreat and drinking the medicine, and around ten locals from Medellin and the surrounding areas, some who have drank the yage before and some, who like me, will be having their first taste of it tonight.

I follow the others down the grassy hill to the long rectangular building. Inside, the shamans are seated in front and we take seats facing them.

My limited Spanish allows me to understand little of what's being said, but luckily Juan David translates the important pieces and every few minutes checks on the foreigners to make sure we understand and to see if we have any questions.

We discuss life and how to find balance between the macro and micro. Juan David explains that there is no time limit and this discussion could go on for hours. I'm worried that I'll begin to fade and be restless and sleepy by the time we actually drink the yage. I'm not really a night owl. I blink my eyes to fight off a yawn. A moment later one of the younger shamans leads me to two bowls ceremoniously placed on an altar.

He demonstrates how to use a spoon, dumping a green powder into his mouth and maneuvering it into the crease of his gums, I follow his lead and quickly my lips and tongue begin to feel numb.

Next, he places a small dollop of thick, black paste on the top of my right hand. He demonstrates a licking motion and I follow suit, dabbing my tongue on the substance that tastes like salted tobacco. I return to my seat and continue listening to the discussion while every few minutes taking a lick of tobacco paste on my hand and adjusting the powder inside my mouth with my tongue. The influence of these two substances is subtle but effective; I am no longer feeling drowsy, but rather like I've just had a cup or two of extra strength coffee.

I'm too reserved and unsure of myself in this new environment to participate in the discussion, but a few of the other gringos do, with Juan David translating their words into Spanish. Everyone is listened to intently and with respect. Following the discussion we stand and everyone joins hands as the music starts. It feels oddly familiar to my distant memories of attending Catholic services with my Mom when I was a small child. As the song concludes the men line up first, waiting in front of Juan David and two other shamans who prepare the yage for consumption. The similarities with religious ritual don't stop with the handholding and song; receiving the yage feels just like taking communion, it is presented in a small cup and after drinking it you turn forty five degrees to face another shaman who gives you a sip of water with which to wash it down. I drink second behind Levi and immediately head outside to sit by the fire and wait for it to kick in. Others come outside and sit or stand or pass by, but no one speaks. It's cold outside and I've wrapped myself in a thick wool blanket that was provided to each of the participants.

Time goes by and the only sensation I'm getting is a hard knot in the pit of my stomach. The fire fades and it becomes difficult to see the faces of those passing between the bathroom, puke buckets, and long house. Occasionally someone comes outside, vomits into the bucket or uses the restroom before returning indoors to lie on a mattress or in a hammock or sit in a chair. For some reason, I prefer being outside, so I've situated myself by the dwindling fire and decided not to move until the medicine starts working.

I don't have a phone or a watch, but I assume at least an hour or two have passed since ingestion. I'm starting to get concerned about why it isn't taking hold. Just then, Juan David comes out from the long-house and walks up to me, exhibiting none of his earlier casual lightheartedness. He's wearing a blank expression and asks simply and directly, "Are you feeling it?"
I answer, "No, nothing."
"Do you want another cup?"
"Yes."
He gestures with his hand for me to follow and I do so. We re-enter the long-house and walk to where the altar stands. He proceeds through the rituals, appearing to bless the yage before serving it. He hands me the cup which I throw back almost as if it were a shot at a bar, but with much more reverence. The taste is what I imagine old, spoiled wine to taste like; nothing overly rancid or offensive but not pleasurable in any way. The second cup hits my stomach like a ton of bricks and I'm sure that I'll end up puking in no time. To avoid soiling the other guests with my anticipated purge, I go back outside and stare at the puke bucket with nervous expectation. But, no, I don't hurl and after another hour or so with no effect I sluggishly walk back inside and curl into a ball in one of the hammocks. My eyes close and I feel like I'm just about ready to catch some much needed sleep when the music starts. And it's entirely different from the simple churchlike music at start of the ceremony. I now understand one of the reasons why there are so many shamans present; they're a band; and no, their music is nothing like what you would hear at Sunday mass. There must be five or six of them playing; guitar, harmonica, drums, flutes and singing. Singing and music like I've never heard before; suddenly, sleep is the farthest thing from my mind. I can't believe the experience I'm living and the memory of having just lost my best friend in a country far from home coupled with the love of my life leaving me due to my own sheer stupidity makes me feel a bit guilty about how deeply I am enjoying the present moment. Now, sitting up in the hammock, smiling, at four maybe five in the morning, attending the

best concert I could have ever imagined in complete darkness while everyone around me trips their balls off and I feel nothing from the medicine but a bulging gut, but somehow I'm deeply content. I enjoy the music and the moment more than I could have imagined, more than feels justified. They play until the sun comes up and shines its rays into the room, naturally illuminating the space as the only light source in this hall that lacks electricity.

The morning sun reminds me that I may have slept for an hour in the last twenty four, and that I should head up to the bunk house to try and get some rest.

Upstairs, I strip off my clothes, shower, and tuck myself into bed. I toss, I turn. I cover my head with the pillow, nothing seems to work. The sun coming through the window, the noise of busy people working to clean up from last night and prepare for tonight's quickly approaching ceremony don't allow me one iota of real sleep.

I lay here with eyes closed but alert, jealous of the snores in the bunks beside me.

I can't take the boredom so I throw on a shirt and sandals and head downstairs. I find Juan David once again seated by the table on the patio that overlooks the property, talking with Gamal. I quietly take a seat.

"Ay, Xavier, how was your night?" asks Juan David, as I sit across from him.

"It was okay, the music was amazing, but, no, I didn't feel any effects," I say.

Gamal asks, "Did you purge?"

"No, nothing. No puking, no shitting. Just a rock in my stomach," I say.

Juan David adds, "That's good, brother. That means it's in your blood now. Tonight you are going to feel it, all of it, just wait."

"Okay, I hope so. We'll see," I say, trying to sound upbeat and optimistic through the tired fatigue weighing heavily on every cell of my body.

I sit back and listen carefully as the two of them continue their conversation.

Juan David speaks casually, but with purpose, while looking around at the beautiful surroundings. "We all have a seat in life and the yage can help you find that seat. First we must learn to sit, then we learn to listen, then we learn to speak. But, the mistake many make is that they never find their seat. They start on the path of religion, then when that gets hard they try yoga, but they get bored, then they come to drink the yage, but eventually leave for another path. There is a time to try different paths in life, but when you find the one that speaks to you, that is when you must commit to it, for life. The yage can help show you the direction, but you must do the hard work back here in the real world in order to carve your own path."

He continues as we listen carefully.

"We know about the sixties and seventies, yes? They used the plants and other substances and guess what, they received the message, too; peace, love, mother earth, brotherhood, but what did they do? They did nothing, they left the teachings in the spirit world and in the years that followed what happened? Destruction of the environment, mental illness, degradation of the family. This is why we have the rituals, to keep us humble and in balance with the sacred plants. To learn from them with respect and to not abuse their power. The hippie generation had no rituals, no system for learning from the plants and that is why they failed to heal themselves, their families and change the world. We have now another opportunity to connect with the spirit world and bring back what we learn and apply it here in the real world, in our own lives; this is how we can heal ourselves and heal the world, by taking the lessons and the knowledge from the yage and living by its guidance."

Juan David stands from the table and asks the two of us, "Who wants agua-panela?"

"I'll take one, thank you," I say, as does Gamal.

Before he returns with the warm drinks, Jean-Paul, one of the two Frenchmen, joins us at the table. He asks us, "How was everyone's night?"

"I didn't feel anything," I say.

Gamal responds that he had a good night, but doesn't offer many details before returning the question to Jean-Paul. "And your night, how'd it go?"

"You mean you didn't hear me crying out in the yard?" he asks, with a friendly but reserved grin.

"No, I didn't, were you okay?" inquires Gamal.

"More than okay. I first reconnected with my deceased parents and was able to forgive; no, forgive isn't the right word. I finally *accepted* the past for what it was and gave no fault to myself or anyone else for how things used to be. The medicine showed me that my parents were deeply wounded by living through the Vietnam War before immigrating to France and having me and my brother. The yage made me feel the love that had been trapped inside them, and I think, inside me too. And I no longer feel abandoned by their coldness during my childhood. It was a beautiful experience."

Juan David returns, accompanied by Levi, with cups of steaming agua-panela.

In what seems to be the usual routine whenever someone appears, Levi is asked, "And how was your night?"

"It was a bit confusing, yea. At first I couldn't understand what the plants were trying to tell me, but after the second cup it all became clear. It was deep, man, really deep," he says, while letting go with a satisfied chuckle. "I felt a connectedness to everything. It was similar to my first time drinking ayahuasca in Peru. I saw that the hand of God has touched every person, plant, thought, animal, all of it, and that we are all living together in a oneness that... yea, words are difficult to describe it, but I felt that we will never die because our impact on the world effects everything around us so we are all kind of one big interconnected organism."

"You were in the weave, Levi," says Juan David.

"Yes, we were all, everything, woven together," he replies.

I drink my agua-panela, then roam about the garden for the next hour contemplating the stories of others and questioning why I was left completely sober after the first night of drinking the yage.

We have lunch and continue to exchange stories. The strange feeling that I've known these people for much longer than a day is striking. I guess it goes back to what I've always said; you can spend years with someone eating cake and sipping champagne, but until you've struggled together, opened up and faced some fears, the connection won't go below the surface. In this place it seems like the surface is stripped away almost immediately.

The day gives way to darkness and cold takes hold of the fading sun. We hear the music coming from down below and make our way to the longhouse for the second night's ceremony. As I enter, Juan David steps beside me and claps a hand on my shoulder. "How are you feeling? Ready?" he asks.

"Yes, I feel good. I'm excited, hoping to feel it tonight."

"Just relax, you'll do fine and remember, if you die you die," he says, before shuffling in front of me to take his seat at the head of the room.

All the rituals from the night before are once again present. We discuss, at length, topics of life and balance; there is music and giving praise before we drink. It's the same batch of medicine as the night before. I drink and again head outside to wait, hoping that tonight I will feel the effect of the medicine. I find a large stone in the garden to sit on while I try to clear my mind of distractions; but I can't, there's a drunken farmer on the next plot of land amusing himself by shouting stories into the wind.

I just wish this guy would shut the fuck up. I'm trying to concentrate and he's bothering me every few seconds with another outburst that he apparently finds hilarious, as each episode of shouting is followed by an equally loud procession of laughter. Just as I'm becoming overly frustrated at this unwanted interruption, the medicine takes hold of me; it communicates directly with my consciousness, explaining that this man's voice is the voice of God. I don't understand how this could be. I begin to listen intently to the neighbor's shouted remarks and even with my limited Spanish it is clear that this cannot be the voice of God, he's just drunk and babbling to himself.

The yage continues, telling me that this is unquestionably the voice of God because God is a part of everything in this world and that by ignoring and rejecting the neighbors shouts I am ignoring and rejecting God.

I welcome the neighbor's voice into my experience and for the first time in my life I am able to hear God speaking through all things in the world, crying out to be accepted and appreciated as their unique addition to the weave of life.

Made in the USA
Columbia, SC
22 September 2020

21267715R00131